STRANGE FREQUENCIES
A SHORT STORY COLLECTION

Published in Standard British English

Strange Frequencies

A Short Story Collection

Richard Clive

STRANGE FREQUENCIES

Published by Sinister Smile Press
P.O. Box 637
Newberg, OR 97132

"On the Other Side of Time" - first published in *It Calls from the Doors* by Eerie River Publishing - October © 2021.
"Rotten to the Core" © 2022
"The God Whisperer" - first published in *Monsters, Monsters, Monsters, Monsters* by Hellbound Books - © December 2021
"The Fever and The Thaw" - first published in *Pandemic Unleashed* by Skywatcher Press - © August 2021.
"Made in Hell" - first published in *If I Die Before I Wake: Tales of the Otherworldly and Undead* by Sinister Smile Press - © June 2021.
"Little Lost Lambs" © 2022
"On Air" © 2022
"Ride the Night" © 2022
"Yesterday's News" © 2022
"It Remains" © 2022
"The Last Gift" - first published in *If I Die Before I Wake: Tales of Savagery and Slaughter* by Sinister Smile Press - © June 2022.

Trade Paperback ISBN – 978-1-953112-38-5

Cover design by Steven Pajak
Foreword by Ramsey Campbell
www.sinistersmilepress.com

Contents

THANK YOU

A very special thank you to Mark Morris for his guidance, wisdom, honesty, and kindness. Equally, I would also like to thank Ramsey Campbell for his incredible generosity and kind words.

I'd also like to thank my beautiful wife and daughter for putting up with me. I love you both. Thank you for believing in me when not many did.

This book is in memory of my grandfather Henry Edward Jones, a writer who loved ghost stories and tales of the uncanny. If you are watching, this book is for you too!

FOREWORD
RAMSEY CAMPBELL

A FREQUENCY OF IMAGINATION

L et me celebrate the fecund talents of Richard Clive! From the opening sentences we can tell we're in safe hands, guided by a writer in enviable control of his material. "On the Other Side of Time" filters an apocalyptic event through a troubled consciousness, conveying both with economical vividness that includes a powerful sense of place. How can such a tale offer any solace? It has surprises to spare. Give it time. It even has enough of that to offer a dark joke, or an optimistic one.

"Rotten to the Core" may evoke the churches of our childhood for some of us—this reader, at any rate. The story barely draws visible breath before launching its first shock. If the general bleakness and theological theme, along with the spareness of the evocative prose, recall Graham Greene, the haunting at its core is in a different although equally honourable British tradition: the Christmas ghost story, explicitly alluded to and brought challengingly up to date.

"The God Whisperer"! There are titles that crystallise unease, and this certainly does so for me. The story generates considerable suspense from revealing the situation and the characters with all the care of a poker player gradually exposing the hand that takes the pot. The author's precise sense of landscape has intensified and brings details of the rural setting to ominous if not unnatural life before we learn how truly spirited it is. The story is a potent instance of the Welsh uncanny, developing the tradition of the occult blended with the scientific that Lovecraft learned from Machen.

"The Fever and the Thaw" only gradually pays out the weirdness of its opening glimpse, which accrues significance as the story does, a classical method Clive turns (here and elsewhere) to distinctly personal ends. Like the released contents of the ice, the story streams in multiple directions. There's more unexpectedness here than in many a novel, but can such a pithy tale resolve so much invention? You won't be surprised if I say yes, but you might be surprised how it does.

May the opening of "Made in Hell" take the palm for narrative urgency? Its fellow contents offer plenty of competition. While the body of the story is incisive about crime and criminals, not to mention appreciative of small-town Americana (a landscape that has colonised many of our minds), we know a hellish denizen is biding his time. Narrative developments keep him at bay until it's opportune to reveal him, and as he carries out his monstrous mission, Clive's gruesome lyricism reaches a peak.

"Little Lost Lambs" returns across the ocean, though the seedy Welsh location it depicts is international in its familiarity. The notion that childhood and the guilt it may bring lie in wait for us all has increasingly found expression in our field, but few treatments convey the terrors youthful inexperience can bring as powerfully as Clive's tale. By the time the monstrous makes itself plain, we've already lived through quite a nightmare, yet the tale has more dread and mystery to deliver.

"On Air" embraces the novella, a form often cited as ideal for horror. Here it provides scope for the narrative to piece itself together in order to accumulate maximum disquiet before revealing how the elements combine. The intersection of contemporary technology and the supernatural is a bountifully fruitful territory for exploration—see Kuttner's "Ghost" and Kneale's *The Stone Tape* and Kiyoshi Kurosawa's *Kairo* for just a few varied examples—and now Richard Clive takes us somewhere fresh. He does throughout his book.

"Ride the Night" confronts ageing. Quite a few of us in the field seem driven to do so, examining the experience from within although it has yet to overtake us (and perhaps again once it has). Mortality and its possible aftermaths are central themes of the field, of course, which may signify that writers in the field are more preoccupied than average with death and its unknown outcome—a healthy concern, I'd say. In a secular sense, the hell that awaits too many of us may be uncaring care in the dusk of our life, but Clive accords his victim of the system a release into a vision born of a culture that has possessed our consciousnesses. It's not the afterlife but some more mysterious displacement, open to productive interpretation.

Age and its imminence haunt "Yesterday's News", which addresses the business of time travel with the succinctness of classical science fiction—"characteristically light and rapid", as Brian Aldiss defined the prose approach. Strictly speaking, the story belongs to the vanished category, once thought useful (and certainly well populated), of science fantasy. As in *The Fifth Element*, an emotion turns out to be a source of scientific power. Take care with salvia divinorum, by the way! Alan Moore once said as much to me. "It Remains" may be seen as a companion piece to "Yesterday's News". Once again emotion wields a heightened power, in this case taking possession of a landscape. It's a dark variation on its predecessor—rather, darker.

Youth and age—"The Last Gift" sums up an underlying theme of this book, and a child's viewpoint has seldom rung truer. His fellow protagonist leads us into the vivid hell of a battlefield, haunted by the guilt many of Clive's characters suffer. Paranoia intensifies the episode, as relentless as any combat vision I've read, until at last all the horrors combine into a magnificently memorable vengeful monster. It isn't quite the last of the gifts this book offers, and they're many and varied. Savour them! I did, and with delight.

Ramsey Campbell
Wallasey, Merseyside
3 September 2022

On the Other Side
of Time

"God," shouts Wright over the din of the helicopter blades. "It's...*beautiful.*"

Mackenzie snaps a magazine into her assault rifle and swallows hard, gazing at the horizon through the chopper's window. The small hairs on her arms prickle. The air feels charged.

Obscured by tendrils of mist, the pyramid-shaped craft hovers above the mountain, inverted so its lowest vertex points down at the snow-dusted peak, the ship gently spinning on its axis by centripetal force.

The craft's three black faces are as smooth as glass, mirroring Snowdon's rugged terrain, and blinding white balls of light orbit the ship in dizzying, elliptical arcs, stitching the sky with bright trails.

The chopper thunders towards the mountain, transporting the three soldiers, the smouldering cities and graveyard towns now miles behind. The villages below, though, lie in ruins. Mackenzie stares down at a collapsed farmhouse and imagines people crushed beneath the building's brick and beams, the blackened bones of men, women, and children buried beneath rubble.

The scale of decimation in the past twenty-four hours is incalculable, and she's almost grateful for the internet dying, for the worldwide blackout. Who wanted to see the destruction of humanity on YouTube? She closes her eyes for a moment to shut out the world because the sky-blue clarity of daylight is difficult to bear. But her mind remains filled with fire and death and screaming.

"Saw a documentary years ago," says Wright, looking at her with his one good eye, the patch affording him the look of a bandit. "The ancient Egyptians, they knew."

She had visited Cairo as a child. But the upturned pyramid that slowly rotates in the sky dwarfs even those ancient tombs. The sheer size and scale of the thing is, quite simply, preposterous...yet it's there, and so is she. Her whole life has railroaded her to this point. She feels her blood pumping, her heart beating hard, adrenaline surging, time ticking...moving further away from the day she lost John...and...

...*the baby.*

The day *her* world had really ended.

Yet when she woke earlier on her bunk at dawn, she was filled with an unspeakable sense of dread. And a strange sense of hope.

A knowing.

Because, she thinks, the universe has clocks, pendulums, mechanisms, and this morning she had felt something click, like teeth interlocking, the gears of a great machine turning, engineering her arrival, bringing her here.

Nearer to the end.

Closer to death.

Closer to John.

"The Aztecs too," says Wright, playing with the silver crucifix around his neck. "Only took four thousand years for the shit to hit the fan."

"You reckon?"

"I know," he says.

"Know?"

"This shit's been a long time coming. You know, this mountain's a prehistoric volcano, and then there're the ancient myths."

"*Myths?*"

"King Arthur...*the Druids.*"

"You sound like someone I used to know."

The chopper passes over a forest and a rocky ford. In the distance, a lake glitters beneath the hazy plumes of drifting clouds that cast thin shadows on the jagged and calcareous cliffs. Snowdon is majestic, the mountain range a stunningly bleak panorama, populated only by the occasional flock of sheep.

"Sorry you volunteered?" says Wright.

"*Volunteered?*"

"*Right*, fucking suicide mission."

"Today's as good as any."

"How old *are* you?"

"Rude to ask a lady her age."

"*Lady?*"

"Fuck you."

He smiles again. "You got balls, Mackenzie."

"Quit flirting," shouts Smith, fixing his helmet cam. "Get ready to rock and roll."

She adjusts her own helmet.

"Put her down here," shouts Smith into his headset.

The copter's pilot obeys, and the chopper swoops low, the ground rushing towards them, Mackenzie's stomach in freefall, the force of air from the rotor blades flattening the surrounding brush. The landing skids touch the rocky ground, and the three soldiers climb out of the chopper, carrying their gear and weapons.

From a distance, much of the tetrahedron's huge form had been visible, but they are now too close to observe its entire shape. Instead, its mass fills the sky, casting the steep slopes in gloom. The craft's smooth surface, though, is even more evident. Mackenzie remembers visiting a shipyard years ago where cranes assembled plates larger than buses, the panels welded together to assure buoyancy. This ship has no such seams, no irregularities, or evidence of construction.

The helicopter ascends, leaving the three soldiers standing at the foot of the mountain. They watch as the chopper fades into the horizon.

"You know the drill," says Smith. "Get up close, get the footage, and report back. *That's all.*"

"Chopper could have taken us closer," Mackenzie says.

Smith pulls out a small pair of binoculars and hands them to her, pointing beyond the track ahead. "*Look.*"

She does. Dozens of small drones litter the uplands like dead flies on a sill. She hands the binoculars to Wright.

"Electrical field. Nothing can get close," says Smith. "With the satellites down, we got to do it the old-fashioned way. But this is a reconnaissance mission. Do not engage with the enemy. We get to the top of the mountain, scout the area, and return to the rendezvous point, *here.*"

Smith sets the pace, marching some fifteen feet ahead, and lazy wisps of cloud drift in, thickening to a white sea as they ascend.

"Where did that come from?" says Wright.

"Weather changes quick up here," Mackenzie says, wiping her nose on her smock's sleeve, pulling the hem up her arm.

"Your tattoo?" says Wright, noticing the ink inside her wrist.

Still holding her assault rifle, Mackenzie turns her left wrist and reads the italic font:

John
02/02/2020.
"John?"
"My…*husband.*"
"You never—"
"Another life."

02/02/2020

"WILL YOU GET A MOVE ON? WE'RE GOING TO BE LATE," SHOUTED JO, throwing her bag in the car's boot. Manchester was a two-hour drive away. The wedding started in two and a half.

No answer.

"*John.*"

Jo marched down the drive, burst through the front door, and found him kneeling in front of the TV, the remote hanging limply in his hand, unconcerned about the creases and carpet fluff he'd picked up on his fresh-pressed suit.

He turned around, wearing a wry if slightly guilty smile. Then he frowned. "This virus," he said. "I'm telling you Italy is in trouble. Feels like the bloody apocalypse."

"If you don't get in the car...*now,* you won't have to worry about the *bloody apocalypse.* It's my sister's wedding. I'm not missing it because *you* didn't get up early enough."

"Need my beauty sleep."

"You didn't look too pretty, way you were snoring this morning. Still had red wine on your teeth," she said. "You can't drink that way once the baby arrives."

He grinned. "You think parents don't drink?"

"Not the responsible ones, not into a wine coma."

"I'll cut back. Months yet."

"*Seven.*"

John walked over and kissed her forehead, rubbing her belly tenderly as he did.

"I'm sorry."

She smiled. "Move it."

"Yes, Sir, Sergeant Mackenzie, Sir."

"That's Ma'am to you, dickhead," she said, trying to contain a laugh.

He switched off the TV with the remote and squeezed past her to get to the door. She playfully slapped him on his backside. She had once dreamed of joining the military, but at twenty-four, she already thought she was too old—not to mention too pregnant. That ship had sailed. The last thing she wanted was to enlist with a bunch of spotty teenage lads who couldn't tie their shoelaces. And John wasn't cut out for military life. While she was punctual and efficient, he was late and scatty, always daydreaming about something or other. His present hangover and dawdling had already cost them a precious twenty minutes, delaying their journey with every subsequent toilet visit and forgotten toothbrush or comb.

When they finally hit the road, the drive was smooth, the expressway clear. They passed a few coaches crammed with travelling football fans, overtook a few long-distance lorries, and that was it. Despite running late, they were making good time, listening to Radio Two at John's insistence, humming along to Fleetwood Mac, Spandau Ballet, and Tiffany. John sat in the passenger seat, nursing his hangover.

"God, you're old," she said, eyes fixed on the road ahead.

"*Thirty.*"

"Old," she repeated. "This music, it's—"

"Better than the crap you listen to," said John. "What's his name, *Stomzy*?"

"Now you sound seventy."

"Respect your elders."

"Could understand if you were even…forty."

He laughed, and she felt irked by his dismissiveness. The least he could do after making them late, after making *her* drive—pregnant—was let her choose the radio station.

"Special day today," he said.

"Yeah, my sister's getting married."

"No, I mean the date."

"Your brother's birthday? *John*, you forgot last year."

"I posted a card," he said. "Think about it, the date."

"February 2nd, *and*?"

"And in numerical terms, that's 02-02-2020."

"So?"

"It's called a palindrome," he said.

"*English?*"

"It means the date reads the same backwards as it does forwards."

"Point?" she said, checking the rear-view mirror.

"Palindromic numbers are said to be significant, that's all. Time… space…everything, it's just numbers."

"What the bloody hell does that mean?"

"Time hinges around the year zero. There's before and after and—"

"Oh, *John*."

"No, there's symmetry in everything. The universe has strange… mathematical consistencies. Take a snowflake—"

"You know what I think?"

"Huh?"

"That you should get to bed earlier."

"No, you don't—"

"I get it. Life, it's all a video game, *right?*"

"I'm telling you: everything happens for a reason. There are some people—scientists, physicists—who believe in the concept of a multiverse."

"How did we jump from your brother's birthday—?"

"Imagine every time you make a choice, no matter how insignificant, the universe splits off in a new direction."

"You stay up too late, drink too much, watch too much—"

"It's like parallel universes. Imagine other versions of you…other versions of *me*."

"One's enough."

"Imagine every choice you didn't make playing out in some alternate reality. Sometimes I wonder—"

"That's dangerous."

"—about that saying: if you had an infinite number of monkeys and an infinite number of typewriters—"

"Go on."

"Well, maybe somewhere we get it right. Somewhere the world's perfect, for all of us."

"Nothing's perfect," she said.

"Apart from you."

"*Creep.*"

"Love you too," he said.

She gave in and smiled.

"I think time's an illusion."

"Tell that to my sister," she said, putting her foot down on the accelerator. "We should have left earlier."

"You know, some physicists believe the universe is tenseless, that the past, present, and future are equally real, that there's no end," he said. "That alternate realities happen concurrently."

"Bollocks."

"Based on science."

"Whose science?"

"I don't know…*NASA*?"

"Based on Sci-Fi Channel rubbish," she said.

"There's a prediction an asteroid could hit us in 2026."

"Six years! You'll be lucky. This virus has its way, the apocalypse is already here," she said, momentarily taking her left hand off the wheel and resting it on her stomach.

He smiled, then changed the subject. "The baby, how big do you think he is?"

"What makes you say 'he'?"

"A feeling."

"See it in the stars, did you?"

"No."

"Ancient Mayan prophecy?"

"It just feels wrong calling *him* 'it'."

"*He's* about the size of a walnut," she said, laughing.

"And you haven't felt him kick?"

"No," she said, checking her mirrors. "That doesn't happen until five months, or so I've read. I've not been pregnant before, you know."

The grey sky started to spit, rain lightly drumming the windscreen. She turned on the wipers. He turned up the radio. Coldplay's

"Clocks" was playing. Maybe it was her hormones, but she was finding the old music increasingly irritating.

"I meant what I said, about the drinking."

John remained silent. The atmosphere changed as if by the flick of a switch.

"John."

"Heard you the first time."

"I know what you're like when you get together with Tom," she said. "The last thing Jade wants is her groom paralytic on her big day."

"Okay."

"I'm not doing this alone. I can't cope with a baby screaming the house down while you're at work all day, and then the second you get home, you—"

"—try to unwind."

"Going to the gym is unwinding, or watching Netflix, or reading a book. Drinking a full bottle—"

"You make out like I'm a heroin addict."

"Maybe you'd snore less on smack."

"I work hard."

"More to life than work and—"

"Let's just leave it, okay?"

Jo bit her lip. The rain was coming down harder now. She turned the wipers to a faster speed.

"This is important, John."

"Can you just drive and get us to the bloody wedding?"

"So you can get sozzled again," she snapped. "Great wedding this is going to be."

"Great wedding, *indeed.*"

She scowled at him, catching his eye in the corner of the rear-view. She checked the outside lane was clear, indicated, and overtook another high-sided lorry. She remained in the outside lane.

"What do you mean by that?" she said.

"By what?"

"Sarcasm doesn't suit you."

"Couldn't think of a better way to spend my Sunday," he added.

"*Our* Sunday," she corrected.

Bill Medley was warbling on the radio about having the time of his life. The music was *really* getting under her skin now, the speaker's hum vibrating in her bones. Wasn't the song from that movie, *Dirty Dancing*? The film sickened her. *Misogynist crap.* And wasn't Swayze playing a man in his thirties, preying on teenage girls at a tacky summer camp? The film should have been called *Dirty Bastard Dancing*, as far as she was concerned. Or—what the hell?—*Sex Predator*.

"You know, you didn't have to come," she said at last.

"Wanted to," he mumbled.

"Sounds like it."

"I just…"

"Just what?"

"Never mind."

"No, John, go on."

"Why would anyone choose to get married on a Sunday?"

"Because it saved them money," she said, sighing.

"And cost *me* time."

"Time…*really*?"

"Yes, really. I get twenty-five days annual leave a year and—"

"And you don't want to spend that time with me?"

"Yes, but—"

"But what?"

"Having to book tomorrow off, I don't get much annual leave, it's—"

"You talk about symmetry," she said. "Pretty ironic. There's a pattern forming here too."

"*Pattern?*"

"Your drinking, your dismissiveness, your utter selfishness."

"*Selfish?*"

"Yes, *selfish*."

"I don't see how that's selfish. I've given up my Sunday—"

"God's sake—"

"Time *is* precious."

She turned and flashed her eyes at him, meeting his.

John's face was cast in a conceited expression of self-satisfaction. Jo felt the thin line between love and hate narrow, and all the things she loved about him became the things she suddenly despised. She risked a second glance, challenging him. His deep blue eyes, usually piercing and honest, appeared self-important and cruel. His slightly large nose, which she usually thought of as endearing and masculine, now gave him the appearance of an ugly and pompous man. For that split second, she resented carrying his child.

"The only thing that's precious is you," she snapped, holding his eyes for longer than she should.

The white van pulled out. Time slowed inexplicably. Jo noticed the thick grime of dust on the van's rear windows, saw the rusted exhaust pipe spouting filthy black fumes; she read the bumper sticker: MILF Hunter Onboard, it proclaimed.

She slammed on the brakes.

Time unspooled, and the world became a series of juddering flashes as the car skidded, righted, skidded—and then thumped into the van's rear, the windscreen exploding in a shower of glass.

"Weather's come from nowhere," says Wright.

Not weather, thinks Mackenzie, wishing for the clear skies and clarity that had been so difficult to bear.

Thick fog rolls down the slopes in a vapour avalanche, consuming the mountain. Lightning pulses, each flash transforming the topography of the pregnant black sky into an unnatural and sinister miasma. Above them, the ship gently spins, its vertex barely visible amidst the storm that seems to spread from the craft with increasing malignancy.

"Keep on," says Smith from behind.

Mackenzie leads, and as they ascend, nearing the mountain's peak, the lower-lying cloud also thickens, and they reach a knife-edged arête. The narrow ridge is perilous, separating the two steep-rising valleys on either side, the traverse requiring them to frequently scramble on all fours.

She sidles along—and sees a figure in her periphery vision. But by the time she turns her head, there's nothing but tendrils of pale vapour drifting over rock. The stress, it must be getting to her, playing tricks on her mind.

She climbs on.

Again, the figure appears, standing at the apex of a distant outcrop of rock—*John*, she thinks—and slips, losing her footing, sending a mini avalanche of rocks cascading below. She steadies her breathing. Looks again.

Nothing.

But the figure's after-image remains stark in her mind, the slight slope of his shoulders, the cock of his head.

John?

She flips down her night-vision goggles and scans the slopes, expecting the thermal imaging to detect a spectrum of shifting orange-red light.

Nothing…

She plants her feet wide apart and unslings her rifle, finger poised on the trigger. Then the sound of loose scree behind her—*a cry*. She turns—and finds the thermal imaging of one man where there should be two.

"*No*," he roars.

She flips up her goggles.

"Gone," says Wright, kneeling over the drop on his right side, his face as pale as the snow. "He was standing right there…I told him. *I fucking told him…The ropes…*We should have used the ropes."

But far below them, where the cloud is lighter, only jagged rocks sneer.

"Shit," she shouts, her heart beating wildly, feeling a pang of guilt for being grateful the sergeant's body is out of sight. The drop at this point is almost vertical, the ground hundreds of feet below. Survival would be impossible. She imagines the shell of his skull cracked and leaking, his limbs shattered.

Wright wipes a glob of snot from his nose. Silence reigns.

They had both lost comrades before, but she had never got used to it; mourning, though, would have to come later.

"Thought I saw someone…*something*…up ahead," she says finally with urgency, pointing. "*Up there.*"

Wright flips down his own goggles, clearly still struggling with shock. "*Human?*" he asks, surveying the slopes ahead.

"I don't—"

"*Sheep?*"

"I don't know…*maybe*," she says, doubting herself.

They mark the spot where Smith fell with a small pile of rocks. Wright says a prayer. Reluctantly they clamber on until the track levels out to firmer ground, their path widening, the inclination softening.

Both soldiers have the high conditioning of elite athletes, yet Mackenzie feels the strain of the climb on her calves. The air is thinner at this elevation, and the constant rush of adrenaline in her blood, too, coupled with a build-up of lactic acid, is causing her legs to cramp. She realises she needs glucose, electrolytes.

"*Refuel*," she says.

They rest, leaning against a shelf of rock where a hardy if delicate-looking species of alpine plant sprouts. Its purple flower is the only colour in a world that is eerily grey and silent.

Lightning, or something like it, continues to pulse above them, but no thunder follows. Both the mountain's peak and the craft's form are now hidden by cloud. Mackenzie gulps down a small bottle of orange juice, feeling its goodness infuse her. She takes two pieces of chocolate from her supplies, feels the spike of sugar replenishing her tired limbs.

"We met at basic training," Wright says, gazing absently into the snow-dappled rock. "He was like a brother to me."

She unwraps another piece of chocolate.

"You were going to tell me about your husband?"

She looks to the ground, says nothing, and when she finally raises her head, her gaze settles on his eyepatch for a split second longer than she'd intended.

"A scratch," he says. "Training Kurdish security forces. IED."

"I see."

"*I don't.*"

She smiles, grateful for his humour; she understands, in some ways, their morale is as implicit to their survival as the laser-sighted SA80 she carries on her back.

A sudden gust of wind brings a thick spume of fog, but the scream that follows is as piercing as it is unexpected, the mountain acoustics causing an unnerving echo, as if rebounding from the deepest gorge.

A shiver creeps up Mackenzie's spine. "*Alive?*" she says, feeling her neck hair prickle with goosepimples.

"*Impossible,*" says Wright.

"*That* word ceased to have any meaning about twenty-four hours ago."

"Come on," he says with a brusque nod.

They hurry, retracing their steps down the mountain slope, loose stones shifting beneath their boots like gravel. They scramble their way back across the ridge and stare into the ravine where they had assumed Smith had perished.

"Sarge?" Wright shouts.

No answer.

"*Sarge,*" he roars.

Only the mountain answers. When Wright's echo finally fades, the silence is eerie. The wind, though, continues to wail like a grief-stricken mother.

"Going down after him," says Wright.

"The ropes aren't long—"

"I'll climb."

"*Think*," she snaps. "You can't lift him out of there, not alone."

"I can try."

"You'll die."

"If he's injured—"

"He has morphine...*supplies*," she says. "You go down there, you're disobeying direct orders. We're talking about the entire fate of the human ra—"

"I can't leave him."

"We're nearly at the top. We get the footage, get back down, get a rescue team. We can be back in hours."

"He might not *have* hours."

"Climbing down there, *if* he is alive, will *delay* him getting proper help."

"No," he says. "You go on, get the footage. I'll take care of Smith."

"I'm not—"

"*Go*," he says.

She watches helplessly as he hurries, fixing his carabiner to the anchor, unravelling the rope from his pack, readying to make his descent.

"You only need to capture a few minutes' footage. Stay low, get what you need, and get the fuck away," he says. "Meet me back here. If I'm not back, get help."

"I can't—"

"*Go*," he says. "Finish this."

And within the flicker of an eye, he's gone. And she is alone, listening to the crumbling scree as Wright descends, lowering himself deep into the mouth of the chasm.

She turns back towards the mountain's peak. She grips her weapon tight and disappears deeper into the fog. Visibility is practically non-existent, and her eyes play tricks, the faint, ethereal shape of a man she once loved guiding her.

She feels the ascent, the strain on her knees, the increased resistance on her tightening buttocks as her muscles work. If she keeps climbing, she'll arrive at the summit sooner or later. But with every step, she fears the edge of some unseen cliff. Again, she imagines Smith's split-open skull, warm blood coagulating on the cold slate.

He had cried out, hadn't he?

Hadn't he?

Something had.

Still the lightning (*not lightning*) flickers, and so do memories in her mind's eye: from a decade before, John's blue eyes, his last lingering glance, regarding her, the second before the car slams into the back of the van, and the cold wind brings a flurry of hail, grazing her cheek like glass.

SHE WOKE COVERED IN FRAGMENTS OF THE SHATTERED WINDSCREEN, pinned to her seat by the inflated airbag, the scent of petrol bringing her around, sharpening her senses. How long had she been out? *Seconds? Minutes?* Time had ceased to exist, yet that confounded radio station continued to blare.

Her head pounded. In the rear-view mirror, the pale, bloodied face of a woman who looked ten years older stared back, regarding her with incredulity.

Ahead, blue lights swirled somewhere beyond the crumpled carnage of the pileup in which she was entombed. The electro-mechanical whine of a short-circuited car horn blared. Her crotch felt wet.

The baby… Oh God… The baby…

Pushing free of the airbag, she turned her head towards John—and saw the ruin of the face she had loved for five years. Both her car's bonnet and the white van's rear had crumpled on impact like accordions, sending a steel rod shooting from the other vehicle's back window like a projectile through their windscreen.

She vomited, spewing the greasy contents of her stomach—the omelette John had made her for breakfast—all over the dashboard.

"Oh God, John... Oh God, no," she whimpered, drooling, acid burning her throat, the stench of puke filling her nostrils. "*John.*"

The scaffolding pole—*the spear*—separated the driver and passenger sides, pressing what was left of John's head into the cushion of the car seat. She could see in high definition the abrasive surface of the rusted steel. And she wondered how many damp days and how many wet weeks and how many miserable months and passing years had caused that corrosion. Decades maybe, the rust thickening, becoming more calloused with every drop of rain.

Time conspired.

Fate was patient.

The pole obscured much of John's face from her line of sight. But along with her vomit, she could smell the copper tang of thick blood, oozing from the ragged flap of skin that hung exposing the layer of yellowish subcutaneous fat of his cheek.

John wheezed, trying to speak. "Lo...love..."

"I know," she said, trying to swallow.

She attempted to stretch and touch his hand, but she was still trapped by the airbag and the suitcase that had flown from the back seat on impact, wedging itself between the dash and the two passenger seats.

Blood bubbled on John's lips. "Together..." he gasped, his words trailing off. "Somewhere together...world...perfect..."

He was dying a terrible death in this sick-stinking car, and his final comfort, it seemed, was the suspect astrophysical theories of dubious internet forums.

Jo was too choked up to speak, tears streaming down her face. She reached again and managed to take his hand. She squeezed.

Oh, God no. Not John. Panic surged through her.

"Help," she screamed. "Somebody, *help!*"

When her husband finally took his last gurgling breath, she sat staring into his vacuous eyes, bleeding from her crotch as they cut her from the wreck. Removing John was a more delicate operation. Flecks of his grey matter had spattered the car's seats. Later she wondered how well they had cleaned up—and how much of her husband's brain tissue, that had once contained his hopes and dreams, had gone with the old Nissan to the wrecking yard.

She bled for two days. When the miscarriage was finally over, she flushed the pre-foetal form down the toilet like a dead goldfish, imagining birthdays and Christmases and bad crayon drawings that would never be.

She drank herself into the worst condition she'd ever been in during a pandemic that was killing people by the thousands. Her kidneys hurt. Her skin was blotchy. Every morning she wiped her sleep-crusted eyes and recuperated just enough to poison her body once more, only to fall asleep drunk and sufficiently numbed until morning.

It was the military that saved her.

Basic training was easy.

She embraced her physical suffering, her blistered feet, her aching muscles. Pain became her. It masked deeper wounds. With exhaustion came sleep, and three years passed in a regimented blur.

After thirty-eight months in the Royal Marines, she was encouraged to try for the Special Air Service. Forty-day marches, sleep deprivation, climbing perilous cliff faces without a harness, it was easy. The hardest part was not swallowing a bullet. Every time she considered it, her memories of John guided her.

On a cold autumn day in October, Joanne Mackenzie passed out for the SAS. Two years later, she was selected for an elite, highly covert squadron reserved for only the most dangerous of missions.

MACKENZIE CHECKS HER HELMET CAMERA IS RECORDING AND EMERGES from the thick fog. The craft darkly glimmers above, its revolutions churning the cloud, the vortex pulsing with white light.

The peaks below are sheathed in a grey sea of fog, and heavenly crepuscular sunbeams fan outwards as the sun sinks below the horizon, the red sky silhouetting Snowdon's crest—where the heads of her comrades are mounted. The spike has pierced Smith's thick head at an angle, hideously warping the features on his blood-drained face; Wright's is a vapid mask, mouth hanging open above the ragged root of his neck.

Then she sees them: seven black shadows circling the decapitated remains. Cloaked in monastic robes, they raise their arms as if in ceremony towards the craft and the whirling vortex above. The creatures' eyes burn as bright as stars from deep within their cowls, and their serrated mandibles faintly gleam, gluey secretions dribbling between labia-like mouthparts.

Pumped with adrenaline, she aims her assault rifle, but a sudden shift in air pressure causes excruciating pain to erupt outwards from her sinuses. Her ears pop. She presses her palms against the sides of her head, dropping her weapon, blood running down her neck.

The air beneath the rotating craft is shimmering like a summer heat haze, and the bright balls of light are orbiting the ship at quicker and quicker speeds, the surrounding storm, too, a cosmic swirl.

Then the thunderclap booms in old-testament fury, the sky shattering as violently as a windscreen in a high-speed crash. Shadows bleed from the hole that has appeared in the atmosphere, ribbons of darkness unfurling like ink in water.

Rock cracks and splits, fissures spreading on the mountainside as if disturbed by a tectonic shift; impossibly, reddening veins of magma appear like branches of arteries, steam rising in the cold air, melting the last pockets of winter snow.

She hears the rhythm of distant drums beating…from beyond the hole in the sky…the mournful sound of a battle horn…*marching…the legion advancing*. She hears this even before the portal's gate is breached and their blasphemous banners emerge at the mountain's summit.

She scrambles on her knees for her weapon, only for it to be kicked away. The seven are upon her, surrounding her, long robes billowing in the sulphur-smelling wind.

Their dialect fills her head like a radio transmission, planting vivid pictures in her mind's eye. She sees ruined cities beneath strange skies; she sees endless rows of towering pyramids and granite-built columns; she sees great lunar-like vistas and endless deserts; she sees boundless, roiling oceans and planets with seven suns. She sees fire, she sees death, she sees whole worlds burning in the flicker of an eye. The creatures push her mind to its limits, manipulating her neural processes beyond the point of sanity.

By the time her bladder lets go, Hell's army is flooding the mountainside, the horde's dreadful percussion louder now than her fast-beating heart. Their tune is maddening, the whistle of their pipes infecting her aspect as nightmarish, birdlike shadows move past her in the falling dark. One soldier plays a wind instrument fashioned from a human torso; another beats a drum sculpted from a head with sticks made from bone.

Her place in the universe feels small, inconsequential; her death will be an irrelevance, and as the hot wind whips up to a human-like scream, she imagines a million others crying out in protest at the planet's annihilation.

The nearest creature unsheathes its blade, eyes glittering blindingly bright, and her only comfort is the long silence she hopes will follow the end of her days.

0Ɛ02/20/Ɛ0

JOHN SAT IN THE PASSENGER SEAT. HE TURNED UP THE CAR RADIO. Coldplay's "Clocks" was playing.

"Do you have to?" said Jo.

"What, the radio?"

"Yes, *the radio*. I can't hear the satnav. Going to be late for the church. The last thing I need is to get lost."

"Loads of time," said John.

The sky was a grey slate, rain spitting at the windscreen with every gust of cold wind that brought a swirl of red and brown leaves.

"I meant what I said," Jo said, watching the road, "about the drinking."

"Haven't touched a drop in—"

"I know," she said, indicating before pulling out. "But I know what you boys are like, especially when you get together with Tom. It's a *christening*, a family occasion, not an excuse for you to go quaffing booze like you're twenty-five. You're forty."

"Don't I know it."

She smiled in the rear-view. "You okay back there, Walnut?"

"Don't call me that," said Will, scowling, his concentration directed at his games console, strapped into the car's backseat. His upper lip was stained with chocolate milkshake, giving him the appearance of a younger boy. He was growing up so quick. Sometimes she felt she lost more of him minute by minute, time stealing the baby they'd made.

Jo said, "Walnut, it's what we called you when—"

"Heard it a million times, Mum."

"*A million?*" she said.

"Six noughts," said Will, looking proud.

"Very good," she said.

"Well, now you've heard it one million and one," said John, flicking through the radio stations. "How many noughts has one million and one?"

Jo watched in the rear-view mirror as Will furrowed his brow in concentration.

"Five noughts and another one," said Will.

"Spot on—and that's a palindrome," said John, turning his head around his seat to acknowledge his son.

"What's that, Dad?"

John said, "It's a—"

"—story for another day," interrupted Jo. "We've a christening to get to. I can't hear the satnav with all the blabbering, and we are running out of—"

"Classic," John said, ignoring her protests and turning up the radio.

Bill Medley was warbling about having the time of his life.

Jo swore under her breath, but she thought she might be having the time of hers too; life was hectic and unpredictable, but on days like this, when the three of them were together, things couldn't have felt more perfect, and if they *were* late, well, it wasn't the end of the world.

ROTTEN TO THE CORE

Father Patrick Tierney believed in the sanctity of confession. He did not take it lightly, nor did he appreciate humour in his church.

"Forgive me, Father, but you have sinned," the child whispered.

It was bitterly cold, and a white cloud of breath billowed through the mesh as the boy spoke. The child sounded young, perhaps no more than seven or eight, perhaps too young for confession at all.

Vaguely recognising the voice, Father Tierney blew on his hands, warming them. *Blasted heating*. Another problem he could do without, especially on Christmas Eve. It was early morning and still dark.

"Don't you mean: Forgive me, Father, *for I* have sinned?" the priest suggested.

The child remained silent, but another white breath bloomed.

Father Tierney squinted, trying to glimpse the boy through the latticed screen. But the light was poor.

"You're supposed to say, 'Forgive me, Father, *for I* have sinned'," the priest repeated. "Then you tell me how many days since your last confession."

This child had been poorly schooled.

Along the corridor, in the church's main chamber, the choir began its carol: "Once in Royal David's City". It was the last practice before tonight's Midnight Mass. The first words were sung by a single chorister. The choir boy sang acapella, his voice a haunting echo between the cold stone walls.

"*My child?*" prompted Father Tierney.

Silence.

The priest leaned in closer, attempting to peek through the mesh, and saw a brown eye pressed up close.

"It is you who has sinned, Father," the boy hissed, saliva spraying through the lattice, hitting Father Tierney in the face.

The priest lurched away in disgust. Despite the cold, he felt a glaze of sweat on his brow. "What...what do you mean?"

No answer.

He leaned towards the mesh and saw only shadows.

He would never usually break the sacred anonymity of confession. But the child was disrespectful. He was not conforming to the order of things. Father Tierney exited the booth and pulled open the door of the adjacent cubicle.

The kneeling mat was there. So was Christ, suffering for eternity on his little wooden cross. He noticed a dead mouse, too, decomposing in the corner. But there was no boy, only the melancholy of the choir, whose sombre carol about a lowly stable drifted in the still air.

It is you who has sinned, Father, spat the voice inside his head.

So much to do and so little time.

Midnight Mass was thirteen hours away, and the clock was ticking.

The cleaner was vacuuming the pews. Gregory was *still* conducting the choir. Father Tierney enjoyed the carols, but there were only so many times you could hear "O Holy Night" before it started to grate.

"Where do you want the tree, Father?" said a bearded man, struggling with an enormous pine.

"How tall is that?" said Father Tierney.

"Ten feet," said the man.

"*Indoors?*" said the priest.

The man dropped the tree, scattering needles on the recently vacuumed floor. The cleaner scowled and muttered something under her breath.

It was a long-held tradition that the tree was put up on Christmas Eve.

"That's the order. *Look.*" The man pulled a scruffy sheet of paper from his back pocket. "Says so right here."

"I ordered a seven-foot tree, and it was supposed to arrive *two* days ago," said Father Tierney.

"What?" shouted the man over the choir.

"Just leave it there," said Father Tierney, gesturing towards the altar.

"I finish at twelve. If you think I'm hoovering all that mess up," said the cleaner, pointing at the fallen pine needles, "you can think again."

It took three of them to stand the tree in the pot. Father Tierney then went into the dusty storage room and retrieved the box of decorations, most of which, he knew, consisted of dog-eared tinsel and ancient baubles that had long lost their lustre.

Thankfully, a middle-aged church volunteer, Linda Murphy, offered to help decorate the tree. Father Tierney unwrapped sheets of crumpled newspaper, revealing a delicate glass bauble, glittering in the golden candlelight. He hung the decoration on the huge tree that now stood next to the altar, noting the church's pervading mustiness had been freshened by the scent of pine.

"There are needles everywhere," said Father Tierney.

"Norway Spruce," said Linda. "It's supposed to hold well."

He nodded and unwrapped another bauble. As he did, the faded print on the tattered newspaper caught his eye.

O'Brien, Noel, 41, passed on 24 December 2016, loving father to Megan and Ethan and husband to Margaret. He will be sadly missed. The funeral service will take place on 2 January 2017.

"*Hung himself*," said Linda, noticing his lingering eye. "Poor blighter."

He stared at the newspaper in disbelief.

"I never knew," he said.

"Family moved away."

"That's terrible."

"I say, poor blighter, but he was a drunk. Or so I heard."

The priest's eyes were fixed on the obituary photo; it was not the boy he remembered. Noel's once cherubic features were a shadow behind the unshaven face of a vagrant.

"You knew the family?" he asked.

"Not really. Cousin did, though. Noel beat his wife. Really put the kids through it."

Father Tierney was still staring at the photo, the paper yellowed by time. He considered how quickly people were forgotten, their lives summed up in a paragraph.

"Come on now, Father," said Linda, touching his wrist. "It's Christmas, so it is."

He hung another bauble on the tree, sprinkling more needles on the cold floor.

"I never knew," he said again.

But deep down, he thought that maybe he did.

"THERE ARE ONE HUNDRED PIES ALTOGETHER," SAID MRS. KELLY. "I'LL bring another hundred tonight."

"That's very kind of you," said Father Tierney, standing under the great arch of the church porch.

"Would you be kind enough to help me with these tins?" she said. "It's rather slippery."

The cemetery looked like a scene from a Christmas card. There was no snow—although it was forecast—but a hard frost blanketed the land, caking every blade of grass. The ice was treacherous on the path too. A robin darted between headstones whilst a menacing-looking crow poked its black beak on the hard ground, searching for worms.

Father Tierney accepted the stack of tins from the elderly parishioner and feigned a warm smile. "Mince pies are my favourite," he said, trying to appear sincere.

He'd struggled that morning since discovering the obituary. He was as accustomed to burying his congregation as he was christening them, yet he always grieved for those who died prematurely, especially when it was suicide.

Such a sad way to go. It was a mortal sin, of course, a violation against the fifth commandment. In the old days, families of suicides were refused permission for a Christian burial. But attitudes had changed. Mercifully, the church now acknowledged the mitigating circumstances of poor mental health, an affliction he thought he could relate to.

"Are you okay, Father?" said Mrs. Kelly.

He realised he was staring blankly into the graveyard.

"Father?"

And it was then he saw it.

The cemetery was a maze of graves. Most of the headstones were worn, dating back to the nineteenth century, weeds wrapping grey stone, shrubs hiding elaborately built Victorian mausoleums. And that was where the boy hid, crouching behind the lid of a stone tomb, peeping.

His plump face was as white as the frost, his piggy eyes black pebbles. The temperature was two below zero. Yet the boy was barefoot and wore only striped pyjamas. But even from a distance, Father Tierney could see his face was somehow...*wrong*. Purple veins branched beneath the temples of his thin skin. He looked deathly. Then the boy smiled—revealing a mouthful of black teeth.

Father Tierney's breath hitched. His chest felt tight.

"Father, are you okay?" said Mrs. Kelly.

His throat was too dry to speak.

Mrs. Kelly turned to him, then followed his line of sight. It was enough to distract him for the slightest moment, but when his gaze returned to the crypt where the boy had stood, there was only that hungry-looking crow.

"I REALLY THINK YOU SHOULD SIT DOWN," SAID MRS. KELLY, HANDING him a glass of water.

Father Tierney stood next to the electric heater in his office. The lights on a miniature Christmas tree flashed on his desk. He was freezing. The cold had seeped into the marrow of his bones. When he looked out the window, he could see the entire cemetery. Dark clouds rolled across the sky. Snow *was* on its way.

"You look like you've seen a ghost," said Mrs. Kelly.

It was the sort of thing people said on television when somebody *had* seen a ghost. What he had seen—*thought he'd seen*—was Noel aged around ten.

"I can fetch you a glass of brandy, Father. I've a bottle in the car. I know what they say, but liquor has its uses."

"Really, I'm fine," he said, knocking back his pills. The doctor had told him his blood pressure was worryingly high.

He searched the cemetery from the safety of the window. Everything glistened in the frost. *White. Crystalline. Still.* But out there in the bleak midwinter, he feared that face appearing again: that white face, those little white hands, poking from the sleeves of striped pyjamas, and…

A smile flashed in his mind's eye.

Black teeth…

"I insist," said Mrs. Kelly. "I shan't be long."

She left him to his devices, and he thought more about the obituary that had been wrapped around the sparkling bauble. He did this whilst absently studying the bowl of fruit on his desk. The clementine had started to turn. The fungal spores had formed a black and whitish glaze on the surface of the peel. He picked up the orange and noticed the one beneath had turned blueish with decomposition. An apple, too, looked rotten to the core. He thought of that boy and his black maw of teeth.

Noel beat his wife. Really put the kids through it.

How had Noel turned out so badly? He'd been such a sweet thing. He tried to shake the thoughts from his mind. He had much to do. This wasn't the time to contemplate the past. It was stress, pure and simple. He'd taken too much on, organising this confounded Christmas service. It was the same every year. He was seeing things, *surely*? Maybe it was food poisoning. Had he touched the fruit lately? What had Dickens written, an undigested bit of beef?

And who said he was to blame anyway? He'd been young too. If it had been a ghost, why would it show itself as a child? Why not an adult? *Forty-one, wasn't it?* Why not fifteen? That had been his age when—he closed his eyes, attempting to bury his thoughts.

Mrs. Kelly returned with the brandy. She left the bottle on the table. *Call it a Christmas present,* she'd insisted before leaving.

The priest took the brandy and drank. The cognac warmed his throat, dulling his mind, infusing his bloodstream, culling the guilt that had resurfaced after so many years.

The alcohol gave him the courage to boot up his laptop, and when he searched online, he found stories dating back fifteen years. Noel had been a good footballer. There were reports of county games where his name was more than a mere footnote.

Then he found the report of the inquest in the newspaper's online archives. The press, local journalists at least, were bound by ethics and law in what they could print following a suicide. He knew from his experience that inquests were often published as a stream of morbid innuendos. Coroners rarely established the cause of death as suicide, not unless the evidence was unequivocal. There were life insurances and other repercussions to consider, and children's lives might be ruined. Better to record the death as misadventure. Noel's inquest, however, had been a much plainer affair. It *had* been suicide.

Man Hanged Himself, read the headline.

Tragedy of Ex-Footballer

Noel had done it at home.

Father Tierney had never understood that. Why put your family through such pain?

Snow tick-tacked against the window. When Father Tierney turned to observe the cemetery through the ghost of his reflection, and the twinkling lights of the little Christmas tree on his desk, he saw the boy. His face was pressed tight to the glass and smiling, revealing blackened teeth and eyes as dark as coal.

FATHER TIERNEY MADE HIS EXCUSES.

Through winding country lanes, he drove, sipping brandy at the wheel. Sixty miles passed, the roads cutting through a blur of hedgerow, the snow now whirling across the windscreen, collecting on the bonnet. Once a tractor had pulled out in front of his spluttering old car, but he swerved and careered forwards, compelled by the prospect of his penance.

Wrapped in a long coat, his face hidden under the peak of an old fishing cap, he skulked into this other church where he was a stranger. He removed the hat and hurried to the confessional.

He knelt. The booth smelt musty. There was a trace, too, of the sweet spice of incense. On the wall, Christ was nailed to a crucifix.

"Forgive me, Father, for I have sinned," he said.

"God listens," said the deep voice from behind the screen.

"It's been two months since my last confession," said Father Tierney.

"You're here now."

"I…I…"

For decades, Father Tierney had sat on the other side of the screen and listened to thousands upon thousands of confessions, men and women who admitted both venial and mortal sin. Those who confessed were often direct. They attended not for counselling but to seek the sanctifying grace of God. But the longer a secret was kept, the harder the priest had to work to coax out the truth. As months became years, the secret would bury itself deeper and deeper, burrowing like a grub in a rotting piece of fruit. Such secrets became entombed. Father Tierney knew this. But it made no difference. The words were trapped deep inside him.

"I…I don't know how," Father Tierney stuttered.

"Anything you disclose is between you and God," said the other priest.

"It was…a long time ago."

"You're safe here," the priest assured him.

Father Tierney stared up at the statue of Christ, the messiah's eyes pleading and mournful.

"Tell me, my child," ordered the priest.

No. He would not let his secret define him. Other people would fail to understand. Speaking of this secret, attempting to articulate what had happened in such frank and unforgiving terms, how might that be perceived by others?

Carnal sin?

Molestation?

Ravishment?

There were other words. But it *had* been consensual, hadn't it?

Hadn't it?

In his mind, Noel smiled again, flashing black teeth in the white of the frost.

"I'm sorry," he said to the anonymous priest.

Father Tierney put on his cap—*church be damned*—pulled down the peak, and staggered out of the booth. He stumbled through the church and into a little girl lighting a candle and, under the accusing gaze of her angry father, hurried out of the old building and into the falling snow.

When he reached his car, he brought the bottle to his lips and glugged more brandy, the spirit burning his throat.

Noel had been seven or eight when he'd first met him. The boy had grown up as part of his congregation. He remembered him on that overnight Sunday school trip, wearing his little striped pyjamas. But nothing—*nothing*—had happened, not until shortly before Noel's sixteenth birthday. He would never have touched an *actual* child. Hell's fires weren't hot enough for such people...for...

Oh God, no...

With the engine of his old car chugging, Father Tierney wept.

"I was lonely," he said to himself. "So young and so lonely."

TWO HOURS LATER, FATHER TIERNEY HAD RETURNED TO *HIS* CHURCH. He felt calmer after the tears and the alcohol that had warmed his blood.

He had to hold it together, get some perspective. What he did —*what they had done*—was sinful, yes, and he would confess. He would. *One day*. But standing amidst the commotion of his church, he was surrounded by sin.

People did bad things all the time, didn't they? Regrettable things.

They confessed, and they went on, inflicting more of their selfishness upon their family and friends. It was the way of things.

Did confessing really make it okay?

It seemed so.

He watched Gregory conducting the choir. The man had cheated on his wife. Many years ago, Sheila had suffered from post-natal depression. Gregory had complained she'd become distant and detached. She'd lost interest in their marriage, and he'd sought out the company of a prostitute, a local drug addict with children and a habit to feed. Yet Sheila was oblivious, *the stupid woman.* And here she was on Christmas Eve, handing out hymn sheets as her grinning dog of a husband orchestrated "Ding-Dong Merrily on High".

Linda, the well-meaning church volunteer, she had stolen many years ago. She'd taken rusks and cartons of baby food to feed her screaming infant. But stealing was stealing, wasn't it? Yet here she was, making hot chocolate for the choristers like butter wouldn't melt.

Paul O'Hara, the young boy who delivered the newspapers, he was here too. He had desires. Forbidden ones. Paul looked like the stereotypical choir boy, his cheeks rosy, blond hair glistening in the golden light. But his hard drive was, no doubt, a murkier place than this candlelit church.

So many others…

At times he had thought himself unfit to lead the congregation. But he was human too.

Father Tierney ducked behind a pillar and took another nip of brandy. He savoured its liquid warmth. He cupped his hand around his mouth and blew, checking his breath. Then he hid the bottle under his coat and took a mint from his pocket.

"Ah, Father. You have returned," said Linda.

She had missed him concealing the brandy by a split second.

"Yes, a small matter I had to attend—"

"Just in time," said Linda. "There's a lady here for you."

Linda nodded in the direction of a woman in her early forties. He recognised her but struggled to place her face. The woman looked tired and drawn.

Linda leaned in closer. "Such a coincidence," she whispered. "It's the wife of that man, you know, from that obituary."

He felt the adrenaline pumping in his veins, his blood pressure rising.

"She wants to speak to you, Father."

"*Me?* Whatever for?"

"She seeks your counsel."

"It's Christmas Eve. I have much to do and—"

But before he could object further, the woman was standing before him, smiling, her eyes now as lively in the candlelight as the little robin in the snow.

THEY WALKED THROUGH THE CEMETERY.

Thick snow now carpeted the ground. It fell in steady flurries through the bare branches of broad trees. Dusk was settling.

"I lost Noel three years ago," said the woman finally.

He nodded curtly. "Yes, I know."

"I wanted to bury him back here, where he grew up," she said. "But there was such a lot to do, and well, I wanted it over."

"Understandable," said Father Tierney. He dared not raise his head and look around for fear of seeing the boy.

"What can I help you with, Mrs. O'Brien?"

"Please...*Maggie*," she said.

He forced a smile. "How can I help you, Maggie?"

"People think Noel was a bad man," she said. "But there was good in him. He was troubled. He had secrets he kept bottled up."

Father Tierney nodded.

"He never told me," she said. "But he would drink. The doctor said he had to stop. His liver, it was damaged and—"

"Addiction is a terrible thing," he said, raising a hand to cover his own breath.

"Noel never talked to me," she said. "Not soberly. He sometimes got cryptic when he was near paralytic."

Father Tierney nodded sombrely, wishing he was out of the cold and away from this woman.

"It's ironic, though, I suppose," she said. "By the end, I could see what was wrong anyway. The secret and the booze diluted the man I married. He was transparent because all that was left of him was the thing that destroyed him."

"What are you saying?"

"I believe my husband was abused," she said with conviction.

Abused, really?

He closed his eyes, shutting out the world. But when he retreated to the blank canvas of his thoughts, even for a second, he found a darker place where the past replayed. The church had been cold back then, too, all those years before, and the boy's hands had been warm.

"I wanted to ask a favour of you," said Maggie, touching his cold hand with her own. "I want you to pray for him, tonight, at Midnight Mass."

"I'd love to help you, but the itinerary for the service, it has already been—"

"Please. My children are with me." She pointed to the road that skirted the cemetery wall. In a little blue car, two children sat, watching with pale faces.

"All they ever hear is their father was a mean drunk," she said. "It wasn't like that. He was consumed by something. He could never look past whatever it was that had happened."

"I'd love to help you. I really would," said Father Tierney. "But I need to prepare—"

"He spoke of you. Often. Usually when he was drunk, but you

clearly had a great impact on his life, Father. It would mean the world if only you could agree. It would mean the world to my children."

"I hadn't seen...*Noel* for years. I really don't think it would be appropriate—"

"Please, *Father*."

And just like that, it was agreed.

Father Patrick Tierney walked back to the church, wondering how he could pray for a man he'd condemned nearly three decades before, a man that haunted the present like the ghost of Christmas past.

THE CHURCH WAS PACKED, THE PEOPLE CLAD IN HATS, SCARVES, AND THICK coats. Outside the snow had continued to fall. But inside the church, despite the cold, candles cast their warm light in abundance.

Father Tierney welcomed the congregation and began his well-rehearsed sermon. But he knew he was struggling to speak coherently because, throughout the afternoon and evening, he'd drunk the entire bottle of brandy. Communion wine had quenched his insatiable thirst since.

From the pulpit, he gazed upon the faces of his congregation through blurred eyes. They watched him: the adulterers, the thieves, the perverts.

The candles that burned beneath him were hypnotic. He fought the booze in his blood that caused him to sway and crave sleep as he interjected the endless repertoire of carols with his priestly counsel.

As the organist concluded the final chords of "O Come, All Ye Faithful", Father Tierney waited for the silence that followed the song.

Hymn sheets and feet shuffled in the pews. People sat. An infant cried out as a mother attempted a quiet lullaby. And Maggie O'Brien smiled from the front row, her arms draped around her two children: a girl aged about twelve and a boy around eight; he looked exactly as his father had as a child.

Could I have been mistaken? Father Tierney thought.

Could *he* have been the boy in the cemetery?

He told himself that maybe he could, the black teeth a trick of the light due to him being unnerved by the strange coincidence of finding the obituary.

Then he realised he had slipped into a trance-like state, staring at the O'Brien family. His congregation were waiting for him to speak.

Father Tierney cleared his throat. "I want to talk about a man who was lost to his family on this day three years ago," he said, knowing he was slurring. "Noel O'Brien was a troubled man, but aren't we all, to some extent or another?"

His voice echoed under the high ceiling, and the church became stiller, the candle flames flickering gently. Amidst the silence of his congregation, the priest became aware of the extent of his alcohol-induced dysarthria. Yet the O'Brien woman gazed upon him as if he was a saint.

"The Devil is in all of us," he said finally. "He can manifest in the best of us. Noel was a man who loved his family. His widow, Maggie, and his two children are with us tonight."

He looked up from his notes and met Maggie's eyes, and she returned a sad smile.

"But Noel found his devil. It's there in all of us, you know, waiting. We must be honest with God. Honest with ourselves. Because if a sin becomes a secret, it then becomes a worm that eats you from the inside."

He nodded at Maggie O'Brien, hoping the congregation hadn't noticed his intoxication...*his hypocrisy*. Without drink, he never would have managed to deliver this service or speak so honestly... It was as close to a confession as he could manage.

"We thank the Lord, though, that Noel has found peace," he said and made the sign of the cross. "Eternal rest grant unto Noel, oh Lord, and let perpetual light shine upon him. May the souls of all the faithful departed, through the mercy of God, rest in peace."

When he looked up again, he saw Maggie was crying, both her children too.

The organist began. Handbells chimed. The choir chanted:

Hark how the bells…
Sweet silver bells…
All seem to say…
Throw cares away…
Christmas is here…

His vision reeling amidst the sea of accusing faces staring up at him, Father Tierney closed his eyes. The carollers' rapid incantations quickened to a pulsing whisper.

The heating was broken. The church was not just cold, it was freezing. People were shivering. Yet he felt a sickly sweat spring from his pores.

Gaily they ring…

His stomach churned.

While people sing…

Acid rose in his throat.

Songs of good cheer…

He belched.

Christmas is here…

He tried to speak, to apologise, for feeling so sick, but realised his voice was unheard under the beat of the carol. He ran, unnoticed by the choir who were lost in their song.

> *Merry, Merry, Merry, Merry Christmas…*
> *Merry, Merry, Merry, Merry Christmas…*

Falling down the altar steps, he knocked into the Christmas tree, causing it to sway precariously in its pot. He hurried past the O'Brien family—and saw the children's faces were blackened and shrivelled like spoiling fruit.

He ran down the aisle, passing the pews, under the watchful eyes of a congregation who'd confessed sins ranging from the triflingly insignificant to the outright criminal.

He crashed through the heavy wooden doors and fell into the snow. Not wanting to be seen, he scurried through the cemetery where he could be left alone with his sudden affliction.

There, consumed by sickness, his palms pressing into the snow, he vomited, splashing the frozen ground. The fetid steam rose in his face. The smell was repugnant. *Worms* writhed in undigested brandy, communion wine, and yellow stomach bile.

He wiped the sweat from his damp brow and noticed he was crouched beside an old grave. Father Tierney looked up from the slab and his stinking mess—and saw the form that loomed over him.

It was Noel, now aged fifteen or thereabouts. He was as naked as that day nearly thirty years before.

The boy was as translucent as a jellyfish. Through thin, blueish skin, his internal organs were fetid sacs, consumed by swathes of swirling black rot that metastasised within. His eyes were black pits filled with writhing nests of worms, his great black wings spread falcon-like, beating the frozen air.

Father Tierney regarded the revenant before him and realised his judgement had arrived. His heart slammed in his chest one final time, and then death swept through him, his blackened soul drifting in the winter night as gently as a sombre carol.

THE GOD WHISPERER

The plan would go like clockwork. That's what Tucker had said.

"Easy money. They're scientists. They won't put up a fight."

But now, sitting in the dark, in the passenger seat, sharing the beat-up Land Rover with two other men, Will had doubts—big ones.

"Fucking dogs," said Tucker, an ugly scowl etched into his thick features. Even in the murk, his knuckles appeared white as they gripped the steering wheel. "Nobody said shit about guard dogs." He slammed his meaty fist into the dashboard.

The engine ticked as it cooled. The headlights were off. Tucker nursed his knuckles. The Land Rover was parked on a hill beside a dirt track, beneath the black bulk of the Grampian Mountains, the car surrounded by a sea of strange-looking toadstools.

Above them the constellations glittered. The farm buildings were scattered sporadically across the valley below, yellow light leaking from the occasional window. The bone-white moonlight revealed two squat shadows patrolling the perimeter of the fences that enclosed the farmland.

Pacing back and forth, the dogs settled their attention on a corner of the fence that was parallel to the car, some twenty feet beneath them. The animals whined and yelped. Then they began to bark.

"They look big," said Jones from the backseat.

Tucker ignored him. His eyes were searching for a way around the dogs. There was none. One narrow drive served what had once been a farm, now protected by a heavy gate and looping barbed wire. The back way was the only way—down the hill and through the fence.

By their boxy-headed silhouettes, Will guessed the dogs were Rottweilers, but it was difficult to be sure.

"Fuck's sake," said Jones. "Will someone throw us a fuckin' bone?"

"None needed," grunted Tucker, producing a pistol from inside his black bomber jacket. "Roll the fuck over, Rover."

On their long journey north, Tucker had proved he was anything but the cool, calculated criminal he'd tried to portray. Despite the intricate planning, the drone footage, and the maps, the man possessed a violent temper. When sheep had blocked a narrow country lane, Tucker's face had turned a furious shade of purple. Then their mobile phones had lost their signal, cutting off their navigation, causing the vein at his temple to pulse. When their route was eventually blocked by a closed road, he had erupted in a fit of incandescent rage, and Jones had narrowly escaped a beating.

Hot temper. Cold steel. It was a bad recipe.

Will listened to the barking of the dogs, took a deep breath, then reminded himself why he was here, and of who depended upon him.

Back in that grubby working men's club, it had been Tucker who had convinced Will to take this job against his better instincts. Because the gig seemed easy. And the reward was twenty fat ones. *Each.*

"Exactly what are they researching?" Will had asked whilst sipping a flat pint of beer.

"Mycology."

"In English?"

"Fungus," said Tucker. "American company. Discovered some rare shit. Look it up."

Will had.

The area was a site of special scientific interest. The facility was a small operation, set up to monitor, conserve, and research the area's unique flora.

The deal: break into the lab, obtain the fungal specimen, and get the fuck out.

Tucker's contact had not divulged the details of what was so special about the fungus. That knowledge was useless, anyway, unless you knew what to do with it.

"So what's the big deal?" Will had asked, tearing pieces from his beermat.

"With the fungus?" said Tucker.

"Yeah."

Tucker scowled. "Who cares?"

"They synthesise that shit, you know, for new antibiotic compounds," said Will.

"I don't care if it's a cure for baldness, bowel cancer, or fucking haemorrhoids."

Tucker was right, Will supposed. *Who cared?* If they got their cut, it was irrelevant. It wasn't even immoral, was it? Because these research companies were in it for the money. They'd sit back and let hundreds of kids die of some rare genetic disorder while they haggled over the price of pills.

Now Tucker fed bullets into the pistol's magazine, his thumb sliding in the ammunition with practised ease. He snapped in the full mag and pulled back the gun's slide, his fingers precise and at one with the deadly mechanisms. For a second, Tucker's hand wavered and the barrel pointed at Will.

"*Christ*, would you keep that thing away from me?" shouted Will.

Tucker remained silent, but his eyes gleamed, as did the gun's black metal, reflecting the dim lights on the dashboard. Will knew nothing about guns. He'd once been to a firing range when he was eighteen or nineteen, but that was a long time ago.

What was that principle—*Chekhov's Gun?* The theory that if you introduced a gun in the first scene of a story, it would go off in the next.

Will briefly closed his eyes and sighed. Bloodshed painted his imagination in crimson shades. "I thought we agreed," he said, finally plucking up the courage to confront Tucker. "No guns."

Tucker looked up from the pistol. His eyes brimmed with disgust. "And how do you propose we reach those labs without being torn to fucking shreds?"

Beyond the dip of the valley below them was a short incline, which rose sharply before the land plateaued. The slope could prove problematic, even for the Land Rover, and they couldn't risk getting stuck, like cavalry in a castle's moat. They had to do this on foot, or not at all.

"Six staff," said Tucker. "Four men, two women. We stick to the plan: cut the fences, *shoot the damned dogs*, and get what we came for."

"How do we know what we're looking for?" said Will.

"I'm sure the researchers will help us out once they know we're serious," said Tucker, waving the gun.

"The fungus, what did you say its name was?" said Will.

"The God Whisperer," said Tucker.

Sounded ominous. But didn't they all? Death Cap. Devil's Tooth. The Medusa Mushroom…Stinkhorn. It was something of a tradition, it seemed, to give fungi names that might appear in a children's fairy tale.

"If you use that gun, they'll know we're here," said Will.

"They *already* know we're here," said Tucker, gesturing to the farm buildings with a nod of his head.

Beyond his pallid reflection in the windscreen, Will saw the front door of the largest building—the farmhouse—was open. A silhouette stood in the doorway. The man was holding a hand to the side of his head.

"And he's on the fucking phone," said Tucker. "We need to get in there, *now*."

Tucker exited the car, slamming the door behind him. Jones followed, clutching his baseball bat.

Will reminded himself why he was here by thumbing the screen of his phone, on which the gaunt face of his sister Jess appeared. Even without hair, Jess was striking, her baldness only serving to make her eyes sparkle all the more. Her three daughters hugged her waist.

Pioneering treatment in America was expensive, but Jess' girls needed her.

He had this.

Will opened the passenger door and stepped out into the brisk night. Soon these valleys would be covered in snow; there was already an eerie stillness to the land. A quiet wind blew, and he could almost hear the gentle sway of heather, the land whispering beneath the cold stars.

Reluctantly, he followed the other two men, all three of them treading on toadstools. These were evidently not the rare specimens they had come to collect—there were dozens if not hundreds of them. The land, Will guessed, must be particularly conducive to fungal growth, hence the presence of the rare and mysterious God Whisperer.

Tucker and Jones were already halfway down the rutted hillside. The grass was crisp underfoot, freezing in the November chill. They staggered sideways down and towards the fence and the raging dogs.

Tucker reached the fence and pointed the beam of his torch at the two muscular beasts on the other side. Their barking had now ceased. Ears back, hackles up, the Rottweilers crouched on their hind legs. The dogs' lips were curled back, revealing salivating jaws. Both animals emitted low growls, occasionally snapping their sharp teeth in the cold air.

Casually, Tucker raised the gun, pointed the barrel through the chain-link fence—and fired. The pistol crack echoed under the brittle night sky. The first dog whimpered and became silent. Tucker fired a second time before the other dog could escape, and the weight of its body thudded lightly on the frozen ground.

Jones was already working on the fence with a heavy set of cutting pliers, his breath frosting while he worked.

Will stood back, watching the action unfold in a dream-like state of disquiet. Two dead animals lay in the grass, bathed in the torchlight, tongues lolling, eyes bulging.

How far would Tucker go?

In the distance, the man in the doorway was still on his phone. Three people dashed from the surrounding white rendered buildings towards the farmhouse.

"Fucking fence," said Jones, struggling with the pliers.

"Hurry," said Tucker. "They're locking the place down."

There was a sharp snap, then another. *"Through,"* said Jones, holding up a flap of loose wire.

Tucker ducked through the gap in the fence, stepping over the dead dogs. Jones followed. Will lingered last in line.

The dogs' blood seeping into the ground appeared black in the moonlight. Will wondered how much more would be spilt before this was over.

This was not how it was supposed to be.

In the distance a lone figure was running for the farmhouse, passing a procession of single-storey buildings that Will understood to be either storage huts or laboratories. A piece of corrugated roofing, a rusted metal drum, and an overturned trailer were the only reminders this had once been a working farm.

"Stop, or I'll shoot," bellowed Tucker.

The silhouette, lit in the gloom by a symphony of strobing security lights, was forty yards from the house's door and the man on the phone.

Tucker pointed the gun at the sky and fired.

The silhouette hit the ground.

Tucker briskly moved forwards, the pistol at his side. "Don't move," he shouted.

But the silhouette did. First, dog-like, it scrabbled on all fours towards the house, and then it was up and running again, arms pumping, heading towards the door, white coat flapping in the wind.

In one sweeping motion, Tucker aimed the gun and fired the semi-automatic weapon three times in quick succession.

The figure collapsed, falling forwards.

The door to the farmhouse closed, shutting out the light from within. A second later, all the lights went out, every window turning black.

Will rushed towards Tucker and grabbed his brawny shoulder, spinning the larger man around. The veins in Tucker's neck were bulging cords. His eyes, though, were dull looking. He might have gunned down a deer, not a human being. For Will, even shooting an animal was a step too far.

"Fucking lunatic! You realise what you've done?" shouted Will.

All Will saw was the flinch of Tucker's thick bicep, and he felt the impact of cold metal striking his head. He staggered and fell as the delayed onset of pain hit him.

"You're either with us or against us," said Tucker, his imposing figure looming over him. The pistol was now at his hip. "*Decide.*"

Lying on the frozen ground, Will's head spun, and when he closed his eyes, the starry sky remained, white dots whirling behind the screens of his eyelids. He patted his temple, feeling for blood—it was dry.

"*Well?*" hissed Tucker.

"You...you *shot* them," said Will, struggling to articulate his words through the pain.

"Not without warning." Tucker shrugged nonchalantly and spat a ball of phlegm into the grass. "Get up—let's get this done."

Unsteadily, Will rose to his feet. Nobody was supposed to get hurt. They *had* agreed to tie the lab workers up, but only so they could make their getaway.

Tucker turned and marched towards the spot where the figure had fallen.

Will was bent over, hands on his knees, catching his breath, waiting for his sight to realign, when Jones put an arm around his shoulder.

"No use going against him," Jones whispered. "Got to stay calm, for all our sakes. Remember, it wasn't you. You never pulled the trigger. Let's get this done, and two days from now, you'll be sipping a cold beer on a warm beach. C'mon, man." Jones pulled him up straight by his arm. Will thought he might collapse. He didn't, but the world quivered.

Stood on the periphery of a sensor that activated a security light, Tucker's figure strobed, his long shadow lurching up against the side of one of the low farm buildings.

This side of the fence, the toadstools sprouted from the ground in even greater abundance. Will noticed their vibrant colours and how they covered the land like coral at the shore of some exotic ocean. They looked somehow alien in this bleak and beautiful land of thistle and heather.

When the two men reached Tucker, they found the girl writhing in the dirt, blood pumping from her thigh. She was in her mid-twenties, wearing a thick fleece over a white laboratory coat.

"Pl...please don't hurt me," she begged.

"We're here for the God Whisperer," said Tucker. "*Where*?"

She shook her head, panting, her breath misting. A strand of her blonde hair was plastered to her sweat-glistened forehead, despite the cold.

"Tell me," said Tucker. "*Now*."

The woman was hyperventilating.

Tucker crouched on one knee, grabbed her hair, and pulled. "Listen, *bitch*. We're not playing games."

"Please, no," the woman gasped.

Again, Tucker yanked back her hair, twisting it violently. The woman's eyes bulged in their sockets, her skin pulling tight against her skull.

Still unsteady from the blow to his head, Will stormed towards Tucker, but the big man threw out a huge fist, thudding into his crotch. Pain seared from Will's balls, spreading to the tops of his legs and stomach. He collapsed onto his knees.

"Won't tell you again. *Last chance*," growled Tucker, cocking the pistol and pointing it at Will. Tucker lowered the gun, turned his attention back to the young woman, and pulled her hair again. "Last chance for you, too, sweetheart. *Where*?"

Her answer was nonsensical.

Tucker pointed to the farmhouse. "*Keys*?" he said, patting her down. He found nothing. "If I have to kick down that door and murder every one of you, I'll do it."

But the woman was unable to speak coherently through her hysteria and pain.

Tucker hit her then with the pistol grip. Her head jolted on impact, and she flopped into unconsciousness. Blood poured from what had been a neat, little nose. He let go of her hair, and she rolled from his arms into a bed of toadstools.

"C'mon," said Tucker, rising to his feet and gesturing to the two other men.

From the cold ground, still wincing from the blow to his crotch, Will stared at the young woman. Left like this, blood leaking from her leg and nose, she'd be hypothermic in half an hour, if not dead from blood loss. Already her skin looked pale and mottled, like marble. Will took off his jacket, knowing he'd be leaving behind traces of forensic evidence, and wrapped it around her. Next, he took off his belt and fastened it around her upper thigh, like a tourniquet. He was conscious of cutting off her blood supply but feared not acting at all. He contemplated dragging her to one of the nearby buildings, but those, he guessed, were most likely locked. His thoughts were interrupted by gunfire.

Tucker was standing before the large farmhouse. It was no fortress, but Will wondered if the small windows and heavy oak door would keep intruders out long enough for the police to arrive. The nearest station was about an hour away.

He'd been stupid and naïve, blinded by pound signs and the promise that nobody would get hurt—blinded by the promise he'd made his dying sister.

Tucker fired a warning shot into the sky. "Open up," he bellowed.

No response.

Again, Tucker shouted, his voice echoing across the valley. "Open up and no one else gets hurt!"

His request was met with silence. Only the cold wind answered, scattering rattling leaves through the carpet of fungi.

Tucker marched towards the cottage door and kicked it with all his weight. The door visibly buckled. He pointed the pistol at the lock. The gun cracked. He kicked the door. It bowed, rattling on its hinges, perhaps still secured by a second lock or chain from inside. But it made no difference. He kicked the door once more, and it crashed open.

Tucker's hulking figure strode into the house, screaming obscenities, waving the gun before him in erratic arcs.

WILL COULD DO LITTLE FOR THE GIRL NOW. THE BEST THING HE COULD offer was to get this done quickly and efficiently. Please let her live, he prayed—and left her in the frost.

Shivering without his coat, he followed Tucker into the cottage and found a dark hall cluttered with sealed cardboard boxes that were stacked four high against the walls.

Tucker was a dim apparition bathed in the residual light from his torch. He stood halfway along the narrow corridor with its three doors, a scowl warping his face. He was pointing his gun at the head of a small, portly man with a thick moustache, who squinted back through the round lenses of his glasses. In his mid-sixties, the man was balding and wore a white lab coat. Behind him, the cowering heads of four of his colleagues crowded in the doorway of a small kitchen.

"We're here for the God Whisperer," said Tucker. His torch skipped across the crudely plastered, uneven walls, the darting beam scattering shadows, terrified faces leaping out of the darkness.

The group shrank away from the torch, their eyes narrowing in the glare.

"Stay back!" shouted Tucker, concentrating the beam on the man in the round glasses. "Where is it?"

The man said, "You're making a huge mistake."

Tucker placed his torch on top of a stack of cardboard boxes, the beam pointing at the fat scientist. He patted the man down, searching him. From the left pocket of his lab coat, he took a jangling set of keys. He held the keys up by the binding ring so the man in the glasses could see them. "You're going to take us on a magical mystery tour," he said, gesturing with a firm nod towards the door and the nearest of the three outbuildings.

Tucker lifted the gun until its barrel was pressed against the dome of the man's head. "What's your name?"

The man looked at him, frightened but quizzical.

"Please, *no!*" screamed a woman from the kitchen.

"Shut the fuck up, or I'll blow his bald head off," shouted Tucker, jamming the gun harder against the man's temple. "*Name?*" he repeated.

"Mackenzie. Dr. Elliot Mackenzie."

"Well, *Elliot*, here's what we're going to do: you're going to take these keys, and we're going to explore that lab," said Tucker, pointing out into the cold night air. "Any games, any at all, and I'll spray your brains in the wind. Do you understand?"

The doctor nodded. "Yes."

"Good. Let's go," said Tucker, picking up his torch.

Lingering near the front door, Jones stepped forwards, gripping his baseball bat.

Tucker gave Jones a brusque nod and pointed to the group cowering in the kitchen. "Stay here. Take their phones. Any one of them causes trouble, smash their heads in."

"Got you," said Jones, readying the bat and directing his eyes at the shuffling crowd of bodies.

Tucker nodded at Will. "*You* are with me."

Mackenzie walked out through the door. Tucker followed with the gun jammed into the small of the man's back. When he passed Will, Tucker said, "I meant what I said. *Last chance.* Now c'mon, let's get this finished."

Tucker patted Will's shoulder, then pinched him hard before letting go.

THE THREE MEN WALKED THROUGH THE DARKNESS, TOWARDS THE LAB.

Again, the wind whispered in the trees, as if conspiring against them, and Will had a strange thought. He wondered if the trees were listening to the erratic beat of his heart, to the thrum of blood in his ears, to the dry rustle of dead leaves. This remote wilderness possessed an eerie, even oppressive silence that was almost symphonic: a beat you could feel, not hear, in the land's inaudible echoes.

Mackenzie led the way, his white coat flapping gently in the breeze. It was obvious he was trying to stall their progress by walking slowly—too slowly for Tucker's quick temper.

Tucker jabbed the gun at the base of Mackenzie's spine, his fingers twitching on the pistol's trigger. Will feared the gun going off; he could see Tucker's teeth were clenched and knew it would take little to irk him.

"Move it," said Tucker.

Mackenzie did.

When they passed the young woman Tucker had shot and knocked unconscious, Mackenzie's mouth fell open. "No, *Jade,*" he cried. He spun around to confront Tucker, who stepped back, but the barrel of the gun remained firm, pillowing into the doctor's soft belly. Mackenzie's face reddened, became a mask of exasperated fury.

"If she—"

"She's alive," said Tucker, barely looking at the girl on the ground.

Will checked, and she was, but her pulse felt faint, although he was no expert.

Scowling and turning towards Will, Tucker snarled, "Your coat—?"

"Was the least I could do," finished Will, meeting his scowl, and that's how they stood for several seconds, eyes locked, the night air charged between them.

Finally, Tucker turned back to the doctor and said, "The quicker we get this over with, the quicker your friend gets help."

Mackenzie stared at Tucker with deep contemplation. Will could see the cogs of an intelligent mind working behind his eyes. After another long second, the doctor turned and walked towards the building.

The laboratory was one of three converted outbuildings. All were one storey, narrow, and crudely rendered in white. The door was PVC but solid.

"Open it," said Tucker.

Fumbling, Mackenzie rattled through the keys, searching for the right one, his eyes wavering momentarily back towards the girl. *Jade,* thought Will. He could almost still feel her gentle pulse on the ends of his fingers.

"Door," barked Tucker, reminding the doctor of his task.

Mackenzie placed the key in the lock and opened the door. He stepped into the darkness with Tucker following closely behind.

"Lights," ordered Tucker.

Inside, Mackenzie pawed clumsily at the wall, searching for the switch, tripping over some unseen clutter as he did. When the light came on, Will squinted against its fluorescence. The doctor's eyes blinked behind their little round spectacles, and Will was reminded of Mole in *Wind in the Willows.*

The lab was one long room: no windows, white walls, polished tiled floors. A stainless-steel worktop ran the length of the room. The worktop was cluttered with expensive-looking scientific equipment, including some Will couldn't identify. What he did recognise was two pairs of binocular microscopes, a plastic bin-shaped container he guessed was a centrifuge, and several laptops. A row of potted plants stood under ultraviolet light. The room smelled of chlorine.

"Fridges?" said Tucker, pointing to a row of three at the far end of the room.

The doctor nodded.

Tucker walked to the first fridge; it, like the neighbouring two, was sealed with a push-button electronic lock.

"Open them," said Tucker, lifting the gun to the doctor's eye line.

"And what if I do? What if I open every damn fridge, and you don't find what you're looking for?"

Tucker prodded Mackenzie's forehead with the gun.

Turning towards the first six-foot-tall fridge, the doctor punched a four-digit code into a security panel before pulling the door open.

The fridge was packed full of glass vials, test tubes, and stacks of petri dishes. Tucker barged the doctor aside and tore into the fridge like a lion into the belly of its kill. Wild-eyed, he searched, checking every label. Glass smashed, and boxes of supplies were tossed to the floor. Unsatisfied, he ordered the doctor to open the other two fridges. When the entire frenzied search was finished, he had still not found the specimen.

Tucker grabbed the doctor by his collar and slammed him against the last fridge, which rocked, tumbling more of its contents onto the hard floor. "Where is it?" he shouted, his face contorted, his feet trampling on a plastic dish, which split underfoot. "The God Whisperer?"

"I have told you—"

"Oh yeah, then we'll tear this whole forgotten shithole apart until I find it."

Mackenzie looked like he was struggling to breathe in the vice of Tucker's grip. At last Tucker eased the pressure, allowing the doctor to catch his breath.

Tucker stepped back, an insane grin splitting his face in two. "How old is that girl, your friend, outside, the one bleeding to death?"

"You bastard."

"My guess—twenty-seven?"

"If anything happens—"

Tucker slapped a hand over the older man's mouth and rolled his eyes upwards in a pantomime expression. He removed his hand, rubbed it on his jeans. "No, I guessed twenty-seven because of the white coat. It makes her look older. Don't you think? Whatever you're doing here, I'm guessing you need a PHD—*right*, Elliot?"

Tucker, still holding the gun, nonchalantly scratched his head, sarcastically miming deep thought. "Do you know what? I'd say twenty-four if it wasn't for the coat. *Christ*, Elliot, she's young enough to be your fucking granddaughter, yet you're going to let her bleed to death, out in the fucking cold, like a pig."

Tucker's brief parody of feigned contemplation had given way to his fraying temper. His skin was flushed, his rage close to the surface.

The doctor blinked again, lightly shaking his head as if the situation had descended into hopelessness.

Tucker jammed the gun into the man's temple. "Okay, you have three seconds to tell me where to find the magic mushroom, fat boy. If you've not told me, I'm going to blow your prized asset out of your head."

"I've told you—"

"One."

"It's not what—"

"Two."

"If it's money—"

Tucker's finger slowly applied pressure to the trigger.

"Okay," said the doctor. "*Okay*."

Tucker widened his eyes in mock anticipation.

The doctor said, "What do you think it is we've got here, some kind of cure for cancer?"

Tucker pressed the gun harder against the doctor's head. "Nice knowing you—"

Will hit Tucker a split second before the gun went off, knocking his aim askew and the bullet astray—it thudded into the ceiling above the doctor's head.

Possessed by rabid anger, Tucker turned on Will, spinning around with the weapon, but Will was quicker and knocked the gun from his grip. The weapon skidded across the polished floor and came to rest some five feet away against the base of the worktop.

The two men wrestled and fell to the ground, fighting amongst broken glass and the contents from the fridges. Tucker's breath was hot, sulphurous, tinged with cigarettes. The big man was trying to throttle him, pressing his thick thumbs into the base of his windpipe. Will's vision greyed out. So, this was it. The last thing he'd see in his brief existence was Tucker's grimacing face as he squeezed the life out of him.

No.

His fingers numb, Will fumbled on the ground and felt something sharp. He picked up the glass shard. His arms possessed the strength of a poorly stuffed scarecrow, but it was enough. He stabbed Tucker in his thigh. The hands that clasped his neck let go. Head spinning, Will gasped, then gulped at the medicinally tinged air of the lab, his throat burning.

Will dived and grabbed the gun before Tucker could recover. He spun around with the pistol as Tucker fell upon him, his hands impossibly large and reaching again for Will's throat.

But now it was Will who had the gun. He pressed the barrel against Tucker's stout neck, dimpling the skin. He put pressure on the trigger, and Tucker backed away.

Using his last reserve of strength, Will kicked Tucker's legs from under him, striking him behind the knees, and Tucker fell to the ground.

Will panted in recovery.

On his back amongst the glinting glass, Tucker said, "You're going to mess this whole thing up."

"You nearly killed me." Will leaned against the worktop. It was then, still gasping, that he noticed the doctor edging along the wall towards the door.

"*Stop*," Will shouted. "Or I'll shoot the fucking pair of you."

The doctor was five feet from the door. Tucker was attempting to push his considerable weight from the floor by his palms when the expression on his face changed. He was now patting the ground excitedly with his bleeding palms, ignoring the glistening splinters of glass.

Tucker had found a substantial ridge in the floor. Will met the doctor's eyes. Mackenzie's wrinkled face was a map of defeat, all at once resigned to them finding whatever it was he'd protected so virtuously.

Tucker was hoisting up a section of the floor—a hatch. When the trapdoor was wide enough, Tucker picked up his torch, which had fallen out of his pocket during the fight. He first pointed the beam at the doctor in the lit laboratory, then jerked it towards the darkness below, motioning for Mackenzie to descend the ladder.

The doctor went first. Still holding the gun, Will went next, so he wouldn't have to turn his back on Tucker. As far as Tucker was concerned, though, the fight was forgotten. He seemed preoccupied only with his discovery.

They found themselves standing in a small room, nine feet square. It was dark but for a blinking security light on the wall next to a heavy looking grey door. Will understood the device and its light belonged to a retina scanner.

Tucker inspected the scanner. "Can you open that?"

The doctor nodded dourly. "I can. But we can't go in there."

"We fucking can, you know," said Tucker.

"Hang on," said Will. He turned towards the doctor. "What exactly *are* you doing out here?"

Despondency darkened the older man's face. He sighed. "Take my word—"

"*Explain*," said Will. This time he was pointing the gun. He had no intention of shooting anyone, but he had to take back some element of control. He sensed the doctor had already accepted defeat.

"You've noticed the toadstools?" said the doctor. "Out there?"

"I'm not blind. But they're not what we've come for, are they?" said Will.

"No."

"The God Whisperer, it's behind that door, isn't it?" said Will.

The doctor frowned. "You need to understand what you're dealing with."

Jess' face flashed in Will's mind. "You've got one minute to tell us."

"The flora in these parts is diverse," said the doctor. "The toadstools you see here are unusual. But the fungi you seek, The God Whisperer, is only found beneath the surface of the soil."

"Just open the fucking door, will you?" said Tucker impatiently.

"Let him finish."

Tucker eyed the gun in Will's hand and scowled.

"Have you heard the term mycorrhizal fungi?" said the doctor.

Tucker fidgeted. "We've not come here for a fucking biology lesson—"

"*Shut up*," said Will.

"In any ecosystem, fungi can be both parasitic and beneficial to other species and plants. Fungi are mostly made up of thin threads, known as mycelium. These threads colonise the roots of plants. But the mycelium doesn't necessarily harm the plants. Instead, often the relationship is symbiotic. The plants and fungus exchange water, nutrients, and sugars."

Tucker blurted, "We need to get the specimen and get the hell out of here before—"

"Go on," said Will, ignoring him, prompting the scientist.

"The fungus forms filaments at the root," Mackenzie continued, "extending the plants' reach and creating an underground network, connecting every plant, tree, and fungi in a radius of miles."

"*And?*" said Will.

"And we believe the local flora is sharing a lot more than nutrients."

"*Meaning*?"

"The God Whisperer's mycelium is supercharged. Science has long speculated that plants share information, a superhighway like the internet, using highly sophisticated electrochemical communication."

"Bollocks," said Tucker.

"*True*," said the doctor. "Experiments have already proved plants activate chemical defences before an aphid attack. Plants connected by fungal mycelium respond when unconnected plants do not. The God Whisperer has colonised this whole area. Haven't you heard it, the land talking, *the whispering*?"

"You're talking shit," said Tucker.

"*There's more*," said the doctor urgently. "We've lost men...and women. If you choose to force your way into that room...unequipped, the consequences—"

"Tell him to open the fucking door, Will."

"So what is it, some kind of pathogen?" said Will. "Fungal spores or—?"

"No," said the doctor. "The fungus has communication...*abilities* well beyond our understanding. The plants, they're connected, and, as natural organisms, so are we."

"What do you mean?" said Will.

The doctor's eyes glistened in the beam of Tucker's torch. "The human brain, the command centre of our very being, the organ responsible for coordinating every sense, emotion, movement, every cognitive thought, is...vulnerable to this fungus in ways we don't understand."

Will's impatience flared, and he grabbed the doctor by the shoulder. "What do you mean?" he repeated. They were face to face, near enough that Will could see beads of sweat on the man's forehead, could smell the sour tinge of his breath. "Tell me," he said, pushing the other man back against the wall.

"Our minds—they're not what we once thought. Science has taught us cerebral function is the result of evolution, over thousands of millennia. But that's not all, not the half of it. Our minds exist far beyond the boundaries of our cranial cavity, far, far beyond." A pause. "We've been running a series of experiments...with the fungus."

Will frowned. "And?"

"*And* we've discovered something incredible. The brain is more than man's faculty of thought. Outside science, there is a transcendent belief we exist beyond the neurological limitations of our human condition—the question of what we are."

"And what *are* we?" said Will.

"*A radio.* The mind is a radio. Everything is connected. *Everything.* Like machines, our minds are electrical. Our minds are radios capable of transmitting thought, emotion, feelings, and so much more. But radios work two ways. Beyond that door is a transmitter too powerful to comprehend, and right now, the volume is turned up loud and the station tuned to Hell. If you go in there—"

The old man's eyes widened into saucers. Then Will felt a sharp blast of pain in the back of his skull, and he hit the floor. The last thing he saw was Tucker, holding the torch he had bludgeoned him with.

FROM THE DARK RECESSES OF UNCONSCIOUSNESS, WILL HEARD AN ALARM. Slowly he opened his eyes, but his head throbbed, the alarm and its infernal bleat drilling into his ears.

The gun was gone, the grey door ajar, the two other men nowhere to be seen.

Will sat up. He was in danger. Tucker and he were no longer allies. The thug might have killed him with that blow to his head.

He remembered the young woman Tucker had shot. By now she was probably dead, had likely bled out in the cold, like a pig, as Tucker had so eloquently put it. His sister too would be dead. Because without this job, America was impossible.

Movement beyond the door caught his eye. A blue-siren light strobed cyclically, hurting his eyes.

Will stood on shaky legs, holding the wall for balance. When he'd steadied himself enough, he kicked open the door and saw the room and every terrible detail.

Lit in the swirl of blue light, it was the size of a basketball court. The walls, floor, and ceiling were insulated with panels that looked like tough black rubber. But the rubber had been penetrated everywhere by thick, interlacing roots that joined in an entwined mass at the room's centre.

The mass was contained in a glass tank the size of a telephone box and mounted on a steel platform. The invasive roots were wrapped around the tank and had caused its glass panels to crack. The chamber was thick with spores that clouded the air like gigantic dust motes.

Will had no doubt he'd found what they were looking for.

The God Whisperer.

The thing was wrapped in a nest of bone-like growths. Its shape was too indistinct to be described as humanoid, but its trailing mycelium fell away from a vegetative mass, resembling legs. If the thing had a head, it was the grotesque flower that bloomed at its crown.

To Will's left, the doctor lay dead, a hole in the centre of his bald head, just as Tucker had promised.

Tucker himself stood before the glass tank. Where his eyes had been were two black holes. His dripping fingers suggested he'd torn them out himself. He stood in a blind, oblivious wonder. On the ground at his feet, next to the gun, were the jellied remains of his eyeballs.

Will stepped forward and picked up the weapon, fearing he needed protection. It was only then that he became aware of a clicking in his mind that was both random, nonsensical, and yet somehow more articulate than language.

But how could he hear anything whilst the alarm thrummed in his ears at such a deafening pitch?

Yet somehow, he knew, another much older sense had been stimulated, a more basic yet refined form of communication, an electrical impulse that all forms of life understood on a molecular level: microbes, viruses, bacteria, insects…human beings.

Will backed away from the tank and the thing inside.

Cracks spread in the glass as the thing sprouted its dreadful fruit, germinating more of its spores.

The spores hung in the air, drifting like thoughts.

Will's mind was filling with sadness. The clacking became unbearable. He thought of Jess and her girls. He thought of the cancer living inside her, the invader that could—*would*—now certainly kill her.

What a terrible world this was, a world where those beautiful girls would lose their mother.

The cracks in the glass tank spread, fracturing like Will's sanity.

Tucker rocked back and forth where he stood rooted to the spot, his hands still dripping with blood.

The siren's light swirled.

Will turned and ran out of the room. He scrambled back up the ladder, missing a rung and scraping his shins.

It spoke to him in the darkest recesses of his mind. Its mycelium had not penetrated the shell of his skull, yet the thing occupied his thoughts all the same, and it knew where his fear and his guilt resided. It told him things.

Jess was going to die.

Will ran into the frosted November night, back towards the Land Rover, forgetting Jones and everything they'd planned.

He reached the vehicle, his breath rasping, and gunned the engine.

The Land Rover thundered along mountain roads. The vast starry sky glittered above, and he pressed the pedal to the floor, clattering through the gears and careering through the winding country lanes, wondering over the infinite possibilities of the thing in the tank.

He turned up the radio loud, attempting to drown the *sounds* that occupied his head. But the God Whisperer played his mind like an instrument, a flute filled with a column of air, the vibrations living in his bones, *talking* to him.

Will stopped the car at a layby on a country lane.

He regarded his tear-stained face in the rear-view mirror. He couldn't escape the God Whisperer. Its mycelium had spread too far.

Will picked up the gun from the passenger seat and stepped out into the cold air.

The night whispered in his veins.

He was part of it now, wasn't he?

He put the barrel in his mouth, tasted the cold metal, and listened to his infected mind talk.

"I'm sorry, Jess," he said, tears streaming from his eyes.

When he pulled the trigger, his thoughts flew free—together with the brains that spattered the frozen ground onto which his body now collapsed. His physical life had ended, but as his grey matter seeped into the soil, his mind went on, leaking into the network of roots, whispering under the cold and lonely stars.

THE FEVER AND
THE THAW

2018

Thirty-four years had passed since Dr. Tom Watkins had last seen the little girl. He was in his mid-sixties now but still remembered the face of the child he'd assumed was a figment of his imagination. Yet here she was again.

The floatplane was flying at low altitude, the glittering lake a shimmering mirror beneath them. When the plane finally touched down, its floats churning the calm water to foam, he looked to shore, and for a glancing second, through the landing spray, he saw the dark-haired little girl. She was wearing a white frock and skipping with a rope. Then the wing blocked his view, and by the time he could see the shore again, she had disappeared.

"So this reindeer disease, do they get it by fucking?" said the pilot, Roy, grinning beneath his thick white beard. "You know, I've always thought they were *horny* little bastards. The way they prance about, probably all queer. Do you get fag reindeer?"

Tom refused to let the incessant bigotry offend him. Throughout

the flight, he'd enjoyed the view, listened to the hypnotic hum of the
small plane as it cruised over the high and snowy peaks and tried to
ignore the pilot. Roy and his irritating questions were white noise,
nothing more.

Seeing the girl, though, had disturbed him deeply. Not since David
and that long-ago day in the park had he felt such a profound sense of
dread. In the cockpit glass, he saw his own dim reflection. His face
was ashen—although not as pale as he remembered David that last
time. That *final* time.

"Did you see her?"

"See who?"

"Little girl, over there?" he said, pointing to the shore.

"You been smoking something?" said Roy, smiling. "We're miles
from nowhere."

By the time the plane neared the beach, though, Tom had put the
sighting down to him being tired and overworked. That's all it was—a
waking nightmare brought on by lack of sleep and travel. *Time to
retire.* After all, what would a little girl be doing out here, alone in the
Alaskan wilderness—skipping, for crying out loud?

Exiting the plane, Tom climbed barefoot onto the amphibious float
and lowered himself onto a rock formation that jutted from the lake's
shore. When the lake was shallow enough, he stepped into the ice-cold
water and walked with tentative steps to the shale beach with his
trainers hung around his neck. On reaching land, he put on his
Sketchers and crouched beside the dead reindeer. It was the first of a
herd of carcasses, lying beside the silver lake that mirrored the white-
capped peaks.

"How many?" said Roy, shouting from the plane over the chugging propeller.

Tom wiped sweat from his brow. "Guessing hundreds."

The sky was clear, and the sun beat down on the dead caribou
herd. Their legs splayed, their many antlers a forest of bone, the dead
animals lay on the barren carpet of sub-Arctic tundra. Apart from the
few remaining glaciers atop the distant Ahklun Mountains, there was

no snow and ice here. It was summer—and a fucking hot one for this far north. Flies swarmed, feeding on the rotting flesh seeping into the brown, lichen-covered ground.

"Shouldn't we be wearing masks?" said Roy, who had now left the plane and was standing at the lake's shore, squinting against the sun.

Tom nodded but thought *suits*—they should be wearing biological suits. He'd made a mistake coming here so ill-prepared. He'd been anxious to follow the ranger's tip and hadn't expected to find what they had.

The scene resembled a massacre.

"Well, don't expect me to come any closer," said the pilot. "Not paid enough for that shit."

Who was? Tom didn't think he was paid enough to listen to any more jokes about "fags" or black people, either. But he'd needed a pilot, and out here, in the lowlands of the Togiak National Wildlife Refuge, even Hicksville was a long way away, never mind San Francisco. Pilots were hard to find, and while he was perhaps five years younger than the charming Roy, he was also too long in the tooth to be bothered teaching the old dog manners.

His handset buzzed in his pocket. Still squatting, he checked—a message from Shaun: *Counting the days till you're home x*

Roy was twenty feet away, but Tom shielded his phone, something he hadn't done in a long time. He resented the pilot for that, for forcing him to hide who he was, but he did it anyway and typed a kiss in reply. He thought he was here for the long haul. California *was* a long way, and the CDC—the Centres for Disease Control and Prevention—had sent him here with a clear directive: find out what was killing the reindeer.

Roy swiped at the flies, then piped up: "So what is it? That CWC thing you told me abo—"

"CWD," corrected Tom automatically.

Chronic wasting disease was endemic in deer species in large areas of North America. It was caused by misfolded proteins called prions that infected up to forty percent of some herds.

"Then *is it*?"

"No, this is…something else."

A warm breeze ruffled the grey/brown fur of the dead reindeer beneath him, carrying the rancid stench of death. The carcass was bloated with the gases of decomposition. The reindeer's tongue lolled from its open mouth. Then the eye twitched. Tom flinched, then saw the eye was infested with maggots. The tiny white larvae were squirming under the membrane and preparing for pupation.

"How do you know?"

Tom heard Roy's voice, but his mind was distant. It was working as he surveyed the scene, trying to fathom what this could be.

"Hey, you listening? How do you know?"

Tom turned to Roy, hearing genuine fear in the old hick's voice.

"That it's not CWD, you mean?"

"Yeah."

"Too sudden. Looks like an outbreak rather than an endemic pathogen."

"Endem—?"

"*Endemic* disease doesn't wipe out entire herds; it tends to maintain a baseline infection rate in a population. CWD is present in urine, in shit, even in antler velvet, so when the animals decompose, the scavengers carry it—the birds spread it. It can infect huge geographical areas. We find it all the time in cattle trails from the Old West. But once it infects an environment, it's difficult to get rid of, and reservoirs of the disease can remain in the soil for years."

"But people *can't* catch it?"

"No," said Tom. "We don't think so."

Roy scowled distrustfully. "*Think*?"

"Similar to mad cow disease. There's research. But don't get too close. As I said, it's not CWD we ought to be worried about. These animals died much more suddenly."

"Lightning?"

Tom shook his head and looked at the hundreds of dead reindeer. "Too many."

Roy wiped his brow. "It's hot enough for a storm, though, hey?"

It was. Hotter than Tom thought it should be, even at this time of year.

"You know, they say the permafrost is melting," said Roy.

The ground beneath Tom's trainers felt boggy and soft, and he imagined the land sick under the blazing sun as if a fever was taking hold. *A thaw.*

He knew that influenza A viruses could spread between species. He had heard stories of American soldiers stationed in Alaska during the great Spanish Flu pandemic of 1918. The CDC had recovered and stored fragments of viral RNA from the lung tissue of soldiers buried and preserved in the Alaskan permafrost. There were other stories too. Other pathogens. Smallpox. Bubonic plague. Who knew what else? Vectors of killer infections sleeping in the ice.

"I read about reindeer in Siberia, infected with some Russian zombie shit," said Roy, "spores or something, released from the melting permafrost. They called it reindeer zombie virus. Killed thousands—and a young boy too."

"Anthrax."

"Huh?"

"It was Anthrax—not a virus. Contaminated soil."

"Right," said Roy, lighting a hand-rolled cigarette and frowning. "You think this could be something like that? I wouldn't put anything past those Russian—"

Before Tom could answer, he heard the rustle of a plastic sheet in the wind. Thirty feet away, ignoring their presence, a long-haired, broad-shouldered man wearing a plaid shirt was dragging a large reindeer by the antlers.

"Hey, stop," shouted Tom, waving his arms in frantic protest. But the man continued to drag the carcass across the ground towards a plastic sheet. "Excuse me. Please, don't touch these animals."

He ran towards the man, and when he reached him, he found him crouched beside the reindeer, trying to free its body from an obstructing rock. The stranger looked up with narrowed eyes.

"You can't touch these animals," said Tom, out of breath and trying to sound reasonable.

The man took a long time to regard him with his dark eyes. He was dark skinned too—native, but when he finally spoke, he had an American accent. "Who says?"

"These reindeer, they are likely contaminated with a pathogen. We don't know it's safe." Tom saw the man had spread out a large sheet of blue tarpaulin on the ground. A quad bike was parked twenty-five feet away. "You're not planning to eat—?"

The man remained silent but suddenly stood, towering over him. Tom was a hair's breadth under six foot, but this man was six inches taller, at least, and broad. *God, he was big.*

"The meat will be rotten."

Still the man said nothing, but simply stood his ground, his long hair blowing in the breeze, his narrow eyes brimming with quiet rage —the promise of violence, brewing like a summer storm. Above, an eagle soared, scouting for prey. Or was it a vulture, looking for carrion?

"This meat is rotten," Tom said again.

"Some of it. My people have been hunting caribou for centuries. You can trust I know what I'm doing. But thanks for your concern."

"Look, I'm sorry. But I can't let you touch these animals."

"Under whose authority?"

"Federal law," said Tom. He had no such power, but the ID card he produced embossed with the letters CDC captured the man's attention. It was a white lie. And he felt a strange sense of shame for his presence here, in this vast wilderness, holding an ID card featuring his Caucasian mug shot. But he knew there was a greater good to consider. And the lie was immaterial because within hours he would ensure public health authorities were informed and a quarantine order was in place for the whole area.

"These parts, we abide by tribal law."

The man was testing him, he knew. He was also still studying the ID card that Tom was holding before him. Then his expression changed as quickly as a break in the clouds, and his furrowed brow relaxed. "You're a doctor?" he said.

Tom nodded.

"My sister, she has a sick child."

"I can't leave this—"

"You're a doctor. You can help."

"I don't have med—"

The man's arm shot out and gripped his wrist like a vice. "We've been waiting for a doctor. No one can come till tomorrow or the day after. My niece—she's coughing blood. She's thirteen." His eyes were wider now, pleading.

Above, the bird of prey circled, its shadow falling over one reindeer carcass and then another. Tom wanted to remain at the site and wait for backup. But what was he supposed to do, chase off wildlife with a stick? What if a pack of wolves arrived, or a fucking bear?

The grip on his wrist tightened.

"Please, *doctor*."

His medical degree and his time in Cambridge now seemed like ancient history. It was over thirty-five years since he'd transferred to the University of California, and then he'd gone on to San Francisco where he'd pursued a career in pathology. He'd specialised in virology. And The Golden State's liberalism had offered Tom more than a thriving career; it had released him from small-minded prejudice—or at least more so than back home in England, where Thatcher's government had enacted legislation that not only legitimised discrimination but instilled it in the narrow minds of colleagues, friends, family...*parents*.

America had offered him an escape. America had given him freedom.

"Hey, don't take no shit from a fucking injun," bellowed Roy from back beside the plane.

The big man let go of his wrist and took two steps forward, nudging Tom out of his way.

"I'm Yupik," growled the man. "Not Indian." He stood with a grimace etched into his majestic, almost regal features.

"Eskimo, Indian, same fucking difference," said Roy, smoking. "All a bunch of alcoholic freeloaders, far as I'm concerned."

A vein at the big man's temple pulsed.

Out here, far from civilisation, goading such a man was a bad idea. Tom looked at the cloud of flies swarming by the lake, saw a ripple in the water as fish fed at the surface, saw the eagle soaring above, saw Roy smoking, his face almost amused that he had riled this stranger.

Who was he kidding? These animals had been dead for days. If the pathogen, or whatever it was, had got into the environment, what could he do?

"I'll take a look at your niece," Tom said, distracting the man from Roy. "As long as you agree to leave that animal here. But first I need to make a call."

The man nodded and said, "Your friend needs to watch his mouth. Name's Nukilik."

"Pleased to meet you, Nukilik. I'm sorry about him."

Nukilik nodded.

Tom made the call.

The village was on the coast, two or three miles away.

Tom was now riding on the back of the quad bike, having left Roy with the plane. He and Nukilik sped over uneven ground, through barren lands beneath the boundless blue sky, the quad lurching and juddering. He'd felt sick for most of the short journey and had already decided he'd walk back to the plane, bears or no bears.

They ascended a small grassy hill and joined a dusty, gravelled track on the far side. The village was maybe one hundred and fifty feet from the roaring ocean. Clusters of wooden shacks were raised above the ground on stilts amongst a maze of boardwalks, grounded rowboats, and powerlines. Archaic-looking, over-sized satellite dishes were mounted on the side of every home. Feral-looking dogs wandered and barked; a ragamuffin boy pulled another smaller, mucky-cheeked child along in a small wooden cart; monstrous-sized bones that Tom guessed to be whale ribs leaned against the side of a house. A little girl spun around, holding her skipping rope at one end so the other end whirled, and two bigger girls jumped and kicked up dust at the outer circumference of their play. He'd seen the game before, heard the song sung in cities and towns and now a village in the middle of the back of beyond.

Helicopter, helicopter, please come down, they sang, jumping and jumping.

While he'd never seen *these* children before, the recent memory of the girl by the lake returned to him as their voices chimed in unison.

"We're here," said Nukilik, killing the engine and pulling up beside a small wooden house with faded, peeling red paint. He dismounted the quad and climbed a short set of wooden steps to the front door.

Tom followed, glad to be off the bike and away from the masculine reek of leathery sweat, but inside the dusky house, the smell was worse.

The wooden-panelled room served both as a kitchen and lounge and was cluttered with the family's belongings—coats piled on chairs, untidy laundry heaped on a battered couch, a table uncleared of plates. An old analogue TV was turned off but reflected the dim light from the half-drawn curtains.

A pot filled with a brown, oniony broth boiled on the kitchen hob next to a plate of flatbread, but the smell wasn't enough to disguise the putrid stench of old sweat and sickness that saturated the itchy-looking blankets wrapped around the shivering girl. She lay on a bed at the far end of the room, her brow damp, her eyes fluttering. She was gasping for every breath.

"This man is here to help," said Nukilik to the woman who sat on the bed beside the girl. "He's a doctor."

Tears sprang in the woman's eyes. Tom guessed she was no older than forty, but her features were haggard and weatherworn.

"Oh, thank you, thank you," she said, tears running down her sallow cheeks.

As Tom approached the bed, he noticed two younger, grubby-faced children, sitting on the floor and playing with a bucket of Lego: a girl aged about six and a boy of eight or nine, building a castle. Each looked up at him with haunted expressions. The boy coughed into his clenched fist.

Tom smiled at the kids reassuringly and stepped around the electric heater that had hidden them from him. The size of a washing machine, the heater reminded him that winter was more than a seasonal inconvenience here.

He crouched before the bed and, without wearing gloves, rested the back of his hand on the girl's forehead. She was burning hot.

"How long has she been like this?"

"Three or four days," said Nukilik's sister. "She's been unwell longer."

"Is she drinking?"

"Small amounts, but she is sick." The woman gestured towards a vomit-filled bucket on the floor beside the bed. The contents were speckled with blood.

"I need to see her skin, her body, to check for rashes."

The woman nodded and peeled the sheets from the girl; she hardly appeared to notice but shivered more violently as her skin was exposed to the air.

Tom saw the rash at once. He searched the room, found what he was looking for, and took the empty glass ashtray from the table. Gently he pressed the glass against the pin-pricked spots on the girl's back; through the glass, the spots remained: the rash was petechial, the girl probably suffering from septicaemia. As he lifted the ashtray from her skin, the girl opened her eyes and gasped, and he saw that death was close. He knew this, and he feared that she knew it now, too, because she'd seen the look in his eyes.

"She needs to go to the hospital—now."

The mother buried her face in her hands and wept.

"I'll arrange for a helicopter," said Tom. "But I need to know: have you been eating the caribou?"

The woman's eyes fell upon the broth that boiled on the stove. The boy coughed again, and the woman sobbed so hysterically she was unable to speak.

Tom marched urgently across the room, past shelves cluttered with smiling family photos, and reached the door, craving the fresh-if-too-warm Alaskan air. When he descended the steps outside, he took several deep breaths, then took out his iPhone and dialled.

The phone took an age to connect. While listening for the ringtone, he watched the girl skipping on the dusty road, the two older girls now turning the rope at either end in steady loops. The girl—the smallest of the three—jumped in the middle with her back to him. The quiet melody of the girls' voices as they chanted their jump-rope rhymes was little more than a quiet hum under the thundering crash of the ocean.

Remembering those squirming maggots in the reindeer's eye and the fermenting stench of death, he was afraid of what he might have uncovered here in the south-western Alaskan wilderness. He recalled Roy's words.

You know, they say the permafrost is melting.

The rope whirled around and around, and the skipping girl turned as she hopped. Tom held his phone tight against his ear, willing it to connect so he could redeem himself and save the girl inside the house who would otherwise die.

The little girl turned to face him as she skipped. And suddenly he realised that he *did* know her. He knew her from a long time ago. At first he thought her nose was bleeding, but then he realised that the blood was black, not red, and that what he was really seeing were flies. Fat and glistening, they crawled from the girl's nose, mouth, ears, and eyes. Her face swarmed with insects, and through them, she grinned.

Tom felt faint. The world spun. He staggered, then fell, waiting to hear the crack of his skull on the hard, dusty ground, but it never came. Instead he fell into a void where years passed in seconds. He fell through time as easily as the cold snow falls in winter, a season he relished now, anything but that feverish sun.

And suddenly there he was. Thirty-four years before.

He sat, waiting on a park bench, looking over San Francisco Bay where David had suggested they meet, the famous Golden Gate Bridge on the horizon. In the foreground, before the bay, Tom watched a little girl on a swing at the centre of a playground. She smiled at him, her long, dark hair falling over her eyes as she swung, her feet pointed and reaching for the sky.

Then all at once David was there, as if he'd simply appeared from nowhere.

"I'm dying," he said.

Tom stared up from the bench at the ghoul standing before him. Even under the thick trench coat, he could see David was thin, his legs narrow as broomsticks, his gaunt face carved from bone. David's lips were split and covered in sores, his eyes burrowed in stretched, bruised-looking skin. Tom's mind skittered like a VHS tape rewinding. And he found the memory: dark room, soft sheets, cool skin.

Two years ago.

"But we—"

David nodded. "I'm sorry."

The park was a riot of play. The playground cacophony filled the summer air like a dawn chorus. Children ran and danced and shouted. A bothersome fly buzzed relentlessly about his face. Somewhere, a dog barked. A basketball thumped against concrete. A skipping rope whipped and whirled, and three little girls skipped and jumped, as the sun dappled on the bay like diamonds beneath the lemony northern Californian sky.

Yet Tom felt locked in darkness. Every second was too long and terrible to comprehend, every word that David uttered from his festering lips indigestible.

The little girls skipped and sang:
Cinderella, dressed in yella,
Went upstairs to kiss her fella
Made a mistake
And kissed a snake
How many doctors
Did it take?
1, 2, 3, 4, 5…

"Are you sure?" said Tom finally.

David's face was a grim mask. He nodded again.

Nearby, a picnicking gang of college kids turned on their boombox: Frankie sang "Relax", which was not easy when the city was caught in the grip of a deadly epidemic where young gay men were dropping like flies.

"When did you—?"

David shrugged. "Not sure, exactly. I got sick."

Tom still stared at David, but now David averted his gaze.

"How long have you—?"

At the unfinished question, David's bloodshot eyes flickered to regard him again. His existence seemed as brittle as cracked glass. He said, "You should get yourself—"

"I feel fine—okay."

David nodded. "Well, I wanted to tell you in person."

The little girl on the swing soared to the heavens. To and fro, she swung higher and higher, the bridge behind her shrouded in a wisp of cloud.

Tom stood and took David into his arms and hugged him because he pitied him and because *he* needed to be held. As he did, two butch-looking jocks approached, tossing a football between them.

"Get a room, fags," said the nearest.

"Don't do that shit in front of kids," said the other. "Not fucking right."

Tom toyed with the idea of giving the two men the finger but then thought better of it. He was still holding David. The man's body felt as light and delicate as a child's, all bones and angles. He thought of the infection in the other man's veins, could almost hear it swimming in his bloodstream, calling for him too: *Tom. Tom. Tom.*

He pulled away from their embrace to look in David's eyes. "I'll be in touch."

"No, Tom. This is goodbye."

Then David walked away along the path. Tom stared straight ahead at the space that David had vacated, towards the bay and the little girl on the swing. Up she went into the sky, a pendulum rising, the rusted chains groaning. When she was at the highest point of her arc, she became a black shape against the sun, and when she fell back down to earth, she drew his eyes again to the three girls skipping. They sang the same words, over and over.

I had a little bird
Its name was Enza
I opened the window
And in-flu-enza

Then their verse became lost in the insectile buzz of flies. That bothersome one had become many, and they were suddenly everywhere. The smallest girl was laughing, but her face was a mask of fat bluebottles, a living infestation that glistened under the hot sun.

WHEN TOM OPENED HIS EYES, HE SAW HE WAS SITTING ON THE DUSTY street, in Alaska, in 2018. The three little Eskimo girls from the dusty road were crowded around him.

"Are you okay, mister? You fell down."

Except he hadn't. Not back in 1984, anyway. He had been tested and was clear. Miraculously he'd been clear. He'd dedicated his whole life to helping people, people like David, and the girl who gasped for breath in her humble wooden home; people like those bleeding from every orifice in a baking-hot shack in Sierra Leone; people who had been infected with SARS, despite their hand sanitiser and surgical masks; people in remotest Peru who died sweating and vomiting, fighting some zoonotic bacteria; thousands of people who, still, in 2018, died of bubonic infections that raged in their lymphatic systems like the black death of fourteenth-century Europe. He needed to understand disease, to know it, to name it, to fight it, to make sense of it.

Nukilik was at his side. "What happened? You okay?"

Tom nodded and saw his iPhone in the dirt. Even from five feet away, he could hear the call handler, her voice tinny and small.

"Hello, hello—is anybody there? I'm going to hang up bec—"

Crawling through the dust, Tom reached the phone. "This is Dr. Tom Watkins. We have a situation up here in Alaska." He was panting, struggling to speak. "Suspected anthrax. Hundreds at risk, but it could be something else, something worse." He thought of dead soldiers buried in the melting Alaskan permafrost, the Spanish Flu frozen in their perished lungs, waiting to thaw. "We have a sick girl."

The three little girls watched him wide-eyed, the smallest swatting at the warm Alaskan air and the fly that buzzed about her face.

MADE IN HELL

1.

F rank D'Angelo hangs upside down in the dark hotel room, eyes focused on the door.

The neon blush of downtown Miami glows faintly from between the Venetian blinds. In the neighbouring room, the headboard thumps, and Frank can hear the thick beat of two hearts hammering towards climax; he can hear every ragged breath. He can hear somewhere, too, a cockroach scuttling for cover; the chink of glasses on the ground-floor bar far below; the distant hum of an ascending elevator.

His heightened senses are tuned to every whisper, scent, *thought*, every rhythmic dilation of a human pulse contained within the high-rise.

The elevator's mechanical doors ping and swish, birthing a rabble of noisy drunks into the corridor maze of the third floor. *His* floor. He inhales greedily, tasting the vaporised currents from the air-conditioning vent: Perfumed skin. Gin-tinged breath. Sweat. It is intox-icating.

He's waited thirty years to kill the old man who will soon emerge from the corridor; he can wait thirty more. Time matters little now. Because back in the void, eternity has its own doors, and Hell is as close as the stifling Florida heat.

The fabric of existence is thin, indeed, like the papery skin of the elderly.

He extends his claws.

The lift's former occupants pass the room by, their echoing voices fading as they trail away along the corridor, searching for another numbered room.

Roosting, one hundred and fifty feet above the city streets, Frank D'Angelo closes his eyes and remembers the faceless boy, remembers Tony La Rosa—the old man he's come to kill—and remembers the life he once lived.

He waits, knowing another familiar name will soon be inked on the scabrous surface of his skin.

2.

17 AUGUST 1991

"SO THE PRICK ASKS ME FOR ANOTHER WEEK," SAID TONY, SNORTING MORE cocaine from the tip of his bandaged index finger. "Kike motherfucker refused to pay."

Frank drove the silver Dodge. Tony told his story from the passenger side whilst Jimmy Pileggi snickered, hanging on his every word from the backseat. All three men wore crinkled suits and loos-ened ties, their faces roughened by two-day stubble.

"What you do?" asked Jimmy.

"What did I do? What do you think I did?" said Tony. "I put his head right through his fuckin' till—that's what. Ka-ching, mother-fucker. The customers, you should've seen their fuckin' faces."

Tony and Jimmy burst into another bout of unrestrained laughter. "Customers? You went when he was open?" said Jimmy, lighting another cigarette.

"He's a Jew. He's always open. Anyway, I said, Jacob, you know the deal. You can sell all the bagels you want, but you don't pay, we can't offer no protection."

"He paid?" said Jimmy.

"Course. Gave the tight-assed fuck a free nose job too."

More laughter.

"Is that how you got the Band-Aid?" said Jimmy. "Trapped it in the Jew's till?"

"No, his kid bit me, ballsy little shit."

"You beat him in front of his *kid*?" said Frank.

"*Kids*," corrected Tony.

"Jesus. Come on, man," said Frank.

"Hey, the kids learned a valuable life lesson."

Frank scowled. "And what was that?"

"Don't fuck with Tony La Rosa."

Jimmy laughed.

"You need to drop the wise-guy routine," said Frank.

"Eh?"

"It's embarrassing," said Frank. "You're a fuckin' cliché. You know that?"

"Bada-bing."

"I'm serious."

"Fuck you."

The car sped west.

Frank's bloodshot eyes bulged in the rear-view mirror. The car reeked of male sweat and cigarettes. In the last twenty-four hours, he'd slept for just three on the car's backseat when they'd rotated drivers.

They had left Brooklyn yesterday morning for a business trip to

Chicago's south side. Arriving late that evening, grouchy and dishevelled, they'd eaten at an associate's restaurant where they'd discussed a potential construction opportunity. But forty-five minutes and two glasses of Valpolicella into that meeting—after a twelve-hour straight drive—the waiter had interrupted their meal. They'd received a call: *Go. Drop everything. Drive.*

Sick of the sight and smell of each other, the three men were still chewing steak and mopping their chins when they got back in the car, but the order had come from the top. And Frank had been made a promise: *do this job, and you'll be made.* It was all he'd ever dreamed of —everything he'd worked towards for two decades. Names on planes, though, could be traced, so they drove—*again.*

The destination? Some hick college town in rural South Dakota. But if the town wasn't familiar, their target certainly was: Lorenzo Russo.

"Way he pinned that hit on Paolo, Russo has this coming," said Jimmy.

"Fucker knows enough to shut everything down," said Tony.

The cops had brought Russo in a year ago. It was a matter of time before they raided every crew member under the Marino family's control. Protection rackets, narcotics, illegal gambling, the pigs would get it all.

"He's cut a deal," said Tony. "Mark my words, Paolo won't be the only guy who gets pinched."

"Then what's taking so long?" said Jimmy. "How long does it take to build a case?"

"The more he's told them, the longer it'll take," said Tony. "But if the pussy thinks he can hide behind witness protection, he can think again." A warped grin spread across his pock-marked face.

Russo had a new name now: Charles Muller. But someone wanted him dead because his location and new identity had been leaked.

It was Saturday morning. Since leaving The Windy City, they'd crossed two state lines and were approaching the Minnesota/South Dakota border after passing the tiny town of Porter.

"Forty minutes," said Frank.

Tony loaded bullets into the cylinder of his revolver.

"We need to talk about his wife and kid," said Frank.

"Talk about what?" said Tony.

"We leave them out of this, okay?" said Frank.

In the backseat, Jimmy fed bullets into his pistol's magazine. Jimmy and Tony exchanged a wary glance in the rear-view mirror.

"I'm fuckin' serious," said Frank. "We go in, we get out. We do this clean."

Silence.

There were rules. You didn't kill a guy's wife and kids. Although special circumstances arose. The reality was, though, innocent people died all the time, and Lorenzo Russo was a rat, the lowest of the low.

"The kid and the wife stay out of this. Do we have a deal?" said Frank.

The other two men nodded. Both avoided his searching eyes in the rear-view mirror.

Frank sighed. "There's something I haven't told you," he said. "If we do this right, I'm going to be made."

Both Tony and Jimmy ceased playing with their weapons.

"No shit," said Tony.

"No shit," said Frank, fixing his gaze on the road ahead. The car's open windows allowed a ruffling breeze, but he felt the air stiffen, the silence grow.

Tony's blue eyes might have turned green; he had similar aspirations, and Frank knew the likelihood of both men being made was remote. It was one or the other. He guessed Tony knew that too.

Jimmy broke the silence. "We can't leave any witnesses, Frank," he said. "You know that, right?"

"Course I fuckin' know that," said Frank. "But we do this right. Okay?"

"Sure," said Jimmy.

They headed west along South Dakota's Highway 30, passing cornfields and the occasional dairy farm. A radio report interrupted

Bryan Adams. A storm was on the way—a possible tornado. All they needed.

At just before ten a.m., they reached their destination:

Brookings, SD. Population: 16,428

They cruised along the town's main street—a succession of low, flat-roofed red-brick convenience stores, sports bars, and sandwich shops. The roads were eerily quiet. Then they headed east and towards the leafier suburbs where Frank pulled over to check the map. The sky was clear, the morning sun already causing the hot air to shimmer above the baking asphalt.

"Can I help you gentleman?" asked the young woman, bending from the sidewalk to the car's passenger window.

Jimmy grinned at the view, acknowledging the cleavage that spilt from her pink halter-neck T-shirt.

"Are you guys lost?"

She was pretty, mid-twenties, and blonde. Everyone was. Every cyclist, jogger, and roadworker was either red-headed or fair-haired. The place epitomised small-town America where the dominant ancestry was clearly Scandinavian or German. The young woman smiled, chewing gum, the sun brightening her golden hair while she stared into the car occupied by the three dark-haired, olive-skinned Italians. None of the men had seen a shower in days. The New York licence plate, at least, was false, but that would attract unwanted attention too.

"We're just fine, lady," said Frank.

"If you're sure," she said. "You guys have a good day."

Tony gave the woman a lewd wink, and she walked on. But Frank noticed she glanced back over her shoulder.

"Every route out of this town is a long road to nowhere," said Frank. "Nothing but cornfields in every direction."

"Point being?" said Tony.

"Someone sees three suspicious wops out here and decides to call the local sheriff's office, there's no way out," said Frank.

They followed the map three blocks east, arriving at a small cul-desac of large wooden houses, built in the typical midwestern style with steep-gabled roofs and overhanging eaves. The pavement was well shaded by enormous elm trees. Of the seven homes on the street, three had American flags mounted on their immaculate lawns.

A small boy rode his BMX up and down the spotless pavement, narrowly avoiding a little dog. A mailman waved at an old lady who was standing on her doorstep with curlers in her hair. A floppy-haired teenager wearing a Guns N' Roses T-shirt skateboarded around the corner and out of view. So far nobody appeared to have noticed the car with the false plates.

"That one there," said Tony, holding the map, pointing to the largest house on the street. As if hearing his cue, a dark-haired woman walked out of the home's front door, followed by a boy aged about eleven.

"That's her. That's Maria, Russo's wife," said Tony.

"You sure?" said Frank.

Squinting, Tony watched the woman and boy get into a red Ford parked in the driveway. The car started, the engine little more than a gentle purr. He nodded. "She's cut her hair, but that's her. I went to the kid's christening. Must've been ten years ago."

"You went to that kid's *christening*?" said Frank.

Tony nodded. "Sure."

The red Ford pulled out of the shadow of the large house and into the glare of the midwestern sun. The woman—Maria—turned and waved back towards the direction of the house. The front door remained ajar. From the shadows behind the door, a hand returned the gesture, then disappeared. The door closed.

"He's in there," said Jimmy.

"We have to do this now," said Frank, watching the red car disappear down the street. The crucifix Frank wore around his neck glinted in the sun, flashing in the rear-view mirror.

The mailman got on his bike and rode away. The old lady patted her curlers and retreated into her home.

"It's broad fucking daylight. Are you out of your fucking mind?"

said Tony, pronouncing every syllable. "We stick to the plan. Scout the place now and return after dark."

"When the woman and kid will likely be back home," said Frank.

Tony scowled. "*And?*"

"And…we leave them out of this, *remember*?"

In the passenger seat, Tony wiped his palms on his knees and pinched the top of his nose. "*Frank…*"

"This is the only way," said Frank.

Jimmy made eyes at Tony, then Frank, his gaze settling on one man then the other. Finally, Tony nodded, conceding defeat but still holding the bridge of his nose as if warding off an aggressive migraine. "Okay," he said.

Russo's house had two adjoined garages. Both were empty—the doors open. Frank started the car and sailed soundlessly up the slight slope of the drive and into the shaded garage nearest the house.

Quietly the three men exited the vehicle, emerging into the cooler clime of the shaded air. Outside crickets chirped. A sprinkler fizzed on the neighbouring lawn. Nearby, children played, their distant voices innocent eruptions in the thick heat. Frank hit the switch to close the door, sealing them in near darkness.

There were two doors at the garage's far end on opposite walls: one leading to the second adjoined garage, and the second into the house. They took the second.

The three men had been here before, not in this town, not in this affluent midwestern home, but in the moment that preceded a hit. Frank's lips were suddenly dry, his knees weaker. But this was their line of work, and fifteen hundred miles away, in the shadow of Manhattan skyscrapers, cops fished bloated, crab-nibbled corpses from the sediment of the Hudson River, discovered bodies rotting under steel stairways amongst restaurant rubbish and rising sewer steam. Most often, though, remains were never found, except by the scavengers of the Catskill Mountains. Death was dealt in silent under-standing. The men understood each other unequivocally, without the need to speak. They communicated with a series of curt nods and eye gestures, moving through the house and its polished floors with deadly stealth.

Outside, a warm wind was picking up; it had arrived suddenly, the still of the day turning, whistling in the pipes.

Despite the house's spacious architecture and high ceilings, Frank rounded every corner with a deep feeling of claustrophobia, his heart thumping hard. His head throbbed. If the police were alerted, this was over. There was no escape from this Godforsaken blot amongst hundreds of miles of corn.

Guns poised, they reached an expansive kitchen with marble worktops where a newspaper lay strewn:

DEVIL-WORSHIPPING RAPIST SENTENCED TO DEATH, read the headline.

Murderer Murphy to face needle after guilty verdict

On the windowsill, in a silver frame, three ghostly faces smiled in a photograph. The picture was bleached white like a negative by a bright shaft of sunlight.

Frank left the kitchen and emerged into a hall. Tony and Jimmy split, veering in the opposite direction to scout the large hallway and other rooms.

Alone, Frank entered a sitting room.

He found the man standing before a large TV, drinking from a mug and smoking. The man turned, and his eyes widened. Coffee trickled on the lush carpet. Back in New York, Russo had been dark-haired and clean-shaven. This man had light brown hair and a heavy moustache. But Russo's features were undeniable. The TV was turned on, the volume low. On the screen, a red-headed woman was forecasting an imminent storm.

Frank aimed his 9mm at Russo's chest.

"Please," said Russo. "I have money. We can talk."

Russo reached for the weapon concealed beneath his jacket, and Frank fired three times. The silencing suppressor did its job, and aside from a dim whistle, the only sound was the dull thwack of the bullets sinking into middle-aged meat. The large man groaned, then collapsed, shattering a small glass table and scattering a Monopoly board and its pieces.

By the time Tony and Jimmy entered the room from the hall, Russo was dead. Tony scowled, looking genuinely aggrieved that Frank had killed Russo before he could.

"We need to go," said Frank, looming over the body, the gun at his side, the silencer still warm against his leg.

As the three men turned to leave the room, the woman stepped through the front door in a wash of bright sunlight. Fumbling with her rattling keys and pushing the door behind her, she stood in the now duskier light of the hall and said, "You wouldn't believe I forgot my—"

Her eyes widened as she saw them through the gap in the door. For the longest of seconds, Maria Russo stood rigid. Then a terrible grimace of understanding formed on her delicate features. While the door behind her was still ajar, it blocked her chance of a quick escape. She darted into an adjacent office.

It was Jimmy who reacted quickest. He followed her with his gun at his side. That mistake was fatal because the blast from the woman's handgun sent Jimmy staggering back from the office into the hall. A second bullet ricocheted above Frank's head, splintering the wood of the door frame. A third skimmed his thigh.

The woman emerged from the office with a wild look of horror possessing her pretty face, wisps of dark hair plastered to her cheek, teeth clenched in fury, the gun's barrel raised as she fired.

Frank raised his pistol and shot.

The woman's head spun as a bullet punched through her neck and severed her spinal cord, splashing the white gloss of the door with blood. Maria Russo fell dead in the doorway, her head hanging loosely by its sinews. Blood spread in a glistening pool on the polished floor, her dead eyes open.

Both men turned towards where Jimmy had collapsed, holding his stomach, white shirt turning a deep red from the blossoming wound. "I'm going to fucking die," he said, panting.

"You're not going to die," lied Frank.

"*Mom*?"

By the time Frank turned, the boy was already crouched at his dead mother's side, a tear running down a cheek as pale as marble; then he looked up at them with inconsolable, questioning eyes.

Tony lifted his revolver, aiming at the distressed child.

"*No*," shouted Frank.

Tony hesitated, the gun dropping slightly. "He's seen us. We don't have time."

"I don't care," said Frank. "He's a fuckin' kid."

The boy stared at them, frozen by grief and fear.

Tony further relaxed his arm, letting the gun drop nearer to his hip, as if Frank had perhaps altered the course of his murderous intent.

The hall grew darker. Outside the wind rose.

Tony scowled. "You know they have the death penalty here?"

The boy was still holding his dead mother, crying.

"We need to get Jimmy out of here," said Frank.

"Jimmy's as good as dead, and he knows it."

Jimmy looked up and met Tony's eyes, the colour draining from his face.

Tony gestured to the dead woman and the cowering boy. "What else would you have us do, Frank? Her shots would have been heard three blocks from here. We need to go."

"He's a child," said Frank.

"*Made man*," said Tony La Rosa, his face a scowl of disgust. "Don't make me fuckin' laugh." He casually lifted the gun, and with the blood-soiled Band-Aid hanging from his trigger finger, he fired, spraying the boy's pretty face across the polished floorboards in an oatmeal plume of blood, skin, and brains.

Frank roared.

Tony turned the gun on the two other men. When he had finished firing, the air was acrid with the tang of propellent. Frank tried to speak, but his chest was too tight, and only blood bubbled on his quivering lips.

Tony grinned his wolfish grin and said, "What's a-matter, Franky boy? Cat got your tongue?"

Frank lay on the hard floor, listening to the howling wind, praying he bled out before the sirens arrived.

3.

TWELVE YEARS LATER

WARDEN JEFFREY OLSON ENTERED THE SMALL HOLDING ROOM ABRUPTLY, looming over Frank, who sat at the table with his hands and feet shackled in chains. "Mr. D'Angelo, I have news."

Frank met the gaze of the silver-haired prison warden in the grey suit. Olson was clean-shaven, in his mid-fifties, and had maintained an athletic physique. The warden sat on the plastic chair on the table's other side. "You're obviously an influential man, Mr. D'Angelo," he said.

"What do you mean?" said Frank.

"Oh, I think you already know," said Olson, squinting slyly in contempt. "*You people* are all the same," he hissed.

Frank shook his head. "What?"

The warden straightened in his chair. "I've been ordered to inform you the US Supreme Court has ordered a stay of execution, following a motion from your family's attorney."

Though Frank heard the words, he almost failed to believe them. He'd refused any legal representation. He'd spent months preparing for this day psychologically, emotionally, and spiritually. He'd sent his final letters, cleared out his cell, put his shit in order. He was ready to die and embrace oblivion; indeed, he welcomed that—anything to escape the waking nightmares the doctors called psychotic delusions. But when they'd moved him from the holding cell minutes ago, his niggling suspicion had grown.

"You can't be serious," said Frank.

"Deadly, if you'll excuse the pun." Olson flashed an insincere smile, then repeated soberly, "Your execution has been stayed."

"*No, please*. I'm ready," said Frank. "I want this over."

"As do I. But I'm afraid that's impossible," said the warden, shuffling a pile of papers.

On the wall, a clock ticked too loudly. The small room smelled of disinfectant. The sterility was spoiled, though, by a fat bluebottle, which buzzed about, zipping into the fluorescent panel lighting. Minutes ago, Frank had speculated that the fly would outlive him if it could avoid the swatting hands of the two correctional officers stationed at the door.

"Why?" said Frank.

"The attorney submitted a petition for a writ of prohibition. It was granted."

"On what grounds?" said Frank.

"Your mental health."

"Fuck you."

"You will *not* be executed today."

He'd escaped death by minutes.

"Most prisoners are pleased when this happens, Mr. D'Angelo."

"Well, I'm not most prisoners."

"Don't pretend you're some kind of...criminal aristocrat. You're a common thug and nothing more. You deserve the needle—worse."

"The only difference between you and I," said Frank, "is that when I say I'm going to kill someone, I fuckin' kill them. And listen to me, you piece of shit...I never killed no one who didn't either try to kill me first or who didn't deserve it."

"Like the boy?" said the warden.

"You *know* I didn't do that."

"Then who did?" asked the warden.

"If I was a fuckin' rat, I wouldn't be on death row, would I?"

The warden smiled benignly. "That's not for me to speculate. But the consensus seems to be you were never fit for trial."

"Bullshit."

"All this, you waiving appeals, acting the lunatic, it's all part of a larger game, isn't it? To avoid justice," said the warden.

"No—"

"The Supreme Court has ordered a re-examination of your case," said the warden. "The attorney has a forensic psychologist attesting you were coerced into carrying out your crimes, that you were manipulated by high-ranking mafioso overlords, that you were intellectually vulnerable due to an existing mental health condition."

"There's nothing wrong with my state of mind, not then, not now. Give me a gun, and I'll do it myself," said Frank. "The only thing that is affecting my mental health is the prospect of having to go through this again. I want this done. *Today.*"

The warden averted Frank's gaze and looked towards the officers guarding the door. "Escort Mr. D'Angelo back to his cell," he said, straightening his paperwork for the third time in as many minutes.

FRANK NEVER WAS "MADE". THAT PARTICULAR HONOUR WENT TO THE bastard who'd left him bleeding out on the floor of the house in that deadbeat Midwestern town. He remembered how that had felt, too, dying. Lying on that polished floor, sirens nearing, the storm building, the smell of blood in his nostrils, he'd watched La Rosa step over him. The motherfucker had then pressed the cannon he'd used to shoot the boy into his limp palm.

It was his senses that had faded first. He'd been vaguely aware of the insectile buzz of a pestering wasp, aware of his tongue resting against the dry roof of his mouth. Then time had ceased to exist. His perception had been reduced to something dreamlike. He might have been lying on the floor minutes, hours, or centuries. He understood now. His brain had all but shut down. He'd been reduced to nothing but his sentient core. In the end, though, nothing mattered. You simply shrank back into the same oblivion from which you were birthed. Then a distant electronic hum had whined on the fringes of his unconsciousness.

Adrenaline.

Clear.

The jolting thud had lifted him from the floor, his senses rushing back into existence, the light flooding his eyes.

Pulse.

The first thing he'd noticed was the smell of latex, the gloves busy about him. The second thing he remembered was the faceless boy. In the blood-stained hall, the boy's *actual* body was covered with a white sheet, as was Jimmy and the woman too. Yet *there* the boy had stood amongst the paramedics, bodies, and commotion, pointing at Frank.

The kid had been shot at point-blank range by a high-calibre revolver. The structure of his face had been obliterated. His mouth, nose, and chin had been replaced by a gaping, ragged hole, the surrounding layers of ruined flesh exposed like an open flower. Despite the pressure of the electrode paddles on Frank's chest, the drip inserted into the back of his hand, the sponge plugging his bullet wounds, it was the grotesquely mutilated boy he'd never been allowed to forget. The boy and his accusing finger.

Everything else had been a blur: his substantial weight—minus three pints of blood—being lifted by a stretcher. Sirens. White corridors. White scrubs. The raging storm outside. He'd died three times on the operating table after he'd gone into hypovolemic shock. But in the end, his life was saved—just so he could be sentenced to death for first-degree murder. The jury had been unanimous, the sentence a modern brand of frontier justice. A deadly solution of barbiturates, paralytics, and potassium would be injected into his veins until his heart stopped.

But twelve years later, Frank no longer trusted the legal system because it had failed to end his misery. Twenty-three hours a day, he sat in his six-by-nine cell at the South Dakota State Penitentiary and contemplated death alone.

He'd considered cutting a deal and ratting on La Rosa. But what good would that do? La Rosa was now a gangland capo capable of extending his considerable influence into any prison in the US. Life without parole, amongst the general prison population—if his lawyer could have negotiated that—would have condemned him to a permanent state of hyper-vigilance. He had family on the outside too. *No.* Frank craved death—but he wanted it on his own terms, not bleeding to death at the hands of some hired convict armed with a toothbrush shiv. Suicide was not an option, not without a gun.

"How are you, Frank?"

Lying on the mattress of his bedstead, Frank glanced through the blue steel bars. The prison chaplain's large frame was a silhouette. It was late, after lights out. Father James Williams stepped into a pool of dim light from a solitary lighting panel. He was a large black man with a shaved head, goatee beard, and little round glasses. He wore a tweed jacket over his black shirt and clerical collar.

"Been better," said Frank.

"You wanted it, didn't you, death?"

Frank nodded.

He had never really accepted Father Williams' religious counsel. Instead, he'd welcomed the big guy's occasional visits and used the allotted time to discuss the Yankees or Giants. The one thing they'd never spoken about was Frank's case, until now.

"I didn't kill the boy," said Frank. "I tried to stop it."

"But you killed the others?"

Frank nodded. "Do you believe in ghosts? In *Hell*?"

"I believe in the Holy Ghost, if that's what you mean."

"I see the boy's face…every day."

"Conscience is what makes us human," said Father Williams. "When your conscience speaks, we hear God's voice."

Frank wasn't speaking metaphorically. The boy's hideously disfigured face was everywhere. When the lights went out, the boy materialised in the shifting patchwork of darkness. He saw the boy's faint, distorted reflection in the stainless steel of his toilet. He saw him in the crackling static of the television. Once he'd reported this to the prison doctor. He'd swiftly been diagnosed with depression and post-traumatic stress disorder, leading to peduncular hallucinosis. The truth was, though, no one gave a shit when the guy on death row was going fucking insane. Not until now.

"No, I'm not talking about God," said Frank finally. "I'm talking about ghosts."

"You have your bible," said Father Williams. "Embrace God, and he will be your saviour. Admit your sins. Find peace. You can be redeemed before the end."

The prison chaplain's footsteps receded down the corridor, leaving Frank alone in the dark. From the hard mattress of his bunk, he stared through the bars of his cell at the space the priest had vacated and waited for the boy; sure enough, the kid stepped forward, his face a bloodied ruin.

He had spent years avoiding the sight of him. If the boy appeared, he'd look away towards the light or close his eyes, and sometimes that small distraction was enough to allow his sanity to prevail. But it had been a long day, one he'd thought would be his last. He'd accepted his fate, and fate had betrayed him.

He decided to challenge insanity. He stared at the hole where the boy's face should have been, between the flaps of rotting skin. The darkness contained by the wound was rich and shifted with liquid consistency, like deep water—like the rippling Hudson River where bloated bodies stared into their own cold oblivion, putrefying.

Peduncular hallucinosis.

Though Frank craved death, he feared that Hell awaited. He understood, too, that all men were doomed. Didn't every man have an execution day? Somewhere, a piece of marble or granite existed for everyone, waiting for a name to be inscribed. The void awaited. You chose your own Hell.

"The priest can't help you," said a gruff voice in the dark. "But I can."

At first, Frank was confused as to where the voice had come from.

Then something fluttered through the bars of his cell like a black moth. The card landed on the floor next to his bunk.

Dwayne Murphy had been on death row twelve years. Only a string of appeals had kept him alive. Despite the two men being separated by mere feet and one thin wall, Frank sometimes forgot he existed. He was reminded by the occasional blatt of a fart or the sound of the other man masturbating. That he didn't like to think about, because Murphy was a rapist convicted of killing three teenage girls.

"I can help you."

Frank picked up the white card. Scrawled upon it in red ink was an equilateral triangle containing an open eye that was surrounded by lines representing rays of light.

"I heard the priest. He's lying," said Murphy.

"Don't fucking speak to me," barked Frank.

"Suits me. But know this: you *are* going to Hell. Might as well embrace it."

Frank looked at the crudely drawn eye on the card, then outside his cell towards the boy that Tony La Rosa had murdered in cold blood over a decade before. But the boy had gone. Only the bars of his cell remained, casting long shadows in the murk of the still, remorseful night.

"HERE, WE'D LIKE YOU TO COMPLETE THIS."

From her plastic chair, the psychologist handed Frank the papers through the steel bars of his cell. The young woman had red shoulder-length hair and was probably no older than twenty-seven or twenty-eight.

"It's a questionnaire," she said, her glasses perched on the end of her pretty nose. "I have a few primary questions of my own before we can begin."

Frank nodded in agreement.

"How is your general health?" said the young woman.

"You have my notes."

"Yes, but I'm asking you for your opinion."

"Fine," he said.

"Many prisoners, especially those on—"

"—death row?"

"Yes—experience depression, anxiety, and stress disorders, that sort of thing," she said. "Do you suffer from chest pains, profuse sweating, increased heart rate, anything like that?"

"No."

"Any recurrent bad dreams or nightmares?"

"No."

She scratched her pen against the form on the clipboard. Then shuffled her papers and picked out another sheet.

"It says here you have suffered hallucinations. You were diagnosed with acute depression six years ago."

Yes, he thought, *because I'm on death row, because a dead boy with a hole in his fucking face follows me around my cell twenty-four hours a day.*

"No," he said. "That was a…a cry for help. I made it up."

"You made it up?" she said, her eyes narrowed in suspicion.

"Yes."

She looked at him as if in contemplation. "I see. And have you ever abused alcohol, narcotics…prescribed pharmaceuticals?"

"Chance would be a fine thing."

The questions went on: Had he experienced physical abuse as a child? Would he change the decisions that had led to his incarceration? Did he have violent thoughts? Did he think about his crimes, relive them, fantasise about the moment preceding him pulling the trigger?

After enduring three months of psychological assessment and screening, he'd convinced half a dozen forensic psychologists and criminal psychiatrists that he was of sound mind.

A new execution date was set. He had three months left to live.

What really clinched it, though, Frank believed, was the letter he'd addressed to the Supreme Court. He'd never been a man of words, and he'd scrawled the testament on a notepad with a cheap biro. It had done its job.

I, Frank Alessandro D'Angelo, confess to killing Lorenzo Russo and Maria Russo in a cold-blooded, premeditated attack at their home in Brookings, South Dakota, in the summer of 1991. I had full possession of my faculties when committing the crimes.

Against his lawyer's advice, he had added:

If I could dig them both up and shoot them again, for nothing but the idle sport of it, I'd do it in a heartbeat.

He refused any blame for the boy.

Frank was taking a shit when the second card fluttered through the bars of his cell. When he picked it up, he again discovered the same crudely scrawled triangle containing the unblinking eye.

"You think I'm impressed by this shit," shouted Frank. But no reply came. His lingering question echoed in the empty corridor.

Later that night, Frank sat in the dark, trying to avoid the sight of the boy. But the sound of a funnelling wind erupted from the bloody hole in the boy's face. In its varying howl, he thought he could hear the faint scream of a child and the low-frequency hum of a wasp, forming an insectile harmonic of words: "*Made man. Don't make me fuckin' laugh.*" Then a racket of gunshots exploded in his ears, awakening his memories like a stirred cloud of bats.

Peduncular hallucinosis, Frank told himself. That's all this was, the slow, degenerative onset of psychosis, his mind playing cruel tricks, his guilt surfacing. But the boy stood resolute, pushed the ruined flesh of his face against the steel bars.

Frank looked away—and saw one of the cards thrown from Murphy's cell. The unblinking eye stared at him from the top of his waste-paper basket. When he dared to look back towards the bars, the boy had disappeared.

"The cards, what are they?" shouted Frank into the unyielding darkness of his cell.

A brief silence.

"Think of it as a calling card," replied Murphy finally, his voice gruff with sleep.

"The symbol?" said Frank impatiently.

"The Eye of Providence," said Murphy.

"What does that mean?" said Frank.

"Depends on perspective."

"Fuck you—and your riddles. Tell me."

"Christians believe the symbol represents the all-seeing eye of God," said Murphy.

Frank remembered Murphy's dishevelled appearance. He was a rapist and a child molester if ever he'd seen one. He remembered hollowed eyes, sun-faded tattoos, and lank hair that stuck to a pallid face so thin it was near skeletal. Murphy had the grizzled look of an outlaw battling a twenty-year dope addiction. He was no Christian.

"And what do you believe?" said Frank.

"The drawing represents the third eye, *the truth*. You're haunted by the past. We all are, by the things we've done," said Murphy. "You crave death, don't you?"

"What's it got to do with you?" said Frank.

"I have a day, too, for my execution. A date with death," said Murphy.

"You deserve it, you piece of shit."

A soft laugh echoed manically in the hollowed architecture of steel and brick. "You have a dark heart, Frank. We are bad men. Nothing good awaits us. But there's a choice."

"What's that supposed to mean?" said Frank.

"I've heard you, talking to the priest, crying out in your sleep. You've already seen Hell, haven't you? It waits for you. Your only hope is to serve it."

"You're a fuckin' lunatic, you know that?" said Frank.

"I can save you," said Murphy.

When Frank lay back on his bunk, movement caught his eye. The boy had returned, his ruined face dripping blood that pooled on the hard floor, coagulating in the cold night air.

He closed his eyes. Hours passed before he fell into a restless sleep.

"I'M GOING TO ENJOY WATCHING YOU DIE," SAID SOFIA GRECO.

When the woman spoke, her nostrils flared and her spit sprayed, like venom hitting the sheet of the Perspex glass that separated them. The woman sat rigidly, her dignity rehearsed, her fury repressed. Her unblinking eyes, though, burned with a fire of hate.

"I have heard of it going wrong, you know, the lethal injection," she said. "One prisoner took half an hour to die. The pain was, apparently, excruciating." She smiled, revealing perfect veneers. "I have a good Chianti in the cellar, a sixty-seven. In two weeks, after I've witnessed your life snuffed like a candle, I'm going to go home, pop the cork, and toast your arrival in Hell."

"Mrs. Greco—"

"Don't interrupt me, you bastard. My sister did nothing to you. My nephew, Leo, he was eleven."

"I'm sorry."

"Are you fucking serious?"

"I never intended to...*hurt* your sister." He sighed. "And I didn't kill the boy...Leo."

"Don't you say his name, you son of a bitch."

"Please—"

"Figlio di puttana," she cursed and slammed her delicate fist against the glass, alerting a watching guard; he did not intervene.

In the Perspex, a familiar reflection appeared from behind him. The lines of the boy's ruined face were a tracing shadow over the woman's hateful scowl.

Back in his cell, he contemplated his reasons for agreeing to meet Greco. Perhaps, after inflicting so much violence on her family, he had wanted simply to allow her to express her anger, to relish in his demise. He thought he was incapable of demonstrating true penitence. Perhaps the last kindness he could offer was to *be* the monster that she wanted to be slain. He'd never felt this hopeless, this alone.

Later Frank lay on his bunk with his troubles. After hours of enduring a sleepless torment, he shouted out in desperation to the neighbouring cell. "You said you could help me. Tell me how?"

A brief silence. "You're a Catholic?" answered Murphy in his southern drawl.

"Yes," he answered, realising the very idea of him being affiliated with any respectable religion was ridiculous. There was no road to redemption; he'd burnt those bridges.

"You're in a kind of purgatory."

"*What?*" said Frank.

"Do you see them, the demons?"

Frank hesitated, then said, "I see a boy."

"The third eye—you see *the truth*, the choices you've made."

"I don't understand—?"

"You carry your sins. We all do. Demons are parasites. They feed on your misery, your guilt. You're being eaten alive. Even a blind man could see there's little left of you."

Frank remembered the last time he'd seen his gaunt reflection. Murphy was right. He looked tired and old, a hollow man with grey skin and whitened hair, his humanity cut out, his lifeforce faded.

"It's a bit late in the fucking day for metaphors," said Frank.

"It's not a metaphor. Men are architects of their own hell. You build it, brick by brick. But that needn't be. You can take strength from your sins if you own them."

"What the fuck?" said Frank.

"Hell needn't be a prison; eternity can be your domain. But first you must confess. *Choose.*"

"Choose what?"

"Darkness."

"What—?"

"You were a gangster, a wise guy?"

"No," said Frank honestly. "I was never…*made*."

"You're going to Hell," said Murphy. "You can either go as a victim and suffer eternal fucking damnation, or you can seek affinity."

"With who, the devil?"

"A deity of many names."

"You really are a crazy fuck, you know that?"

"I'm offering you a chance," said Murphy.

"Why am I even talking to you?"

There was a brief silence.

"Because," answered Murphy finally, "I've seen the boy too."

Frank lifted his head from his flat, unfluffed pillow. For a fleeting second, he dared to glance in the direction of the bars of his cell. Indeed, the boy was there.

"He's standing at the bars outside your cell," said Murphy. "He has no face."

"You can see him?" The words left Frank's lips desperately.

"His face is gone," said Murphy, "and in two weeks, you will be gone too."

Am I sane? thought Frank. The possibility terrified him.

"I can help you," said Murphy, his voice a thin whisper. "Eternity waits for the anointed, for the ordained."

Frank had no idea what he was talking about—perhaps Murphy was even crazier than he was—but he had little time for contemplation because a metallic prang startled him. He looked to the floor where the noise had originated and saw Murphy had tossed an old tobacco tin through his bars; it was painted with the Confederate flag. Anxious that a guard could have heard, he peered out into the corridor outside his cell: Nobody. Nothing. Only shadows…and the boy. Always the boy.

He picked up the tin and opened the lid. Inside was a bare hypodermic syringe and a small plastic bottle containing a dark liquid.

Ink?

"Frank—D'Angelo, that's *your* name, right?"

The rapist addressing him by his full name made him somehow uncomfortable. "Yes," he answered.

By then Murphy had already begun his canticle. His voice was near indecipherable from the other side of the cell wall, but the chant was delivered in a pitch several octaves lower. By the prosody and precision of his intonations, Frank guessed the crazy bastard was reciting classical Latin verse.

"What are you doing?" said Frank.

"Do you remember the names of the people you've killed?"

Lorenzo Russo. Maria Russo. There had been many more: scores of them. But he'd never killed indiscriminately. It had always been with cold, business-like efficiency. He was assigned. It was professional. There was a name and a bullet. Rarely had it been personal. Most deserved it.

"Well?" harried Murphy.

"I guess I could remember most if I—"

"Inscribe the names of your victims on your body."

"What?"

"Every one of them. I have heard a lot about you, Frank. I know there were many. Leave your face and hands until last."

"Are you insane?"

"I can see the boy, Frank."

"Tattoo myself?"

"Confess. Own your sins."

"With a dirty needle?"

"Worried about infection?" Murphy sneered. "You'll be dead in a fortnight."

Frank picked up the needle, inspected it.

"There's something else," said Murphy. "You must not sleep. Wait until they pump your veins with poison."

"Are you serious?"

"You must purify your soul. You came into the world naked. You'll leave in the same skin. Pledge yourself. Free yourself from mortal concerns, its trappings. No food. No sleep. Conceal the needle. Recite the names. Work at night. Prepare for sacrifice."

Again, Frank dared to glance at the faceless boy on the fringe of his cell, blending to the shadows.

How could Murphy know?

Whilst the prospect of insanity had terrified him, that fear was insignificant compared to eternal damnation. He'd never believed in the prospect of Hell. But that was then, and this was now when his imminent death was a stark fact:

I can see the boy, Frank.

On the other side of the wall, Murphy's bizarre chant continued.

He remembered visiting a church as a child, the books, the crude medieval paintings, the depictions of Hell: naked humans entwined by serpents; horned demons lancing bodies; cauldrons of screaming sinners cooking in flames.

A ridiculous fairy tale…

Perhaps the doctors were correct in their diagnosis: he had simply succumbed to mental illness after years of solitude and regret. But maybe insanity was all Frank had. He tore off the crucifix that hung around his neck and tossed it to the floor.

He rolled up his trousers. He unscrewed the top of the ink bottle, dipped the needle, and began to carve names on the meat of his calf. As he did, he imagined a hundred rotting eyeballs rotating in their cadaverous sockets, looking up from the tenebrous murk of the Hudson, stirring from the depths in acknowledgement of their killer. The sharp pain of the needle, though, was a comfort. That at least was tangible, something real he understood, to pin down his scrambling sanity. He recited the names, whispering as he worked, owning every life he'd taken, making his confession.

And one by one, they did appear. The corridor outside his cell became busy, filled with those he'd butchered and maimed, faces that had haunted his conscience for decades. As if summoned by the ritual of his litany, they pressed wet flesh against the bars of his cell, wounds smearing, filling his nostrils with the rank stench of decay.

His world was a grey place. But there were still two distinct sides: good and evil; Heaven and Hell; darkness and light. Frank D'Angelo had chosen darkness. The anointment took minutes, and that night he was ordained, made a member of The Order Abaddon.

By morning's dull cast, thirteen days remained until the lethal injection. Already black ink scaled his shins like ivy, crawling up his limbs towards his beckoning torso.

Made man, said Tony La Rosa from the deepest recesses of Frank's sleep-deprived mind. *Don't make me fuckin' laugh.*

He'd never been *made.* That honour had been stolen, the initiation that set you for life. But there were other ceremonies—Murphy had promised—ceremonies that set you for eternity.

With each night, the needle punctured, the pigment spreading like sepsis, his blackened soul poisoned beyond antidote.

The air soured, and something that blended to the dark whispered unseen in the quiet of his cell.

The nights passed in a frenzied blur, Frank's soul in utero.

"WHAT THE—?" THROUGH THE BARS OF THE CELL, THE WARDEN STARED at Frank's naked body, his eyes wide with amazement.

Buttocks bared, limp cock shrivelled, rib cage exposed, Frank stood in the cold confines of his cell with his arms at his side. He'd completed his work with seconds to spare, leaving his hands and head till last as Murphy had instructed. He'd worked by night and in stealth, and every inch of his reachable body was now covered with the names of his victims. On that final night, he'd shaved his head with a blunt razor and tattooed his pale skull. Rivers of blood ran down his face, blinding his eyes. The needle had been so blunt he might as well have carved the names with a spoon. The pain, though, he'd savoured; it had kept him awake.

An overweight guard opened the cell door, the sliding mechanism like sudden thunder. The warden entered, followed closely by a correctional officer with his hand placed on the taser attached to his belt.

"My God, you're fucking insane after all," said the warden, Jeffrey Olson, squinting, circling Frank, and bending to read the words on his graffitied body.

Olson turned to his inferior officers. "Look at him. Has nobody been watching him?" The men shrugged in apparent confusion.

"You know that's contraband, don't you?" said Olson, pointing to the empty bottle of ink and the needle that Frank had placed carefully in the tobacco tin on the floor a minute before.

Frank ignored his question. He staggered with exhaustion, wiping blood from his lips. He'd left his eyelids and tongue till last. That had been a delicate job for his butchered, bleeding hands because he shook with the effects of sleep deprivation and hunger. He'd feared to press too hard, in case the needle—even blunt as it was—penetrated the thin skin of his eyelids and blinded him.

"*Names*?" said Olson, reading the words scrawled on Frank's body. "What is this, a confession? Stalling tactics? You have been a busy boy." He sighed. "If you think this will delay things, you *are* out of your mind." He tapped an expensive-looking wristwatch. "Twenty-four hours."

The itinerary had been planned with military precision. Frank was given a clean white uniform. He was escorted to a holding cell. He'd refused final visits with family and friends. Even though hunger burned in his gut, he'd refused his last meal too. He spent his last mortal day on earth sitting on a bunk in a bland room fighting sleep, regarding his uncut, brittle nails, and reciting the names of the dead.

At 9:20 a.m. on Saturday, 20 September 2003, the door to the holding cell opened. Frank was dressed in a white gown and slippers, handcuffed, and led down a sterile corridor.

His head spun. He swam in a sea of nausea and dizziness. With every step, his heart pounded in his ears. He feared dying but thought it might be a relief, to finally sleep. He was so tired. He'd refused the sedative they'd offered, but his reflexes were out of kilter, and every second unwound too slowly. His blurred, watering eyes burned. Colours appeared too stark. And when he looked up from his chained and shuffling feet, he saw the dead, the buzzed heads of the prison officers mutating into the butchered faces of his victims.

They arrived at the death chamber.

Dressed in grey shirts, three correctional officers led Frank into a small white room, together with the warden. The air smelled clinically tinged. The walls were bare apart from a simple clock. In the centre of the room was a padded gurney with unfastened straps next to a small medical table. A black phone stood on a second table in the corner.

Father Williams stood in his clerical clothing, clutching a Bible and staring at Frank's newly tattooed face. The priest nodded curtly as he passed.

Frank caught sight of his reflection on a large mirrored screen. He was unrecognisable. He was a bald, thin man, older than his years. He'd not slept for so long, and he knew that caused him to hallucinate because the tattoos covering every inch of his sallow skin squirmed like maggots. The ink shifted and reformed, the words reading as others than the names he'd scrawled.

He was uncuffed and helped onto the gurney where he lay flat, his heart hammering in his chest, his breath escaping him in desperate bursts. His arms placed by his side, the officers fastened buckled straps at his wrists, torso, and ankles. He was trapped. He could blink, and that was all.

"Try to relax," said the officer nearest, his sulphurous breath tinged with coffee. *Didn't prison officers receive standard-issue toothpaste?* He was living out his final moments, yet that was the thought that occurred to him. These were *people* putting him to death, people with petty concerns and small lives. What qualified any of these wage slaves to end his life with such medical meticulousness? It was true Frank had craved death, but now the moment had arrived, he resented these people. He thought he'd prefer a more brutal death, something less intimate—a firing squad, maybe—because this clinical façade somehow made it worse.

A female officer clipped something to his gown. "A microphone," she said. "For your final words." Her voice was soft and maternal. Another officer taped a heart-monitor sensor to his tattooed chest.

A man wearing a white coat entered the room from a second door and put on latex gloves. "Stay calm," he ordered, his kind blue eyes sparkling. The man took a sachet from his pocket and tore it, producing an alcohol swab. He wiped inside the hinge of Frank's left arm. Frank stared at the ceiling, the jaundiced, unnatural light blurring his tired eyes. He was terrified.

A sharp prick.

The doctor sighed.

Another sharp prick.

"Vein's constricted," said the doctor. "This man's dehydrated." He gripped his arm hard and tried again, face lined in a frown. "There, all done," he said, patting Frank's arm as if he was a young child frightened by a tiny needle. He inserted an intravenous tube, taping the drip secure. The doctor repeated the process, inserting a second IV into his right arm. This time, two goes was all it took to find the vein. Then lines were attached from behind Frank, feeding into his arms from the room with the mirrored screen.

The officer at Frank's rear turned a mechanism that altered the angle of the gurney from nearly flat to forty-five degrees. He now faced a second screen concealed by a mechanical curtain, exposed in his gown for all to view, his dignity and absolute vulnerability laid bare.

Apart from Father Williams, only two officers remained stationed at each end of the gurney: the woman and the man with the bad breath. Everybody else had cleared the room.

Up the curtain went, revealing a second mirrored screen he knew concealed the witnesses who looked on: Sofia Greco waiting to watch him die.

He faced his tattooed reflection.

"Frank Alessandro D'Angelo, you have been sentenced to death for the murders of Lorenzo Benito Russo, Maria Francesca Russo, and Leonardo Antony Russo on August 17, 1991," the female officer said with unwavering authority, all trace of maternal warmth gone. "Now you have the opportunity to make a final statement before we proceed to carry out your sentence."

Frank tried to speak, but his lips were too dry. He wet them with his sandpaper tongue. "Tony La Rosa," he croaked, desperately trying to catch his breath. "I'll see you in Hell."

There was a brief silence, and the gurney was lowered back down so he was again horizontal. He was staring at the ceiling, his heart beating so hard it felt like it might burst out of his chest. Here he was —this was the time. The end had come.

"Release Syringe A."

He felt the sedative enter his veins. Immediately his heart slowed, and his thoughts became muggy and thick, his fear dissipating. Father Williams bent over him and put a firm hand on his shoulder. But in the blurring glare from the ceiling's light, Williams' head morphed. The priest's face became that ruined atrocity of the boy's, ragged flaps of skin hanging around a cavity that resembled some huge, bloodied maw.

Frank felt himself receding, and his eyes closed.

"Syringe B."

The pain arrived in a bolt of agony, like acid burning every molecule in his body, abruptly waking him. He writhed in his binds, convulsing in frenzied spasms.

"He's still conscious," shouted the doctor who was again at his side. Panic filled the room.

The mechanical curtain descended, obstructing the witnesses' view of the ensuing chaos.

Another blistering stab of pain hit Frank, and he felt his muscles tighten as if his body might enter a seizure. And that's how he died, facing sin, staring into the gaping wound of the boy's face that had become a cavernous black hole where a storm raged within. The void swallowed him like a tornado. His memories flew around him within the vortex amongst whirls of debris.

In the great, iridescent gloom of the sky, the moments of his life were projected on the sullen clouds by eruptions of sheet lightning, every gentle moment, every act of wickedness lit in violent fulmination: baking oatmeal cookies with his mother; kissing a pretty girl; beating a man to death with the bloodstained butt of his revolver; watching as Tony La Rosa killed an innocent child.

Deafening thunder roared with Old Testament fury. He roiled in eternity.

When the storm abated, Frank found himself kneeling in the hot sand of a vast desert where fires burned on the horizon. It was dusk. He watched the flames lick the air, backlighting endless rows of inverted crucifixes. In the distance, men screamed amongst the incessant hum of swarming flies.

Somewhere, he knew, Sofia Greco toasted his arrival with a glass of vintage as blood red as the crimson sky. But not Frank. No crucifix awaited him. Damnation was a blessed kiss. He was ordained.

Made Man—Don't make me fuckin' laugh.

It would be Frank who would have the last one.

4.

THE MIAMI SUNRISE PAINTS THE HOTEL ROOM IN A LUMINOUS HAZE, THE light beaming through the Venetian blinds, illuminating constellations of swirling dust motes.

The alarm clock reads 6:38 a.m.

In the long corridor, two drunken figures stagger, falling into doorways and clipping a fire extinguisher, knocking it on its side. Frank detects their meandering approach from the hotel room with sonar-like precision.

"I can do this thing with my tongue," says La Rosa, his voice thinned by age.

"Shush," says the girl, hiccupping. She sounds like a child. "You'll wake the...*sleepy people*."

Laughter.

"Fuck them. If they're not awake now, they soon will be, way I'm going to make you scream."

The girl laughs. "Well, we're not breaking any laws...as such."

"Not yet, sweetheart."

The girl giggles. By the smell of her, Frank surmises she is young enough to be La Rosa's granddaughter. He can smell the Jack Daniel's on La Rosa's breath. He can smell the ink on the thick wad of cash contained in the old man's wallet. He can smell the banana-scented condom coating that clings to the girl's labia from the last client she'd fucked.

The handle turns, and the door opens. The old man stands on the edge of the room, the hooker a foot behind, the sunrise now blinding the room in a wash of warm light.

Squinting, La Rosa pauses for a second as if he's caught the whiff of danger, a rat sniffing poison.

Hidden by shadows, Frank remains poised on his powerful haunches, an apex predator waiting to bring about death, waiting for the prize of La Rosa's tarnished soul.

Finally the old man enters the room in an arthritic shuffle. The Tony La Rosa of 1991 had never walked like that. But Frank has no doubt that this is the same man who shot him and left him bleeding out so many years before.

"Welcome to my humble abode," says La Rosa, gesturing for the prostitute to enter the room, a manic grin scarring the grey flesh of his elderly skin.

Frank moves like a glitch in time, a stir of flickering shadows ghosting in the glare of the burnt hue of dawn. He propels his solid mass towards the door; it slams, sealing the old man in the room. He grabs La Rosa by the lapels, throwing him across the floor like an unwanted toy, tearing the jacket of his expensive suit.

La Rosa falls against the bed, bones audibly snapping; he cries out in pain. The girl is knocking on the door's other side, oblivious.

"You okay, Tony? *Tony?*"

Cowering, pissing his pants, La Rosa looks up.

The names of the dead scroll Frank's skin like digital rain, and he looms over the old man, his huge wings extended, his horned head casting a forked shadow across the brightly lit room.

Shaking, La Rosa regards him with narrowed eyes, a glint of recognition forming. "*You,*" he says and produces a revolver from inside his jacket. He points it uselessly, his aim wavering.

At seventy-eight years old, La Rosa no longer resembles the ruthless killer who put so many men to death, and in his last moments, his sharp wit and quick mouth fail him. He looks frightened and old.

Frank rams his fist down the old man's narrow throat, rips his tongue from its root, and holds his glistening trophy aloft.

La Rosa's bloody body lies still on the floor, a brittle pile of bones. His soul, though, is a heavier thing burdened by decades of hate and murder and sin.

In the lonely, barren desert, where the sky is scorched red, a cross waits for La Rosa, a cross and a faceless boy whose ragged flaps of skin surround a hole as black as the darkest of hearts.

LITTLE LOST LAMBS

The gaunt man put Kevin's cup of tea on the table, met his eyes, and said, "You found me."

"Wasn't as hard as you think."

The greasy spoon was empty apart from the two men. The café reeked of fried food. The walls were slick with grease. The gaunt man serving him had once been his friend—back then, Brian had been chubby-cheeked and freckled. But now his face was pinched. His faded red apron was tatty and stained, his eyes tired, older than they should've been, but they were blue—the glint he remembered gone.

"What happened to my brother?" said Kevin.

The other man sighed, shook his head. "Long time ago."

Kevin nodded and stared at the man who was now a stranger.

Brian averted his eyes, holding a ketchup-stained plate at his waist. Finally he said, "Thirty years…*more*."

"When did you get out?"

"Two weeks ago." He wiped grease from his hand into his thinning hair.

"This job?"

"Better than being stuck in—"

"—a medium secure unit."

Brian nodded. "Part-time."

"I see."

"Always been a feeder. Thought I'd enjoy it, working as a cook." Brian stood rooted to the spot, but his eyes, though still tired-looking, became avian-like and busy, darting to the café's door and back to the plastic table where Kevin sat. "If the boss comes back, I'd appreciate it if you kept that to yourself, about the—"

"—secure unit?"

"Yes."

"*Prison?*"

He nodded.

"Well, that depends." He saw something stir in Brian, not anger, but an agitation behind eyes that were soulless.

"Look, please. I'm doing okay. Been hard."

"Hard, really?"

"Yes, really. Youth detention and prison were bad enough, but you any idea what it's like being held on a hospital order?"

"*Sectioned?*"

Brian closed his eyes and nodded.

"Then I guess I've no idea."

Brian again looked to the door, turned back to Kevin, but kept his eyes averted. He said, "At least in prison, you know there's an end game, a definite sentence to serve. Back in that place, you never knew how long."

"You appealed, though. *Tribunal?*"

"Waste of time."

Looking at the man standing before him, it was easy to see why any judge would go with the doctor's advice. If a man couldn't even remember to zip his fly, what chance would he have holding down a job, sticking to the rules, resisting the chance to abduct little kids whilst screaming *they* were coming for him—again?

Brian scratched his bristled face. Kevin noticed the grey-black rim of dirt under the man's nicotine-stained fingernails. Mud? Dead skin? He'd read once that finger-nail dirt was usually keratin debris—from scratching. Or perhaps it was something worse—maybe shit? What-ever it was, Kevin decided to leave the steaming cup of tea where it was on the yolk-stained table.

"I want you to tell me what happened to Joe."

Brian did look at him then. "You wouldn't—"

"Something was in those woods with us. *What?*"

Brian shook his head.

"That was my eight-year-old brother we lost out there."

"And we were ten-year-old boys. You know what I told the police, what I told the doctors."

"Yes, that you knew nothing, that you didn't do it."

"I wasn't locked up for that, for what happened to Joe, and you know it."

Kevin did. The police believed Joe had drowned, had fallen in a fast-moving river nearby, his body never recovered. But Brian *had* been locked up for attempting to abduct two smaller kids right after, and then a third when he'd been paroled as an adult. None of the kids had been harmed. Instead, the doctors believed Brian was recreating Joe's disappearance, that his brain had misfired and was struggling to cope with misplaced guilt.

Kevin had other ideas.

"You *know* something, and I've waited over three decades to find out what. Not easy to talk to a guy when he's locked up in one institu-tion after another."

Even when Brian had finally got out, he ended up straight back inside again, such was his obsession.

Brian shook his head as if in denial.

"You led us out there, to the forest. Didn't you?"

"Look, you can't blame me. I was a child. I've paid for—"

"—the crimes you committed?"

"I—"

"For attempting to fucking kidnap children—"

"I—"

"Was Joe not enough for you? I read about it—on parole, you tried to abduct a nine-year-old boy, you fuckin' maniac—*again*."

"The doctors—"

"I can't believe they've let you out."

"The meds, they've stabilised—"

"What happened to Joe?"

"I wouldn't—"

"What happened to Joe?"

"I didn—"

"You, *you* led us there."

"I wasn't well."

Kevin scowled at the man in disgust. "*You!*"

"I was a child," Brian shouted and threw the plate he was holding. Porcelain shattered. Shards scattered amongst the crumbs on the filthy tiled floor.

Kevin stood up and shoved the man in the chest. He felt his palm strike bone.

"Get off—"

Kevin walked towards him slowly. "My parents were never the same. I didn't just lose Joe but everything. Do you know what's worse than losing your little brother? I'll tell you, you fuckin' monster—it's waking up every day and wondering what happened, wondering if it's my fault, if I could have done anything." He grabbed Brian by the neck of the T-shirt he wore under the apron. Even in his fury, he was disgusted to discover the shirt was damp with kitchen grease or sweat. He slammed Brian against the wall.

"*Tell me*," he growled.

"I'll do better," said the gaunt man with cigarette breath. "I'll *show* you."

1988

THE THREE BOYS ARRIVED AT A SMALL CLEARING IN THE WOODS.

"We'll stop here—eat something. If we keep heading through those trees, we should find the footpath," said Kev, throwing his body on the ground in a heap of sweat and exhaustion.

"Only thing on the menu is us," said Brian. Gnats swarmed around his freckled face. He slapped at the bug cloud, chubby cheeks rippling. "We got food left?"

"Some chocolate," said Joe, emptying the rucksack on the ground next to his older brother's head; Kev didn't flinch. Pathetically, a Marathon bar, Coke can, and rusted Swiss Army knife fell into the long grass, together with Joe's inhaler. They'd eaten the rest of the food—packets of Space Raiders and sickly sour penny sweets—as they'd walked, further and further into the wooded hills, searching for the promise of a couple of dirty mags. Kev thought those older boys had lied to Brian. There was no hut—no magazines—no tits in these woods, apart from Joe. But Brian had insisted.

Joe had persuaded Kev to let him join the expedition by agreeing to carry the rucksack and not grassing him up. Shameless blackmail was what it was.

"I can't walk anymore," said Joe, moaning again. "My feet hurt." He took his inhaler from the ground, gave himself a blast, and slumped next to his older brother.

"Stop whining," said Kev, noticing Joe's right trainer had split. Mum would go ape. The trainers were new. The last thing Kev had wanted was Joe slowing them down, but he'd made the mistake of boasting two weeks ago he'd watched both Rambo movies on Bobby Davies' Betamax. If his parents found out, which they would if Joe acted on his threat, his chances of seeing *Robocop* would disappear quicker than the path they'd lost two hours ago. The path *he'd* lost. Still, this had all been Brian's idea, not his. *Brian's*. And even considering the blackmail, it'd been Brian who'd vouched for the little shit in the end too.

"We'll share the bar," said Kev. "Once we've rested for five minutes, we'll head off."

They split the chocolate and guzzled the Coke, although they'd lost some when it fizzed. They had been lucky to get any. Joe had nearly broken the ring pull—he was yet to get the hang of peeling them. They'd sucked every drop of Coke from a pin-sized hole; the jagged edge of which had cut Kev's lip. Blood smeared the can, but Joe drank it anyway. Kev didn't blame him. The heat was unrelenting.

They sat, resting. In the trees, birds twittered. Bugs glided in the sun-cooked afternoon air. You didn't see bugs like these in the garden. They were bigger, juicer looking. Their shells and wings glistened with the sheen of health. Two prehistoric-looking beetles fought in the grass, mandibles twitching and threatening cannibalistic violence. Grasshoppers chirped, the air alive with their song. Other things chittered by in the breeze. The woods were an insectile metropolis, an alien world of eat-or-be-eaten.

Brian and Joe were sunburned on their noses and cheeks. Kev felt his face prickling too. His hair was damp with sweat, and his eyes stung. God knows how burnt they'd be if not for the cover of trees. But the blasted things obscured everything. If the path *was* ahead, the trees hid it.

"Are you sure that's the way back to the trail?" said Joe. "Not sure—"

"The path is past those trees," said Brian. "Has to be."

"Come on," said Kev. "Keep going."

They marched. The trees again became thick, the terrain tough. The fallen leaves of one hundred bygone autumns carpeted the forest floor, the detritus hiding uneven ground and old, bulging roots that tripped them and scuffed their now filthy trainers. Branches scratched and pulled at their bare limbs. Above, the sun was a white-hot ball that strobed between the canopy of leaves. Ankles bleeding, they stumbled through stinging nettles and the barbs of thistles. Ahead, the gnarled bark of an old oak scowled at their trespass into wilder territory. The tree's girth suggested a great age. Kev turned from the tree, spooked for no obvious reason but their isolation.

They emerged from the thick forest before a field enclosed by wire fences. Another two hours had passed.

No path.

Kev scanned the field where a dozen lazy sheep grazed. Brian lingered thirty feet behind, his podgy face tired and damp with sweat.

"Fuck," said Kev, studying the line of trees that surrounded the field on three sides. On the fourth side, the field bordered another field and another and another. As far as he could see into the distance, each field was separated by more wire fencing. He couldn't see any gates.

"Shit."

Joe narrowed his eyes. "You swore. Mum said—"

"Not the time."

"We're lost—"

"Not now."

"If you hadn't made us take the short-cut—"

"*Shut it*, Gaylord."

"I'm telling Mu—"

"If you don't starve to death or die of thirst." Kev gave his little brother his best action-hero scowl. Secretly, he'd rehearsed the pose in the mirror, modelled his narrowed eyes on Harrison Ford's in Indiana Jones. But how dare the little shit blame him! *Brian* had brought them here, but time for blame could come later.

Tears welled in Joe's eight-year-old eyes. Kev felt guilt rise, but the emotion was soon quelled by irritation. "*This* is why I didn't want you to come. Stop being such a spaz. Tell Mum what you want. Until we find a way out of this, I can swear as much as I want, *capisce*?"

Joe's face was a blank mask of confusion.

"It means—Okay—*understand*—*capisce*—it's what gangsters say, in America." He sighed.

Joe nodded, seemed to get it, wiped the sweat from his eyes, nodded again. "Caprish," he said, conceding defeat.

Kev shook his head at the mispronunciation but noticed his little brother looked younger than he had an hour ago, like a baby, like a little lost lamb.

Brian emerged from the woods behind and pointed to the trees on the other side of the field. "We should head that way. The path's gone."

Cupping his hands to shield his eyes, Kev surveyed the landscape, imagining he was some reluctant war movie hero—Arnie scouting the enemy lines from afar, face streaked with black paint, hulking torso wrapped with rounds of ammunition. But there was no enemy in sight, only grass and more trees shimmering in the heat. And flies. Everywhere. Clouds of them: gnats, midges, and juicy-looking mosquitos, fat with blood, buzzing about their perspired faces. Deep down, Kev knew this wasn't a game. They'd been out in this for hours. It had been hot when they left, but nothing like this. And the last can of pop was gone.

"The fields will be easier," said Kev.

"Not with those fences," said Brian, shaking his head.

He was right, of course. The barbed wire looked savage. The wire was bound tight to thick wooden posts, each spaced twenty feet apart. Snagged on cruel, crisscrossing squares of wire, tufts of wool blew gently in the warm breeze. The field smelled of shit.

The sun beat down on their hot heads.

Kev wiped his brow. "Okay. We'll stick to the trees. Give us cover from this heat." He knew, though, they were more likely to find a farm or house or road if they followed the impossible lines of fences into the heat-shimmering horizon. But the fences were imperious. Endless. Climbing one without shredding a limb would be a task, never mind half a dozen or more. But crossing the field, they would have to climb only two.

Brian said, "We'll find a log and crush the wire down."

"Don't know. Those fences look solid."

Brian pointed. "Look, weak point over there, where the fence has...*buckled*."

A fence had been damaged. The wire trampled down. It looked easier to climb.

"C'mon," said Brian. "See what we can find in the forest."

The two boys turned towards the forest. Joe should have been there, standing behind them, but he had disappeared.

"Little shit," said Kev. Spinning around, he scanned the fields. His heart quickened—Joe was nowhere to be seen. "Joe," he shouted. He looked again, all around, but his brother was gone.

Usually, he didn't worry about Joe, and certainly, his anxiety didn't spike so quickly, but this wasn't *usually*. They were lost. This predicament—the unrelenting heat, their isolation, their lack of provisions, of drink—fuelled his fear.

"Joe," he shouted again. His voice sounded lonely in the midst of the land's great expanse, his cry carrying a slight edge of desperation. A wave of adrenaline rushed through his veins, his mind snatching at wild thoughts of his brother's demise: the metal teeth of an animal trap breaking bone and mutilating the meat of his younger brother's thin legs; Joe lying in the long grass gasping for breath, his trusted inhaler out of reach; *a stranger* with a hard-on for murdering little kids, out here, following them, throttling his little brother in the trees as they bellowed his name under the hot sky.

"Joe," he shouted.

Nothing.

They searched for another twenty seconds, a time that felt far longer. And Kev saw a ribbon of colour amongst the brown, grey, and green of grass, trees, and wood. Joe's red shirt gave him away. Anger replaced worry. Joe knelt, struggling with something tangled in the wire fence some sixty or seventy yards away. *An animal?*

The two older boys jogged, calling Joe's name, but he ignored them. The younger boy was concentrating hard, fighting with the thing caught in the fence, his hands covered in blood. Kev realised then that Joe's T-shirt had been white, not red. *White.*

The lamb twitched. Its back legs kicked, stopped, kicked.

Joe pulled at the animal's front legs, furiously trying to free it from barbs of wire. The head was caught in the cruel mesh. One eye was a jellied ruin. Kev could smell the metallic scent of blood—and shit. The animal, in its last throes of life, stank.

Joe looked desperate and breathless. The lamb fought, although Kev couldn't work out from where the blood originated—maybe from the gouged eye.

"Leave it," said Kev. "The thing's as good as dead."

Joe barely acknowledged him. He was pulling on its wool, trying to free it from the barbs. The lamb opened its mouth and gave a throat-rattling scream. The one good eye rolled.

All three boys flinched at the sound. Lambs bleated, not screamed.

Kev shivered with revulsion. "I said *leave it*." He pulled Joe's arm away from the struggling lamb. Joe fought him, and Kev grabbed him harder. They tussled until Kev lost his footing and fell on top of the wounded animal. The lamb's head was stuck, angled awkwardly in the web of wire, and the force of Kev's landing on its back broke its neck on impact. The animal went limp.

In that second, the near silence of nature was amplified, the chirping grasshoppers a distant chorus in the warm breeze. As Kev listened, he could almost hear the ticking of his brother's mind, a bomb about to go off.

A crow swooped down and landed on the fence twenty feet away, feathered wings ruffling.

From the hard-baked ground and dry heather, amongst sheep shit and thistles, Kev lay bleeding. He'd caught his right arm on the fence. But the worst thing was the lamb underneath him. Its blood was all over him. He jumped up, repulsed by the animal and the wet warmth of its blood.

Joe's face tightened. "You…you…"

Kev wiped his bloodied arm on the grass while Brian watched. He didn't think sheep carried diseases that humans could catch, but the lamb's blood and his were mixed. He felt his stomach surge with anxiety and revulsion.

Joe babbled incoherently. "You…you…"

"—did it a favour," said Kev, scowling.

"You killed it."

Kev inspected the wound on his arm. It was deep enough. Rivers of blood trickled down towards his wrist.

Brian walked over to check it out. "Looks nasty."

"Be fine," said Kev, but he wasn't sure. He remembered Rambo out in the wilderness, evading military police and sewing up wounds on his own bulging bicep with a needle and thread.

Joe sat sullen-faced next to the dead lamb.

"We need to get cleaned up. Get this blood off us," said Kev.

Joe was covered in so much blood, he looked mortally injured.

"Joe, you listening?"

But his younger brother stared at the ground, his eyes sharp with fury, face streaked with gore.

"We're going to get across this field, but we need to find a way over that fence." Kev pointed to the first of two fences that blocked their way to the trees. He knew by now how to manipulate his younger brother. "We'll need your help."

Joe looked up then. Kev could feel the heat of his brother's eyes. Joe was angry but tempted, torn between two evils. He wanted nothing more than to be equal to the older boys. By asking him for help, Kev knew he was offering him recognition that was hard to turn down. Joe stared, caught between anger and the want of acceptance.

"The lamb was as good as dead anyway," said Kev. "You tried to help it, did your best. It's out of its misery now." Kev spat on his hand and tried to wipe the blood from his arm, but it only smeared. "We're going to find a log and try to push down the barbed wire."

"Over here." Panting, Brian was already dragging a small log behind him. "We can use this."

Kev acknowledged Joe and smiled. "C'mon, what do you say?"

Joe sighed, got up. "Don't suppose I've much choice."

One log was not enough. After nearly half an hour of searching the forest floor, they'd found three logs that looked sturdy enough to take their weight, but they bolstered their engineered bridge with branches Brian had cut with the Swiss Army knife's saw. Joe had found some ropey vines too. The construction was anything but solid. Together, they lifted the logs, placing one end on the ground and the other against the barbed wire of the fence. The boys did this at the weak point where it appeared the fence had already been compromised.

"I'll go first," said Kev.

Tentatively, he walked up the log sideways. He could feel the bridge buckle beneath his feet and the wire starting to give under his weight. Wire and fence creaked. He knew that to climb to the top of the makeshift bridge was to risk it collapsing and him falling into the barbed wire. The dead lamb and its mutilated eye flashed in his mind. His plan was to get three-quarters of the way up and jump.

Kev counted to three and leapt.

He made it, but only just. He landed on all fours, one hand grasping the prickly spine of a thistle, the other a handful of sheep shit. But he'd avoided the barbed wire. Pulling himself from the ground, he picked thistles out of his left hand. Joe was already following him up the makeshift bridge.

All the boys made it over the rackety construction, although Joe cut his shins when his short legs failed to clear the mesh. His trainer had caught in the top wire, and he'd face-planted the grass. Kev's arm still bled too. He'd tied the wound with a piece of frayed rope he'd found hanging from the fence, more for the look of it than anything else. He thought the rope gave him the appearance of an apocalyptic nomad, like a character from *Mad Max*.

The field was far larger than they'd anticipated. Stubborn rows of gorse hampered their way, and an hour after they'd climbed the fence, the sky had darkened. Brooding clouds gathered in a dark mass. The air felt charged, the stifling heat threatening to erupt. The boys kept plodding towards the line of trees.

"Looks like rain," said Joe.

Kev looked up at the sky. "No shit."

"The trees aren't far," said Brian. "If we can make it, at least we'll be sheltered."

"Aren't you supposed to stay away from trees in a storm?" said Kev.

Above, the rolling, ominous clouds spread in the darkening sky.

"Don't know," said Brian. "But I'll take my chances. We're exposed out here. C'mon, keep moving."

In an eerie trick of the light, Kev noticed Brian's eyes gleaming with a purple hue, the imminent storm reflected in his eyes.

On they walked towards the trees, Brian dragging their makeshift bridge behind him, ready to climb the second and last fence.

Lightning flashed, exposing dark segments of pregnant clouds in pulsing, silver bursts. Thunder erupted. Rain arrowed down, stinging their faces and limbs.

The boys ran. The rain hissed. The storm rolled across the sky, like tumours swelling, spreading, turning day into night as it consumed.

"Get the bridge against the fence," shouted Kev.

Standing before the barbed wire fence that blocked their way to the trees, the boys looked for a weak point—found one. Yet again, they discovered wire that had been compromised and not repaired.

Thunder roared. The sky strobed.

Brian and Joe positioned the bridge against the fence. But the bridge had been damaged on their journey across the field, and the wood was wet, making it slippery to climb.

"I'll go first," said Kev.

He climbed up, this time almost on all fours. When he reached the top of the bridge, he stood upright and leapt but slipped on the rain-greased wood. His left foot caught on barbed wire, and he felt serrated teeth rip at his flesh. He tumbled to the ground on the other side of the fence, his foot tangled.

By the time the two other boys had made it to the other side of the fence, Kev had realised his foot was trapped, mangled in the mesh of wire. He lay on the wet ground, the flurries of rain and hail hitting his exposed skin like nails.

"You have to pull your foot free," said Joe, shouting over the storm.

"Can't. Hurts too much."

Joe used a stick he'd snapped from a tree and tried to separate Kev's foot from the wire. No good.

Brian stood transfixed, staring at the unyielding coils of wire mesh around Kev's injured foot.

Kev's foot was wet; he wasn't sure if it was rain or blood.

Brian looked down at him, his face illuminated by the pulsing storm, his expression dull yet possessed with morbid fascination. Again, lightning lit the field and Brian's sun-pinked, vapid face. The forest was twenty feet away, cloaked in darkness, yet it looked inviting from the midst of the buffeting storm, which snatched at hair and flapped wet T-shirts.

"You two get shelter," said Kev. "Go."

"No," said Joe. "We can't leave you."

Brian said nothing. His gaze was still focused on Kev's foot.

"Brian," Joe shouted over the rampaging wind, "what can we do?"

Brian remained silent.

A new light danced on the periphery of the field, flickering to its own symphony of colour, on the horizon and then all around. The light pulsed in coordinated bursts that suggested a pattern of intelligence.

Not lightning, thought Kev, and for a moment, it was as if he was watching this other light not from the ground of a wet field but from somewhere else entirely. The dancing light seemed like a weird form of communication, like Morse Code.

Joe's lip quivered.

Brian's eyes were bright, lit with that purple hue Kev thought had been the essence of the storm, a reflective trick of the light. Brian grinned, but his eyes didn't smile. "I brought them to you," he whispered, his words almost lost in the violence of the storm. "For you," he said. Kev read his lips more than heard him.

From the wet grass, Kev knew something was wrong, that Brian had led them here. He'd been set on this path since they'd left early that morning. *The fences*, he thought. *He knew where to find the damaged fences*. It should've been day, yet it was night. The storm's darkness had suffocated a hot summer day, but this other unnatural light flickered on the field's every side now too.

He became aware of something in the trees.

His heart hammering in his chest, Kev was the only one to see it. Joe was oblivious, frantically trying to free his brother's leg like he'd tried to free the lamb. Brian was dead-eyed, delirious, staring at the dancing lights on the horizon and all around.

The figure moved amongst the trees. Its gangly form shuffled, a silhouette against what was now a wall of white light behind the foliage. Other things were moving within the trees now too—shadows, smaller things, their large heads bobbing. Kev was sure that the things were watching them. They crowded in the trees.

Joe turned, saw them, and screamed.

"Run, Joe, *run*," shouted Kev, wriggling on the ground furiously, trying to free his foot.

The tall figure stepped out of the trees and began to move towards them.

"Go," said Kev.

Joe was crying. "I can't leave you."

"Run," said Kev. "You have to go, now, *capisce*?"

Joe's eyes fixed on his, a look of grim acceptance growing on his face as their eyes held. Never had Joe kissed him before, but he did then. He hugged him hard and fast and kissed him on the cheek. Their faces, wet with tears and rain, pressed together.

And Joe ran.

Kev lay in the grass, willing his brother to get away.

Brian was still grinning, staring into the furious storm.

Kev tried again to pull his leg free, ignoring the pain.

The thing from the trees turned its attention to Joe, its elongated head following the direction of his little brother's escape. Joe was a silhouette, backlit from the almost blinding light in the trees. The other things in the forest stirred. Despite the storm, their whispers grew in Kev's ear like the mutterings of distant, excited children.

Joe ran, but there was nowhere to go. The fence was on one side and the trees on the other.

A line of figures emerged, blocking Joe's path. The white light from the forest behind spilled around their child-sized forms. Joe stood before them.

They closed in.

The world blinked, and Kev fell into a vacuum of blackness. He felt his mind plunge into a void. He fell amongst the voices of his parents, of his little brother calling those words, *I can't leave you.* They echoed from the deep recesses of his unconsciousness. And they never left him, not then, not more than thirty years later.

—*I can't leave you.*

Kevin drove. He left the window open, though, didn't want his car infested with the smell of café grease and stale sweat. The cold, sobering air rushed in and caused their breath to fume.

Perhaps fearing his boss would be informed, Brian had shut the café and left a note. If he'd refused, Kevin would've told the café owner about his criminal record, about his mental health, about prison and the attempted kidnapping he'd read about—he'd have told him everything. But he didn't need to. This had been Brian's idea.

Brian sat in the passenger seat, wearing a tattered, bobbly fleece and a cheap pair of aviator shades. The sunglasses looked ridiculous. Bent and out of shape, they perched crookedly on his nose, the gleaming lenses serving only to accentuate a face that was tired and pale. But even though it was a cold day, the sun was bright.

"You know, I've not been back there since," said Kevin.

Brian remained silent, rocking gently in his seat.

"For fuck's sake, put on your seatbelt."

"I don't like them."

"Tell you what I don't like, your head smashed against my dashboard. I've just had this car cleaned."

Brian ignored his request.

They drove deeper into the country hills, leaving behind the Welsh seaside town where Brian worked in the down-trodden cafe, leaving behind the well-maintained roads of more urban areas. The car careered through narrow country lanes, only slowing to navigate blind bends, where thick hedgerow scratched the Ford's paintwork. Kevin winced. He'd never married, never had children. His car was his baby, but it seemed of small importance now, even when the suspension rattled when the car slammed over potholes.

The roads gradually steepened, took them high above the rural village where they'd both grown up and spent long summers together. The village was the nearest settlement to the path they'd lost all those years ago. It looked abandoned, not a village at all but a small collection of houses. Kevin had not been back since leaving. His parents had moved away after everything—to a busy town. His former childhood home looked small, grubby, and forgotten, not how he'd remembered it.

After another two miles, Kevin found the lay-by which he knew was near the path they had walked all those years ago. The footpath began a few feet from the road that was rarely used but for tractors and farm vehicles. The area was thickly forested.

Kevin parked the car. For a moment, the two men sat in silence, the soft tick of the cooling engine the only sound.

Brian took off his shades and said, "My life has been a disaster."

"If you're expecting sympathy—"

"I'm not."

"Then what?"

"Even back then, I was lonely," said Brian. "I used to walk. Alone. For hours. The week before we all went, I'd been there before."

"Where it happened?"
"Yes, further."

"What do you mean, further?"

"I'll show you." Brian lifted his gaze from the pristine floor of Kevin's car and looked him in the eye. Brian's eyes looked milky, which Kevin found disconcertingly repellent.

"I knew what I was doing, but it wasn't me."

"What the fuck's that supposed to mean?"

"That I knew what I was doing but couldn't help it."

Kevin felt an intense hatred for the man sitting beside him, the man who looked pathetic and vulnerable and much older than his years. He hated the pungent smell he emitted, hated that even now he refused to be held accountable. It was everything that was wrong with the world, personified, this lunatic who had been responsible for his little brother's disappearance.

"You're a poor excuse for a man."

Brian nodded.

"They looked everywhere for Joe," said Kevin.

"I know."

"You know where his body is?"

"No."

"Then—"

"I can't explain till we get there. But I want you to know coming here has been the catalyst for everything that went wrong in my life—all the madness, the voices in my head. I honestly couldn't help it. The police couldn't pin Joe on me because it wasn't me, not really. Because of what I'm about to show you, I've spent my life in constant psychiatric care."

Kevin pulled the keys from the ignition and put them in his pocket. "If not you, who?"

"I've dreamed of this for over thirty years, coming back here. I still wake to the sound of my own screams, covered in sweat and fighting for breath. Coming here again was the last thing I wanted. But now, I do want it—*relief*."

"I wish you'd get to the fucking point."

Brian looked at Kevin, and for the first time, Kevin saw something of his old friend in his eyes. It was as if they were children again.

Perhaps it was the murk of the light, the trees obscuring and casting shadows and causing optical illusions.

"Look, Kevin."

He shivered at this man using his name.

"I fear for you, bringing you here. But I realise you want closure too."

"I've wanted it for so long."

Brian looked at his reflection in the car mirror and nodded. "*Yes*, so long."

"Take me there," said Kevin.

FINDING THE PATH WAS EASY, LOSING IT HARDER. THE TWO MEN WALKED through trees. Leaves fell. Winter was on the way, and the day was brisk. The afternoon, too, would be short. It was late November, not summer. The heat from that long-gone day was hard to imagine. The sun, though, was bright, glaring when the trees allowed it. Brian wore the cheap shades. Kevin squinted. They walked amongst the skeletal trees, wading through the crisp, fallen leaves. Twice, they got lost. But Brian soon found his way again.

"It's this way," said Brian. The forest looked familiar. An old tree with a grim face scowled, and Kevin had an inkling he'd trodden this path before, although there was no real path, not now.

When they arrived before the fields, they found the wire fences, but the barbed wire was gone. Back on that day, under the sweltering heat of the sun, this journey had taken half a day. Brian claimed he hadn't returned here since, but they found the fields in little more than an hour and a half.

The new fencing was easy to climb.

They were up and over in seconds, then walking in silence across the fields. Kevin checked his phone and saw he had no signal and that the time was nearly four p.m. It would soon be dark.

Feeling the early winter chill of dusk, Kevin climbed the second fence and stared at the place where he'd caught his foot all those years ago. The barbed wire was gone, but he knew the spot.

Something cracked underfoot.

Brian was still climbing the fence when Kevin lifted his shoe to see he'd stood on something grey. Plastic. Dirty and forgotten. Joe's inhaler had waited here for so many years. He picked it up and inspected it.

I can't leave you.

"This way," said Brian, who had overtaken him and was walking towards the trees.

Kevin dropped the inhaler where he'd found it, noticed the sun was going down, and followed.

They walked another fifteen minutes from the second fence and the field. Brian stood in a clearing. In the centre of the clearing, a black rock jutted from the ground. The rock was flawlessly rounded at its edges, like a pebble.

"This is what I wanted to show you."

Kevin walked closer. Three feet in height, the rock gleamed like black porcelain.

"You've brought me all the way out here to show me a rock."

"Don't you think it's unusual?"

It was, highly.

"Not enough that the police took any notice. They searched this whole area."

Brian nodded. "Come closer."

Kevin did.

"Touch it."

Sighing, shaking his head and fighting with thoughts of throttling the man who had the look of a junkie with a twenty-year smack addiction, Kevin approached the rock and touched the surface.

The rock was cold, far colder than it should have been.

"That's it," said Brian. "Hold your hand there."

Deep in the wood, where the light was now failing, the two men stood, and the rock gleamed, not enough that it was reflective, but almost. Kevin thought he could see the rock's surface darken where his faint shadow was cast. This intrigued him. He stared harder at the rock and felt sure it was warming to his touch too.

He looked at Brian and saw he was smiling.

He stared back at the rock and its shiny surface. He thought now it *was* reflective, that he could see his image in the ebony lump of mineral protruding from the ground.

It was faint at first, and distorted—like the dim outline of an inquisitive face reflected in the back of an old spoon. The face peered blindly back at him from the surface of the rock.

And then Kevin realised with a shock that the face wasn't his.

It was Joe's.

"*Joe,*" he said. Tears sprang in his eyes. His heart pounded. Kevin looked up at Brian, who'd taken off the glasses. His eyes were bright and purple like the sky.

"I'm sorry. They must feed," said Brian.

"*Feed?*"

Kevin looked at the rock, tried to see the dim apparition of the reflection that had been there a second before—an apparition which his logical mind told him had surely been conceived by poor light and thirty years of mourning.

Lights danced on the horizon, and a symphony of colour lit the late-autumn evening. By the time the tall figure emerged from the trees, the two men were surrounded. The others hung back, gathering amongst the trees, shadows that, if not for the size of their heads, might have been children.

On Air

SATURDAY, JULY 25, 1987

D*ear Diary,*

Today I met the coolest guy ever—Ollie Bernard. When I'm older, I want to be a radio DJ, just like him.

The ward is so boring lately. But that German doctor (or is he Danish?) won't leave me alone. He treats me like a kid. Doesn't he realise I'm fourteen? He keeps asking about my thoughts. But he said a diary might help with my head and stuff. So here it is! He promised nobody would read it. So…if you're reading this and your name is not Jimmy Simpson, KEEP YOUR BIG NOSE OUT!

I can tell the doc thinks I'm schizo. Perhaps the springs will uncoil and pop out my head like those Garbage Pail Kids. Just call me Loony Lenny!

Anyway, tonight I was let out to visit the adults' communal room to watch TV, and Ollie came right over. I didn't recognise him at first. But he looked a bit like Face from The A-Team—he even dressed a bit like Face from The A-Team, which was weird because that's what we were watching!

I couldn't believe it when he told me he runs the actual hospital radio station. And guess what? He gave me cigarettes, and not those shitty Silk Cuts Mum smokes either. He gave me fucking Marlboro...and my own lighter. Whoa! Ollie (he said I can call him that) said he has big plans for FM-85 and big plans for me too.

Anyway, Ollie says he's going to make me a mixtape. That way he can talk to me and play me music even when the station is off air.

To think, I can count Ollie Bernard as an actual friend!

Anyway, got to go. I've got a tab with my name on it. If you don't know, tab means cigarette. It's what Ollie calls his smokes.

Later Alligator,

Jimmy Simpson

1.

"PEOPLE CALL THIS PLACE THE LOONEY BIN," SAID RYAN. HE WAS SITTING on the bed, sketching superheroes, his bulky headphones wrapped around his slender neck.

Will's heart broke a little. "Look, son—"

"I think terrible things, all the time—"

"That would make anyone—"

"*Mad?*" said Ryan.

"No. Unwell."

"You don't know my mind...the horrible things I think about people," said Ryan.

Will shook his head. "*Just* thoughts, son."

Ryan looked at the floor. He was too thin. The stark line of his jaw and the dark rings around his eyes were exacerbated somehow by the hospital bed and the tightly folded sheets he sat on. He was a grey ghost in a white room where the warm air was tinged with iodine antiseptic.

The posters he'd put up—*Fortnite*, Kevin De Bruyne, *Avengers: Infinity War*—did little to disguise the clinical nature of the ward.

"The doctor wants to up my meds," said Ryan.

Ryan was picking up the vocabulary of psychiatric nurses, psychologists, and doctors. He was fifteen, for crying out loud. Will felt sure his son had got worse since being admitted too. Since being sectioned.

"We'll get through this," said Will.

Ryan looked up from his pencil sketch and stared out of the small window where grey clouds sailed across the August sky like invading warships.

"Give yourself a break."

"Hard, Dad."

"I know."

"You don't."

Ryan returned to his drawing. He'd captured Black Widow in incredible detail.

The drowning silence was interrupted only by the sound of the radio leaking from Ryan's headphones.

Then there was a knock at the door.

"Hey, Ryan," said Sonny, sloping in, his entrance abruptly lifting the room.

Sonny held up his palm. Ryan gave him five.

"Mr. Wallis," said Sonny, nodding.

The ageing hospital porter briefly left the room through the now open door and returned pushing a rattling trolley piled with dirty plates and cutlery. Ryan's plates remained where Sonny had left them an hour before, now cold on the tray table beside the bed, the chicken curry and sponge cake untouched.

"Man, you have to eat something," said Sonny in his soft Caribbean lilt. "What is it with kids today? No one wants to eat."

Sonny pushed back a grey dreadlock. Thirty-five years working on the ward hadn't dented his enthusiasm or wicked sense of humour.

"You need to take that down," said Sonny, pointing to the poster of Manchester City's Kevin De Bruyne.

"And replace it with who?" said Ryan.

"Ronaldo," said Sonny with a mischievous glint in his eye.

"United suck," said Ryan.

"Keep your eye on the poster," said Sonny, clattering Ryan's plates onto his trolley. "I may stick it in lost property."

"You dare." Ryan was smiling. So was Will inside. In many ways, Sonny had helped his son more than the scores of doctors, psychiatrists, and mental health care professionals.

"And what's this?" said Sonny, picking up the old radio beside Ryan's bed.

"Dad brought it. My phone's broken." Ryan produced the smashed Samsung from his jeans pocket.

"We'll get it fixed," said Will.

Ryan said, "I usually listen to the radio, podcasts and stuff on my phone."

Sonny said, "Kids today—"

"—don't know they're born," finished Will. "Music is so throw-away these days."

"What do you mean?" said Ryan.

"Digital music, you can download or stream it whenever you want," said Will. "It takes away the novelty. Back when I was a boy, I'd save for weeks with my paper-round money. Once I bought a record, I'd force myself to like it."

Ryan feigned an exaggerated yawn.

"True," said Will. "When we bought a record, it was for keeps. Nothing is quite like vinyl. Movies too. Every Saturday, I'd go to the corner shop and choose a video to hire. It was a big deal. These days, you kids pick a film from Netflix, and if you don't like it, you choose another."

Sonny smiled. "When *I* was a kid, we thought radio was magic."

Ryan laughed.

Sonny said, "Serious. Do you know how radio works?"

Ryan shrugged.

"Radio waves are electromagnetic," Sonny said. "Sounds are changed into invisible radio waves that can travel through space in different frequencies. That radio receiver transforms the waves back into sounds."

"You're a scientist?" said Ryan, smiling.

Sonny laughed. "You can learn a lot through radio. The frequencies, they're nothing more than vibrations, you know. There are good vibrations and bad ones. Our brains are electrical, too, like this radio. Good stuff happens when we tune into the good vibrations."

"And what about the bad ones?" said Ryan.

Sonny smiled. "We let them be."

Sonny high fived Ryan again and pointed to the pills left in the paper pot by the nurse. "Take your medicine."

Ryan washed the pills down with a glass of water and put on his headphones.

2.

"FUCKING CONTRAPTION," SAID THE MAN, HITTING THE BUTTONS ON THE coffee machine. Finally, the machine responded and spurted out a milky-looking liquid into the plastic cup. "You drink this?"

Will nodded.

"Tastes like shit," said the man.

Will smiled.

The man picked up his coffee and sipped, then pulled a face as if he was about to vomit. "Dear God. Disgusting." Under the harsh corridor lighting, the man's eyes were dark, the bags heavy, the bristles of his beard speckled with grey. "Can't help myself. Need the caffeine."

Will knew that feeling. There was something about the confines of the ward that brought about a need for coffee. Or was it simply that even the weakest caffeine buzz offered a short-lived distraction from the despair of reality?

"I've seen you with your boy," said the man.

Taken aback, Will said nothing, slotted his own coins into the machine, and hit the cappuccino button.

"Ah, you don't want the steamed milk, mate," said the man. "Tastes like fucking goat semen."

Will laughed. It was a relief. Smiles were in short supply lately.

"I'm here with my girl too." The man nodded towards the small room that neighboured Ryan's.

The door was ajar. The girl was sitting on her bed, brushing her long, dark hair in elegant strokes. Even from the corridor, Will could see she was thin. *No*, Ryan was thin. This girl was emaciated. Her head was too large for her body, her cheekbones razor sharp. But she was pretty, her eyes accentuated by her frailty.

"Milly won't eat," said the man. "Started on one of these crazy teen diets. At first, we were pleased when she was eating so much fruit. But that's all she ate. She collapsed a month ago. Insists she's too fat. Swear she's worse since she's been cooped up in here."

"I'm sorry."

"We'll get through," said the man. "Name's Kevin." He stuck out a hand.

Will shook. "Will."

"I only volunteered to get the drinks to get out of that poky room," said Kevin. "Bloody hospital radio all day."

Will had heard. He'd considered asking the nurses to request the music be turned down. Looking at the teenage girl sitting on her hospital bed, he was glad he'd refrained. Ryan listened to the same radio station, but at least he did so with his headphones.

"I wouldn't mind," said Kevin. "But the station just plays eighties trash. The sound quality is abysmal too. The music sounds, I don't know, warped."

Will had put down the distortion to the unreasonable volume and the echoing acoustics of the hospital corridors.

"I've told her to listen to Ed Sheeran like a normal kid," said Kevin. "Milly's always been obsessed with old music, though. She plays the piano. Top of her class. But that DJ wants shooting. Calls himself The Sultan of Synth—*tosser*."

Will smiled. "If it keeps her happy."

"Your boy okay?" said Kevin.

"As you say, we'll get through."

"You will," said Kevin, nodding.

Still holding his drink, Kevin picked up the two other plastic cups that waited on an adjacent table by crushing the three together, splashing hot coffee on his hands. He winced. "See if I can't get Milly to drink this." He smiled, winked, and carried the cups precariously towards his stick-thin daughter. She was still sitting on her bed in the little hospital room where the lead singer from the band Berlin wailed "Take My Breath Away" as if 1986 had never ended.

3.

"RYAN IS SUFFERING FROM SOMETHING CALLED PURE OCD," SAID DR. Petr Jensen, a tubby Dane with grey hair, kind blue eyes, and an effeminate manner.

Will and Sue sat in the doctor's office outside the children and adolescents' psychiatric intensive care unit, drinking the goat-semen cappuccinos.

The office overlooked the grey hospital car park. A water machine and a stack of paper cups stood in the corner. A bookcase was crammed with medical journals. The consultant sat at the other side of a desk that held a computer and a plastic tub of stationary.

"I want him home," said Sue. "We've learned to live with Ryan's...obsessions."

When Ryan was small, he'd obsessed over symmetry and order. At five years old, his little shoes were always straight, left meticulously in the same corner of the porch, his jacket placed on the same hook. Always. In stark contrast, his visiting cousins had thrown their clothes on the floor in a scatter of hats, coats, and trainers. This had bothered

Sue. She'd complained her own sister had failed to instil discipline in her children. But Will knew kids were supposed to be carefree. Back then they had joked about how their little boy's penchant for neatness might be employed around the house.

But what started as a tendency for order gradually became an obsession. Ryan had developed tics and habits. He had made odd gulping noises, beat his chest like an ape, and developed an eye twitch. He became obsessed with certain numbers: four, eight, sixteen. Will and Sue fretted that their boy would be bullied and made fun of. But he'd been small, and what was normal anyway? Small children had imaginary friends, picked their noses in public, and went out shopping dressed as Iron Man. One habit had replaced the next until, around age eleven, they'd stopped.

Their boy was normal.

A phase.

Then two months ago, his mental health had taken a turn for the worse. They had accidentally found the drawings under his bed. Ryan —who loved Manchester City and Marvel comics and dreamed of one day becoming an artist—had sketched hundreds of scenes featuring gratuitously depicted suicides. The identity of the unfortunate lad in every picture was obvious: the artist and boy were one and the same.

He'd been in the hospital a month. His days were spent in a Valium trance, listening to the hospital radio. Despite his glum mood, and even whilst his intrusive thoughts persisted, Ryan promised his parents his suicidal fantasies had ceased.

"Ryan has gone downhill since coming here. He promises the drawings were fantasy," said Will, gripping his wife's cold hand. "We're inclined to believe him now. We think he'll be happier at home with his family."

"I can't allow your boy home until he's completed his treatment," said Dr. Jensen.

Sue scowled. "Are you saying we're incapable of looking after our own son?"

"I'm saying you don't have the expertise to deal with a complex medical case, Mrs. Wallis. I have worked on this ward for over thirty years. I have seen a lot of young people come through these doors. Ryan still needs round-the-clock supervision."

"Look," said Sue, straightening in her chair. "We appreciate your help, but we feel Ryan would be better at home where he has his room, his things, and his family and friends."

"We'll endeavour to get Ryan well and home—"

"Being here is making him worse," Sue said. "Constant poking and prodding, being stuck in that blasted room all day, it's unhealthy."

Dr. Jensen stood and faced the window, gazing over the drab hospital car park towards the grey horizon where the rain clouds thickened. "I have a difficult job, Mrs. Wallis. The last thing I want is to let you down. If I let Ryan go home now, I would let you all down."

Will said, "The thoughts he complains of—"

"Are manifestations of his anxiety," said the doctor. "When was the last time you noticed Ryan acting out his compulsions?"

"His habits?" said Sue.

"Um-hum."

"Seems to have grown out of them," she said.

"*Seems?*" said Dr. Jensen.

"What do you mean?" said Will.

The doctor said, "Sufferers of OCD experience obsessions and compulsions, checking behaviours, that sort of thing and—"

"Ryan has stopped all that," said Sue. "Before he went to big school, we were worried he'd get picked on. But the summer holiday before, he stopped doing them. He's been okay for a long time—or *had* been."

The doctor turned back towards the window in a slow moment of contemplation, then faced them. "Outward signs of OCD are more easily identifiable in children because they're more obvious. Older children and adults often become adept at hiding compulsions."

"You're saying he's still doing these things secretly?" said Sue.

"Possibly. The other perhaps more difficult symptom of OCD is intrusive thoughts," said Dr. Jensen. "It's exactly these intrusive thoughts that cause someone suffering from OCD to carry out their rituals in the first place. Sufferers believe, or half believe, they can banish upsetting thoughts or ward off their worst fears by acting out compulsions. Rituals give relief."

"The habits help?" said Will.

"Not in the long-term. The more a person performs a task, the more they feel the urge to repeat it. It spirals," said the doctor.

"Like an addiction?" said Will.

The doctor nodded. "In a person suffering from *Pure* OCD, the obsessions are internalised. The rituals become less important. Instead, obsessions can manifest themselves as even more intrusive, leading to even more disturbing thoughts. There's no relief because there are no rituals, only the obsessive thought itself—and the consequential guilt."

"What are you saying?" said Will.

The doctor gently smiled. "Ryan's unpleasant thoughts are largely directed at those he loves or cares for. It's a great cause of anxiety to him."

"He says he feels numb," said Sue.

"Since we have medicated him," said the doctor.

Will tightened his grip on his wife's hand.

Dr. Jensen continued. "Ryan is simply unable to control his response to his thought processes. His fears are the root of the problem. Everyone suffers from disturbing thoughts. It's part of being human. People think of doing horrendous things all the time, inappropriate things, *violent* things. But it's a fleeting thought, nothing more. Most people accept that and move on. It's not talked about. But Ryan is so distressed the thoughts spiral, like his earlier compulsions. The more he attempts to resist the thoughts, or performs the compulsion to expel them, the more the thoughts are reinforced."

Sue wiped a tear. Will was relieved. Finally, they had some kind of diagnosis.

"If I were to say to you, don't think of a big red button, that would be the first thing you'd think of," said the doctor. "But the problem starts when you can't *stop* thinking of the big red button."

"Can this be cured?" said Sue.

"We can treat him. Pure OCD is sometimes difficult to completely erase," said Dr. Jensen. "Cognitive behaviour therapy can be effective, but the problem is it can initially heighten stress in patients and the likelihood of—"

An alarm shrilled.

"Excuse me," said the doctor. He rushed towards the door, banging his thigh on his desk and knocking over a pot of pens.

Will rose from his chair and followed the doctor out into the corridor.

Then the doctor swiped a card in a security access terminal and pulled open the door to the adolescents' psychiatric intensive care unit. Anxious because his son was on the ward, Will caught the door, followed, and held it open for Sue, ushering her through.

They stepped into chaos.

A young nurse was crying hysterically. Tears streamed down her cheeks, a glob of snot hanging from the end of her nose. A tall male nurse was holding her tight, trying to comfort her.

White coats flapped, dashing back and forth. The alarm drilled the air, rattling skulls. Doctors and nurses barked urgent instructions.

Will saw his son then. He was standing outside his room, holding his Nintendo Switch at his side. Ryan looked around at the ensuing mayhem as if in a slow-motion dream.

It was then they brought her out.

Two male nurses carried Milly from the small room that neighboured Ryan's. The two men lifted her onto a hospital-trolley bed. She was unconscious. Wearing a blue hoody and jeans, her baggy clothes hid her skeletal form. But her attire did not hide her bone-white face and hands—nor the cord that trailed from her neck.

"She's stopped breathing," said a young doctor at the business end of her trolley.

"Ligature cutters, *now*," said Dr. Jensen. A nurse handed him a scissor-like tool. He attempted to cut the cord. Failed. "Too deep," he said. "We need surgery. Go."

Pushed by the team of doctors and nurses, the trolley rattled towards Will and Sue at hurtling speed, crashing through the security doors at the same split second another nurse swiped her ID card.

As the trolley passed, Will stared at the furrowed abrasion around Milly's bone-thin neck. While the trailing cord was visible, the noose itself was deeply embedded in the teenager's throat.

The rush had stirred a breeze in the stagnant air, and Will could smell Milly's sweet perfume. He had smelt the vanilla scent before in the corridor. But it was her bulging, dead-looking eyes he thought he'd always remember—her eyes and Bananarama singing about a cruel summer, the words floating from Milly's empty room like cotton candy in a light wind tinged with iodine antiseptic.

4.

AFTER THE TERRIBLE COMMOTION ON THE WARD, ANOTHER KID HAD screamed in their room for over half an hour.

Ryan had never heard anyone scream for that long. He wondered if the girl—he was sure it was a girl—had damaged her vocal cords. Every wail had sent shivers down his spine and caused his head to feel like it might explode.

A young nurse with reddened eyes had come to see him. She had given him more of those pills.

He wanted to forget the whole thing, had tried to lose himself in his art. But he'd given up on his latest sketch of Captain America. Lying on his hospital bed, he could think of nothing but the stick-thin girl and that cord wrapped around her neck.

He put on his headphones to drown out the thoughts. Music helped calm his nerves. Since being admitted, he'd discovered the hospital radio—FM-85—quietened his mind, as if the frequency modulated the faulty wiring in his brain. The music was kind of cheesy, but without the radio, his mind was filled with white noise, the static he associated with his creeping insanity.

Now, though, the radio played a song called "Mad World" by a band called Tears for Fears. The lyrics, about dreams and dying, were in poor taste. He guessed the DJ was oblivious to the incident on the ward because the song felt somehow inappropriate. So did the radio talk show that followed. The interview was both clumsy and crass.

"You're listening to FM-85," said the velvet-voiced DJ in his trans-Atlantic drawl. "I'm Ollie Bernard. We're taking some time out from the music to delve into something serious. Did you know suicide is the second leading cause of death amongst teenagers? Shocking! Well, as promised, today I have with me a young chap who has been there. How are you doodling, Jimmy?"

"So honoured to be here, Ollie."

"It's a privilege, Jimmy. Tell us what happened."

"Well, it was such a long time ago—"

"—that you decided to kill yourself?"

"Yes, I was determined to," said Jimmy.

"Tell our listeners what that felt like?"

"Well, I was locked up for being different, by the doctors who were supposed to help. No one understood me."

"I'm sure we have listeners who know how *that* feels," said the DJ.

"I felt so alone," said Jimmy. "I had no friends. I had been bullied at school. Inside I was…dead already."

"Wasn't there anyone you could talk to?" said the DJ.

"Only one," said Jimmy. "But there was no way out. Suicide was the only answer. I thought about death and suicide all the time. When I imagined dying, when I imagined suicide, the thought gave me this…this warm feeling, as if all my troubles would just melt away."

Suddenly the boy on the radio—*Jimmy*—began to laugh hysterically.

Ryan shivered, unsure why this odd interview had unnerved him so much.

"Such a sad story," said the DJ. "Well, we're going to be right back with Jimmy in a minute, talking more about this important subject. In the meantime, here's 'True' by Spandau Ballet—back in a jiffy."

Suicide…

Ryan never would have attempted it. His drawings had been an escape from reality. Nothing more. Now, though, the thought of taking his own life did hold some morbid appeal. At least he would no longer have to suffer the endless humiliation of being stuck on the ward.

The rain was so heavy he could hear it over his headphones, pitter-pattering against his window, like fingers tip-tapping Morse Code:

You, too.

You, too.

You, too.

He turned up the volume on his radio, closed his eyes, and drifted, feeling himself fall towards sleep. Kaleidoscopic patterns whirled on the screens of his eyelids as fractals of symmetry.

The rain beat like a soft drum.

Black flowers blossomed…

He walks down a long corridor, searching for the door to a secret room. There are other doors, of course. But when he opens those, he finds people standing behind. Family, friends, doctors, nurses, they wait like vampires in coffins, staring blankly and smiling stupidly. Ryan runs along the corridor, searching for the one special door, but it eludes him. It always does.

He searches frantically, lost in a maze of doors.

Somewhere there *is* a door…

He woke, sweat glazing his brow. But as the seconds ticked by, the memory of the dream evaporated as quickly as his perspiration.

His father stood at the bed's foot. "You okay?"

Ryan rubbed his eyes. "Bad dream," he said, taking off his headphones.

"I turned off the radio. I could hear your music six feet away —*Wacko Jacko*?"

"Huh?"

"The music. You were listening to Michael Jackson, you know, 'Man in the Mirror'?"

"Don't know that one, Dad."

"Hospital radio?"

"Yeah, all I can get."

His father raised his eyebrows. "Do you want to tell me about the dream?"

Ryan shook his head.

His father walked closer and squeezed his shoulder, and Ryan thought, *Drop dead, fuckwit*. The thought was a reflexive response over which he had no control. A rush of guilt followed. But this was how it was. Kindness spawned projections of hatred, at first towards others, then towards himself. Because the second another person expressed affection towards him, his sick mind would bite, and he would be left to deal with a legacy of remorse for something he could not take back and certainly never admit.

His conscience haunted him day and night. His fears were so intertwined with his existence he sometimes felt he was nothing more than a biological extension of his inner dread: a puppet of meat. He wondered if living in this permanent state of anxiety would lead to eventual insanity. The perpetual war of anger and guilt was too much. If it wasn't for the Valium…

Ryan said, "The girl?"

"Milly?"

Ryan nodded. The deep ligature wound on her neck had both appalled him and filled him with morbid fascination.

"She'll be okay," said his father.

Ryan hoped so.

Sonny knocked on the door. "Ryan, how we doing?" The porter walked into the room. His smile was as bright as a Caribbean morning. "You okay, big man?"

The thought—*the word*—it arrived in Ryan's mind as convulsively as a sneeze.

It was a forbidden word, a racist word, a vile, disgusting thought he could not repress.

A deep feeling of shame washed over him. He was not a racist. He'd never said *that* word aloud in his life. Yet the thought came from nowhere. It was always worse when he liked the person.

"Looking a little pale," said Sonny.

Inside his head, Ryan's inner voice screamed, trying to drown out these evil thoughts, but that word came again...and again...and again...

Ryan winced, holding his hand to his head as if warding off a crippling migraine. He *loved* Sonny.

"You okay, son?" said his father.

Ryan remained silent. For all his inward protests, the hateful voice shouted louder. He was overcome by an overbearing need to leave the little hospital room and get away. Back at home, his mental health had been delicate. But here there was no bedroom retreat where he could *really* be alone, no escape, no private suicidal fantasies to punish himself.

Instead, his mind had been carved open, the wounds exposed for all to inspect. There was only the torment of doctors prodding and prying, the acid-trip nightmares of sleep...and the distraction of the hospital radio.

"You okay, champ?" said Sonny, punching his arm playfully.

Again, that word...that awful word...

Ryan swung his legs down from the bed. He ran towards the door, slipping on the mopped floor, and knocking over a clutter of plates piled on Sonny's catering trolley. Porcelain smashed.

He ran through the corridor.

The ward was locked. Entry was granted either through a buzzer on the wall or a security card. But fate intervened. A middle-aged woman wearing a red jumper—a visitor—saw Ryan running towards the door and held it open for him. He ran out and towards the fire escape, heading up the stairs two steps at a time.

The psychiatric unit was old. The original building was an

imposing three-storey Victorian asylum with twin conical-roofed towers at each end of its expansive design. The rear had been extended, though, with a modern wing where there was access to a flat roof.

Ryan hurtled up two flights of stairs. When he reached the third floor and the steps to the roof, he found the door was locked with a thick padlock. He kicked the door in frustration, rattling it on its hinges.

He had no idea why he'd craved the altitude of the roof. He'd been cooped up for so long. Perhaps he needed fresh air. Perhaps he wanted to blow away the cobwebs. Or perhaps his torment had finally driven him towards the appeal of standing on the edge and looking down at the hospital car park and the prospect of absolute oblivion.

You, too.

Instead, he turned left into an older part of the building that was evidently no longer in use. The long corridor tunnelled into a darkness broken by a shaft of dim light at the far end. Although the lights were out, electricity hummed. Pipes rattled. Echoes stirred in the cavities behind the old Victorian walls where Ryan imagined mice and scurrying rats.

His shameful thoughts followed him down the dusky passage that was empty but for a few plastic chairs and a collapsed, soiled-looking wheelchair. He walked towards the slanting light cast by the lone window—and found another corridor, then another. Haunted by the hollow echoes of his own footsteps, deep within the network of the old asylum's architecture, Ryan arrived at the foot of a short spiral staircase. At the top of the stairs was a door.

His heart fluttered. His palms sweated. The foreboding sense of history and place somehow exacerbated his sense of solitude. Away from his little hospital room, a dank mustiness prevailed, scarring the air with the whiff of neglect and century-old sickness.

And it was then he heard it: a quiet sobbing, the rise and fall of ragged breaths.

The sound was unmistakably female. It was coming from above him, from the room at the top of the stairs, beyond the door.

Gripped by inquisitiveness, taking hold of the bannister, he ascended the steps. Once he reached the top, he pushed open a creaking wooden door and emerged into a musty storage room.

Milly sat on the windowsill, silhouetted against the filthy glass, still wearing the baggy hoody and jeans. As he neared, the dull light from the window lit her pale face amidst an ethereal galaxy of floating dust motes.

She turned her head towards him and wiped a tear from her cheek. The ligature wound around her thin neck was a cruel abrasion on her otherwise flawless, marble-like skin. The groove was abraded and deep. She wore the black and yellow bruise, though, with an empowered dignity.

"What do you want?" she said, her voice trembling, her dark eyes smeared with mascara.

Ryan remained silent, transfixed by her tragedy.

Judging by the steep gradient of the ceiling above his head, he guessed he was standing in one of the original asylum's twin towers. The room was the size of a large loft, which was kind of what it was.

The brick walls were exposed, the wooden beams cobwebbed, everything coated in thick dust. A discoloured white sign with bold black letters was screwed into the wall: **Lost Property**, it read. The room was piled with bric-a-brac: a black umbrella, an old rotary dial telephone, a traffic cone.

A single bare bulb dangled from the ceiling from a frayed-looking wire.

"You're the boy from the room next door?"

Ryan nodded.

"Are you okay?" he said. It was all he could muster. While the girl was pale and thin, she was also beautiful: soft eyes, glossy hair, full lips.

She nodded.

"How did you get—?"

"Same way as you," she said, her voice firmer.

His eyes veered to the wound on her neck, and she raised her hands self-consciously. He averted his gaze and flinched as if he'd been caught looking at something he shouldn't. But he had lived in the darkness of depression all his young life, and while he knew the wound around her neck might have repulsed others, for him it held a strange allure, affording this wraith of a girl a dark mystique.

After a time, he dared to look at her again, and she held his eyes with her own.

"I'm Ryan."

"Milly," she said.

"I know."

It was then the red neon sign fizzed, flickering in the gloom. The sign read *On Air*. It was perched haphazardly at an angle above a small door in the room's darkest corner. Her cheeks still damp, Milly turned towards the red glow, and the pallor of her skin was inflamed by its illumination.

"Do you like music?" she said, her smile a thin scratch.

"Course."

"Over here." She hopped down from the sill and stepped over a stack of cardboard boxes with yellowed Sellotape. She walked beyond some wooden shelves cluttered with VHS cassettes, an old desktop computer, and an archaic-looking bright yellow stereo covered in black scorch marks.

Ryan followed.

The small door was low, and Milly had to bend to enter the tiny room. Ryan watched from beside the door.

"Look at all these old records," she said.

The space was the size of a broom cupboard. Dozens of infrared lights pinpricked the darkness like tiny red eyes, dust swirling amidst the dim phosphorescence. The cupboard space was jam-packed with old radio equipment: a mixing desk with dozens of knobs, faders, and meters; two sets of turntables; a cassette deck; a large furry microphone coated in dust; speakers, and boxes full of vinyl records and tapes.

"It all still works," said Milly, pulling out a record from its dust-covered sleeve. She placed the record on the turntable and fiddled with its prehistoric mechanisms. "Come in here."

Ryan did.

The record turned. The needle scratched. The speakers crackled. "The band is called A-Ha," said Milly.

They were squashed up close.

"I think my Mum likes them," he said, remembering an old VH1 music video in which pencil-sketched comic book characters came to life.

"They say music is like a drug," she said.

"They do?"

"Scientific fact," she said. "I read this article that said music makes us feel the same way as good food, wine, or you know."

"*You know*?"

"*Sex*," she whispered, her breath brushing his cheek.

He felt his face flush as red as the neon sign.

The music played. While the record was clearly warped and scratchy sounding, the song's drum machine popped, and the synthe-siser swarmed, filling the air with a thick fuzz that was distorted yet whole: a wall of sound flawed by its own purity. Ryan remembered his dad preaching about vinyl and how modern digital recordings could never replicate the charm of analogue. He understood now. Somehow, in that dark little room, the synthpop tones and the singer's falsetto range filled the darkness as completely as water would a glass. Maybe it was the Valium, but the music was oddly tangible, the song's lyrics camp incantations. It was, Ryan thought, like magic.

Milly's eyes glistened.

Touch me, pleaded the singer.

"Well, all those things—food, wine, drugs, sex—*music*, they help release something in the brain called dopamine," she said. "It makes us feel good."

"Oh, yeah?"

"Yeah. It's related to the psychology of desire and satisfaction."

She was close enough that he could smell her breath; it was warm and sweet.

"There was this old guy, a composer," she said. "His name was Leonard Meyer. He said it was all about the payoff."

Ryan shook his head. "*Payoff*?"

"When we listen to music, our minds anticipate a series of patterns, you know, sonically. And when our minds predict the patterns, or when we don't, we either feel rewarded or frustrated. The music causes neuro...*transmitters*, I think they're called, to release dopamine. And that makes us feel good."

"Wow," he said.

"It's kind of a dance of reward and expectation when you think about it," said Milly.

"So music influences our emotions, I mean directly?" he asked.

"Totally. We connect to it on a deep level."

"Weird."

"Not really," she said. "Imagine you're a caveman, and there's this huge sabre-toothed tiger that's been eating all your family. So, you're out hunting a woolly mammoth or something. Then you hear this almighty roar. Instinct tells you to be frightened. You're programmed to be frightened. It's genetic memory. Sound has a direct influence on how you behave. Music manipulates that by playing with those patterns of expectation. There are people who believe that consciousness is generated outside the brain. They believe the brain is simply a receiver."

"Cool," said Ryan.

She was so clever.

"Some people think music could even be responsible for *shaping* the way our brains evolved," said Milly. "Something to do with our auditory cortex. We play music, and the music plays us."

"Music can control our minds?" he said.

"Yeah, I suppose."

"Wish I could control mine," he said.

Milly pointed at a record at the top of a pile next to the turntables; its dusty old sleeve featured a man in a leather jacket playing the guitar. The record's title was *Wired for Sound* by Cliff Richard. "That's it!" she said. "We're wired for sound, all of us."

"Never thought about it that way," he said.

"It fascinates me," she said, "the way music makes us feel."

Amidst the twinkling LED lights of the antique equipment, Milly's eyes shone, and Ryan felt the weight of expectation to say something profound. "And how do *you* feel?" he said. The words were out before he could take them back.

The spell was broken. Even in the dark, he noticed her eyes change, like a drifting cloud blocking the sun.

"I have to go," she said, blinking rapidly. "I shouldn't be here."

Attempting to stall her, he looked around the cupboard-sized room for something to talk about—anything—and pointed to an old framed photo on the wall. "Who's that?"

The good-looking man was sitting in the same tiny studio, challenging the camera with his confident stare. Sunglasses were perched on the top of his head, holding back his slicked-back, glossy hair. He wore a white jacket with the sleeves rolled up and a T-shirt embossed with the MTV logo. The photo was autographed in gold pen. The signature was difficult to decipher, but Ryan thought the scrawl read *Ollie Bernard, The Sultan of Synth*.

"Is that the DJ from the radio?" he said. It wasn't so much the name he remembered but the alter-ego: *The Sultan of Synth*.

Milly remained silent, and Ryan looked around the tiny studio. But whoever was broadcasting now surely wasn't doing so from here, using this archaic equipment.

"I...I have to go," Milly said again, brushing past him and chewing her nails, arms raised to hide her neck. In the space of seconds, all her playful flirtatiousness had disappeared.

Ryan watched Milly step over the clutter and walk towards the tower's exit. He let her go because he knew how it felt to be trapped in the darkness when all you wanted was to be alone.

She opened the door, letting in a dim shaft of light, regarded him with her dark eyes, and left.

Ryan stood alone in the doorway of the little studio, the record turning, the needle scratching, the speakers fuzzing with static, the music reaching its crescendo.

Above his head, the neon sign fizzed as electricity surged in its tubes. The erratic voltage was probably caused by corroded connections or rat-gnawed wire, he supposed.

The sign gently pulsed, its radiance scarring the darkness in intermittent, wounding throbs: *On Air...On Air...On Air*.

5.

"HOW HAS HE GOT OUT OF A LOCKED WARD?" SAID WILL.

"We don't know, Mr. Wallis," said the young nurse. "Look, try not to worry. We'll find him."

Will was standing next to the coffee machine. Posters on the wall denoted a range of mental health conditions: anxiety disorder, bipolar disorder, obsessive-compulsive disorder, post-traumatic stress disorder.

How had this happened to his boy? When Ryan was born, fifteen years ago, Will had gone for a quiet beer with two of his closest friends and boasted his son would one day play for Manchester City. It was banter, of course, three young blokes jesting in a smoky pub. He didn't care what Ryan chose to do with his precious life so long as he was happy. That's all that had mattered.

Yet Ryan had ended up here. But for the first time maybe, Will acknowledged that his son needed special care. Of all those damned posters on the wall and their collage of psychological sicknesses, one word appeared more boldly than any other: suicide.

Will massaged his temples, wishing he'd pursued Ryan out into the corridor, wishing he'd followed more quickly.

The nurse placed a gentle hand on his wrist. "We are checking the car park—"

It was then Sonny burst through the ward's locked doors with his arm around Ryan. "I found him in the old hospital," said Sonny, "in Lost Property."

Will rushed over to the orderly, clapped him on the shoulder in gratitude, then hugged his boy ferociously. "Why, Ryan?" he said, pulling away from the embrace and clasping his son's shoulders perhaps a little hard. "Why?"

"I needed to be alone," said Ryan, mumbling.

Drawing him in close again, Will held his son tight. "Promise me you'll never do that again."

But Ryan pulled himself free, shrugging his father away. He walked, head down, towards his room.

Sonny put his arm around Will. "Let him be," said the older man, his dark skin creasing into a weathered frown.

Reluctantly, Will did.

6.

DR. JENSEN SAT ON A PLASTIC CHAIR, SQUINTING THROUGH HIS HALF-moon spectacles as if Ryan was some laboratory specimen.

Ryan had his feet up on the bed, had been listening to the radio and thinking about Milly until his dad had taken away his head-phones. His father stood at the foot of the bed next to his mother, who sipped coffee from another plastic cup.

The panel lighting in the hospital room was harsh, causing his father's scalp to gleam under the thin hair of his crown, and Ryan noticed too his mother's crow's feet and the dark bags under her eyes. She looked old. They both did. Old and pathetic. He realised for the first time they had winged this—parenthood. They were responsible for him being imprisoned here.

"Ryan, you need to take your pills," said the doctor, pushing a paper cup on the bedside cabinet towards him.

Ryan folded his arms.

"When you left your room earlier, were you planning on hurting yourself?" asked Dr. Jensen.

Ryan remained silent.

The doctor said, "Can I ask you why you felt the need to—?"

"*Escape*?" finished Ryan.

Dr. Jensen said, "You're not a prisoner—"

"Well, it sure feels like it," Ryan spat. "I wanted to get to the roof, see the view."

His mother covered her face with her hands and let out a low, muffled moan.

Ryan had lived with guilt for years, was sick of tiptoeing around, feeling bad for everyone else, for things he had never done but only thought. He resented them for burdening him with guilt, for caring, for making him care. Well, maybe he no longer would.

"Maybe I wanted to jump, end it all, splatter my brains all over the hospital car park," he said, his voice laced with spite.

His mother wept. The sight of her made him sick.

"*Ryan,*" warned his father.

"No, Dad," he said. "You have no right. None of you. It's my life, not yours. *My* head. *My* thoughts."

"Nobody has disputed that," said his mother. "We just want you home."

Years of pent-up anger seethed inside him. They had fuelled this rage by locking him up like a lunatic.

"We want what's best for you," she said, touching his arm.

He flinched, pulling his arm away.

Old whore.

Ryan fought the thought, feeling the pang of instant satisfaction and the wave of guilt that followed, the emotions colliding like wasps, swarming in a nest full of venom.

Whore, whore, whore.

The thoughts were unbearable when he was angry; because they came so freely, his angry mind gave credence that the thoughts *must* indeed be his true feelings. The guilt was worse due to this semi-endorsement.

"You had no right to look in my head in the first place," said Ryan.

"Nobody is looking in your head, Ryan," said his father from under the halo of his gleaming scalp.

Bald prick.

Inside, Ryan recoiled. "Then why did you look at my pictures?" he said.

"You know that was an accident," said his mother.

"You looked in my head, and you didn't like what you saw, and so you've locked me in this place. And now you think you have the right to take away my things," said Ryan, directing his gaze at the headphones clasped by his father.

"What is it with these headphones and that bloody hospital radio station?" his father said.

The doctor frowned as if confused.

Ryan said, "Music has healing power—"

"That may be so," his father said. "But—"

"I'm not the only one who thinks it," said Ryan. "The radio makes me feel better. Milly says so too."

"We don't have a hospital radio station," said Dr. Jensen, interrupting.

Ryan ignored him. "Music, it's science. She showed me. It's true. Music plays with the patterns of reward and expectation in the brain. It's all to do with psychology—desire and satisfaction. The radio makes me feel better, and you've taken my headphones away."

His father carefully placed the headphones on the bed and raised his hands in a placating gesture. Ryan snatched them up.

Dr. Jensen leaned forward in his chair. "You've spoken to Milly?" he said.

"Yes," said Ryan.

"When?" said Dr. Jensen.

"An hour ago. In Lost Property. In the old radio studio."

"That's impossible," said the doctor.

Faggot.

"No, it's not."

Faggot, faggot, faggot.

Ryan wasn't a homophobe, yet the words kept coming, seeping from his mind like a battery leaking acid. He had images flashing in his head too, of his fist pummelling the doctor's fat face.

The doctor scowled. His father was also frowning.

Dr. Jensen said, "What you saw earlier on, it's enough to disturb anyone. Even trained doctors and nurses with years of experience can suffer trauma after witnessing such…incidents. Several of my staff have already been referred for counselling."

"What are you getting at?" asked his father.

"Maybe we can have a quick word outside, Mr. Wallis."

"No," said Ryan. "Don't treat me like that. I'm old enough to make my own decisions. If you've got something to say, say it to me too."

The doctor shot a questioning glance at his parents; they both nodded solemnly.

"I wouldn't usually break patient confidentiality," said Dr. Jensen. "But since this matter has a direct link to Ryan's health, I can tell you Milly's not faring well at all."

"What do you mean?" asked his father.

"She's in a coma," said the doctor. "She has been since she left surgery this morning."

7.

THE WORDS PLAYED ON REPEAT, IN RYAN'S HEAD, ECHOING LIKE A WHISPER
in a deep well: *She's in a coma.*

It was dark. He was alone. The lights were out. He'd taken the
pills, not only those in the paper cup but half the plastic tub he'd
stolen from the nurse's medicine trolley. The little hospital room roiled
around him. He felt sluggishly drunk.

He was listening to the radio. George Michael was singing that
there was no comfort in the truth because all you'd find was pain.
Ryan could relate to that. He checked the door. Every fifteen minutes,
the nurse would poke her head into the room and check he was still
breathing. Little did she know he had more pills, lots of them.

He'd heard what the doctor had told his father. They *had* gone
outside—all three of them—in the end. His parents had stood in the
corridor and listened. The doctor convinced them their only son was
experiencing delusional ideation, that he could be suffering from a
complex blend of OCD and paranoid schizophrenia, or maybe post-
traumatic stress disorder.

Meanwhile, Milly, Jensen had claimed, was in a coma, was having
tests to determine the extent of the damage to her oxygen-starved
brain. She might never wake up. She was hooked to one of those
bleeping life-support machines that kept her from dying.

Shadows lurched on the walls. Distant voices echoed along the
corridors. Ryan turned up the volume on his headphones.

Had it really been Milly? Or an imposter?

A ghost?

No, Milly was still alive, even if her brain tissue was as cognitive as
a bowl of instant jelly; he'd read once that the consistency was similar.

Poor Milly.

"You're tuned to FM-85, the home of your favourite hits," said the DJ.
"Are you feeling a little glum today? I know we usually keep
things upbeat, but here's a tune to help you revel in your misery:
'How Soon is Now?' by The Smiths."

The song opened with a tremolo guitar. The singer warbled about
sadness and needing to be loved.

If this was life, Ryan didn't want it, not anymore. It was all too much. The Valium he'd taken made it easy to ingest the rest of the tub. And the stolen painkillers. Any resistance to the idea of ending his young life had been eroded. He popped the lid and emptied the contents into his palm. Sonny had left a jug of orange cordial by his bedside. Ryan poured a glass and swallowed the pills, gratefully tasting every acrid capsule.

In the dark, he closed his eyes and listened to the radio. The music played, and Ryan drifted. He found Milly in the airwaves, in the frequencies of sound where music had brought them together.

8.

WILL WOKE TO HIS MOBILE RINGING IN THE NIGHT, THE PHONE'S URGENT glare assaulting his eyes in the dark of his bedroom where Sue slept beside him. His hands fumbled for purchase on the smooth screen. He answered.

"Mr. Wallis?"

"Speaking."

"Hello, I'm sorry to wake you. My name is Mandy Gilbert. I'm a nurse on the children and adolescents' psychiatric unit."

He knew her. "*Yes*?"

"It's Ryan, I'm afraid. He's been transferred to the general hospital, to intensive care. He's taken an overdose."

They dressed quickly, silently, too afraid to speak. Will drove, hurtling through the suburbs, under the flickering glow of streetlights, each strobe wounding their tired eyes in jaundiced throbs.

At his side, Sue wept, clutching a bag. The sports bag had been packed the previous day and contained Nintendo games, Ryan's favourite hair gel, and his beloved Sharpie pens. A terrible thought occurred to Will: what if these favourite things had already been used for the last time? The nurse's words echoed over and over in Will's mind: *overdose*.

Bleary-eyed, they ran through the bright hospital corridors, navigating each sharp corner as they followed the signs towards the ward nobody ever wanted to search for.

Breathless from exertion, they arrived at the intensive care ward where a nurse escorted them to a small room, and they were introduced to the shocking sight that was their beloved son.

Ryan resembled a fresh corpse. He lay bare-chested on the bed, propped up by pillows. Two IV drips fed into the backs of his hands. A monitor measured his heart rate, blood pressure, and oxygen. A clip was attached to his finger and adhesive patches fixed to his chest. He looked small, young, and vulnerable, his mouth a thin slat filled with a serpentine tangle of plastic pipes.

"My boy," said Sue, breaking into tears.

A tall and elderly doctor entered the room. The doctor's thin hair was combed back over his liver-spotted scalp. He wore glasses and a thick moustache, his expression dour. "Mr. and Mrs. Wallis?"

Will nodded. Sue sat at the bedside, holding their son's limp hand.

"My name is Dr. Barker. I'm sorry to inform you your son has taken an overdose."

Will said, "How—?"

The doctor shook his head dismissively. "There will be an investigation," he said. "But I can't speak on behalf of—Dr. Jensen has been paged. I'm expecting him shortly."

Will said, "Is Ryan going to be—?"

"We are monitoring him, carrying out tests," said Dr. Barker. "We will know more in an hour once the bloodwork returns. For now, he's stable. I'll be back to update you soon, but we need to carry out a brain scan."

Will said, "What are his—?"

"I'm afraid I don't know anything more at this stage," said the doctor. "The quicker we carry out our checks, the quicker I'll be able to give you more definitive answers."

Will nodded, and the doctor abruptly left.

They sat with their son, crying, holding each other, and watching him sleep in his chemical-induced coma, praying for his precious life.

9.

"I'm sorry about your boy."

Will turned from the coffee machine on the intensive care unit to see Kevin standing behind him. It was shortly after five o'clock in the morning, less than twenty-four hours since they'd first talked about the goat-semen cappuccinos. Yet the man appeared ten years older. His greying beard looked like it had grown out a week. His bloodshot eyes were dull in their sockets, his hair greasy and unkempt.

For a second Will said nothing. Then he said, "How's Milly?"

Kevin shook his head and swallowed as if stifling tears. "They don't know what's wrong with her."

Will thought that was an odd thing to say. It was obvious: Milly had attempted suicide and starved her brain of oxygen. He wondered if the man was suffering from denial.

"She's had tests. The doctor said coma patients usually have minimal brain activity, but Milly's brain is…overactive."

"*Overactive*? Surely that's a good thing," said Will.

"She won't wake up. We've put the radio next to her bed. I've read it can help, you know, the music. She loves that bloody radio station."

Will nodded.

It was obvious Kevin was in a deep state of shock. He pitied him, but right now he needed to preserve every ounce of strength for his own family.

"Your boy?" said Kevin.

"They've taken him for a scan. He's had blood tests," said Will. "He's due back shortly."

Sue waited in the little hospital room, and Will was anxious to return to her before the doctors arrived.

He heard the shouting from along the corridor. He entered Ryan's room to find Dr. Barker standing at the foot of the bed. Dr. Jensen was with him.

Sue was angrily berating the Dane. "How was my son allowed to swallow all those pills?" she shouted.

"I can assure you, Mrs. Wallis," Dr. Jensen said, "we're investigating—"

"And what good will that do if my son dies, doctor? What good will that do him then?" She pointed to where Ryan lay, a nurse reattaching various monitors following his round of medical tests.

Dr. Barker said, "Mrs. Wallis, maybe it's best if you sit down."

Will took Sue by the arm and escorted her to the chair beside Ryan's bed. She sat down. Will remained standing.

Outside, the sun was rising, the birds chirping, a crow cawing, welcoming a warm summer morning. But there was nothing to savour on a new day when his fifteen-year-old son could slip away as easily as daylight that distant evening.

Dr. Barker said, "Are you aware your son may have dabbled in any substances, apart from those prescribed, I mean?"

"*Drugs*?" said Will.

The doctor nodded.

"He's never taken drugs," said Sue in urgent defence.

Will put his hand on Sue's shoulder.

The life-support machine continued its bleeping, every short, sharp pulse punctuating the seconds with the reminder that death was real, that it was close.

Dr. Barker said, "I'm not accusing your boy of anything. We have a bit of a…strange situation on our hands, and I'm trying my best to get to the bottom of things so we can help Ryan. I have your son's medical notes, of course, but can I ask, has your son suffered at all from any illness recently, apart from his mental health? Or a head injury, anything like that?"

"No," said Will, looking at Dr. Jensen. "*You* have his medical notes. What are you getting at?"

"Ryan's bloodwork is fine," said Dr. Barker. "Despite the overdose, his hepatic and renal levels are okay when you consider the number of pills Ryan consumed. What is rather...baffling is the brain scan."

"What do you mean?" said Will.

Dr. Barker said, "Although Ryan scores low on the Glasgow scale—"

Will said, "*Glasgow*—?"

"It's how we measure coma patients' level of responsiveness," said Dr. Barker. "Ryan is currently relatively unresponsive, which is to be expected, yet his brain activity is off the scale."

"I don't understand," said Sue.

"Perhaps it's best if I show you in my office," said Dr. Barker. "If you'd follow me, please."

Will and Sue left Ryan in the care of the nurse and followed Dr. Barker out into the corridor. Dr. Jensen followed too but had remained silent since Sue had berated him. They passed Milly's room and saw Kevin sitting sullen faced next to his comatose daughter; he was fiddling with a radio as if trying to get a better signal.

Dr. Barker led them into a small office and shut the door. The office was much like Dr. Jensen's in the neighbouring psychiatric hospital with a large desk, water machine, and various medical journals stacked on a small bookcase. But this room had two large monitor screens fixed to the wall.

Will and Sue sat down. Dr. Jensen leaned on the edge of the desk.

Dr. Barker stood between the monitor screens. "I have been practising for nearly forty-five years," he said. "I've worked in intensive care for twenty-five. I'll be honest with you: I've never come across *anything* like this before."

Will gripped his wife's hand.

"Neurons," said Dr. Barker, his expression indicating he was resigned to explaining something they would never understand, "are the cells that make up your brain. Your brain has around eighty-six billion."

Sue scowled. "He's brain-damaged, isn't he? Oh God, no."

"Let the man speak," said Will.

Dr. Barker regarded them with a sideways glance and turned to the monitor furthest to his left. He touched the screen, and it flickered on, showing numerous files. The doctor tapped a file, which opened. He then clicked, tapped, and swiped until a video played.

"This is a normal functioning human brain," he said, pointing to a blue-on-black computer-generated image of a brain. The brain spun on its axes and was magnified, revealing hundreds of thousands of interconnected spidery, web-like cells.

"Every time we think, a chain of electrical impulses begins, one neuron sending a message to another, and so on, and so on." Dr. Barker tapped the monitor where tiny pulses of light travelled from the branches of one neuron to another and another in a self-perpetuating electronic wave of information. "With every thought, eighty-six billion neurons communicate like this. These electrical impulses travel at incredible speeds—one quadrillion synapses happening at once."

"And?" said Will.

"And that is how a normal human brain functions," said Dr. Barker. He tapped and swiped the second monitor screen to the right. "This is what Ryan is experiencing."

On the second screen, another computer-generated map of a human brain appeared. Again, the image was magnified. The tiny pulses of light passing from one neuron to another were still visible, but new lights appeared. Flashing like fireworks in indiscriminate eruptions, the new lights were brighter yet totally random. There was no pattern of intelligence, no logic, no symbiotic association between one neuron and the next. Instead, the pulses of light flashed so brightly the other lights appeared inconsequential.

"The images you're looking at are computer-generated," said Dr. Barker. "But the synapses we're seeing have been identified using neuroimaging, or brain scanning. That is, we've mapped the brain function by identifying where neurons are firing—where glucose has been used in the brain. These vastly simplified computer-generated images simulate the brain activity your son is experiencing."

Dr. Barker continued, "The messages, or ions, you saw being

passed between neurons in the first video is how the human brain works—*a chain reaction*. The mind is electrical, and our thoughts develop that way—"

Will had some understanding of the workings of the brain. He'd read several articles on how the brain's various segments operated. And in Will's own mind, those synapses fired, too, forming their own chain reaction and carrying memories stored in his temporal lobe to the problem-solving prefrontal cortex.

Ryan's words echoed in his head: *The radio makes me feel better—*

He remembered Sonny's words: *The frequencies, they're nothing more than vibrations—good vibrations and bad ones—*

Dr. Jensen's words: *We don't have a hospital radio station—*

Kevin's words: *She loves that bloody radio station—*

The radio... The frequencies... The vibrations...

Will remembered, too, how the station had sounded: *warped*, like an old record.

Dr. Barker was still pointing at the erratic lights flashing on the computer-generated simulation of his son's comatose brain. He said, "The random lights you see on the second screen are inconsistent with the biological mechanics of thought—"

"I spoke to Kevin," said Will, interrupting. "Milly's dad."

Dr. Barker frowned.

"Milly's the same, isn't she? Her brain scan, I mean?"

Dr. Barker hesitated for a long second, then nodded.

Will turned to Dr. Jensen, who remained perched on the edge of the desk in apparent passive contemplation. "What did you mean yesterday when you said there wasn't a hospital radio station?"

Dr. Jensen scowled, looking perplexed. "Exactly that. We don't have a hospital radio station, not since—"

"*Since?*" urged Will impatiently.

"August 1987."

"That's very exact."

Dr. Jensen nodded. "The station was shut down."

"Why, doctor?"

"It was a long time ago," said Dr. Jensen.

"Please, *tell*," said Will.

"There was a patient," said Dr. Jensen, sighing. "As part of his care plan, he was permitted to operate a radio station, for two hours a day. The station was monitored, of course. But things…well, they got out of hand."

"What do you mean?" said Will.

"It was a long time ago. I don't see how this is relev—"

"*How?*"

"The patient's name was Oliver Bernard," said Dr. Jensen. "He had some strange…"

"*What?*" said Will.

"*Delusions,*" said Dr. Jensen.

"What kind of delusions?" said Will.

"I don't see—"

"*Doctor?*"

Dr. Jensen exchanged a look of caution with Dr. Barker. Dr. Barker nodded, prompting the Dane to continue.

Dr. Jensen sighed deeply and said, "There was a boy. He died."

10.

22 AUGUST 1987

JIMMY SIMPSON SNAPPED SHUT THE CASSETTE TRAY OF HIS BRIGHT YELLOW boombox and hit **PLAY**. To think, the cassette marked *Mega Mix 87* had been compiled especially by Ollie Bernard—AKA The Sultan of Synth.

Kate Bush sang about making a deal with God, filling his little hospital room with operatic lunacy. Jimmy had been busy diligently writing in his diary; with all these drugs in his system, he made a point of writing down everything, just like the doctors had told him.

"Not too loud," said the nurse, popping her head around the door.

"Okay." Jimmy turned the volume down a notch.

"And don't forget your pills," said the nurse.

Fat chance.

He hated the hospital. Scratch that: he fucking despised it. The looney bin, that's what people called it. The doctors said he was schizophrenic, but he'd never killed anyone in his fourteen years, tempting as it sometimes was. If he was going to hurt anyone, it would be himself, he supposed—that was why he'd been admitted after all.

"Jimmy, how are we doing?"

The doctor walked in without so much as a knock. Nobody respected his privacy in this place. He closed his diary and pressed **STOP**. He didn't want the doctor to see his journal or hear his mixtape. He flung the diary in the drawer of his bedside cabinet where he kept it.

"Have you got time for a few questions?" asked the doctor.

Like he could say no. Jimmy nodded.

"You've been going over to the communal room, in the adults' unit?" asked the doctor. He was a Danish fellow with blond hair. *Jensen*, his name was.

He nodded again. "Only on Saturdays."

"I see."

"The nurse said the kids won't be allowed to go over anymore."

"That's right," said the doctor.

"Why?"

A brief silence.

"We've bought a television set for the children's ward," said the doctor. "Makes more sense. No more boring news, hey."

"Was that all you wanted to ask me?"

"No." The doctor cleared his throat. "When you've gone over, to the communal room, have you spoken to any of the adults?"

"Only to ask if I could watch TV. When *The A-Team*'s on."

"And that's all? You haven't spoken to any of the grown-up patients?"

"No," lied Jimmy.

When Jimmy grew up, he wanted to be a radio DJ, too, just like The Sultan. He was so cool: the way he wore his hair, the way he rolled up the sleeves of his jacket, a cigarette hanging limply from his lips. Okay, so Ollie was only the DJ for the hospital radio station, but big things were ahead of him.

"The man who runs the hospital radio station, he's a patient. Did he talk to you?"

"No."

"Good-looking chap? Gelled hair?"

Jimmy shook his head.

He and Ollie chatted regularly, about music, the station, and life. Ollie had told him what the doctors were trying to do—see inside his head. He must not let them. Once they got their meddling fingers into your mind, it was over.

The nightly two-hour radio show, though, was the only good thing about being in the hospital. But the days were long. Last week—what now looked like his very last week visiting the communal room—Ollie had slipped him the mixtape, together with another packet of Marlboros. It was their secret. Jimmy would have played it sooner, but his boombox had chewed his *Thriller* tape beyond repair. It'd taken him ages to untangle it from the cassette deck.

"Very well," said the doctor, smiling.

"Why do you ask me?"

"Nothing important. I'll leave you alone. What are you listening to, anyway? Anything groovy?"

Groovy.

An acidic glob of vomit rose in Jimmy's throat, such was his disgust. He tried to stifle his scowl. Failed. "Nothing much," he replied.

He waited for the doctor to leave. When the door closed, he plugged in his headphones for privacy and pressed **PLAY**. The song ended. Bernard's smooth voice soothed the headache brought on by the doctor's line of interrogation.

"Hey, Jimmy," said Bernard in stereo. "Hope you're enjoying the sleek sounds I've prepared for you!"

Then a steady beat grew amongst synthesisers and rock-pop guitar, and Kim Wilde—*what a fox*—sang to some unknown lover, accusing the man of not loving her. *How could someone not love Kim Wilde?* Whoever he was, Jimmy hoped he was banged up in the nuthouse too.

But the more he listened to the song—"You Keep Me Hanging On" —the more he thought he understood Kim Wilde on a deep level. Her lyrics resonated with him, seeped into his core. What a bastard that man was—and Jimmy knew how Kim felt, too, because nobody loved him either. If his parents did, how come they were fifty miles away and he was stuck here?

Jimmy was sitting on the floor, next to his stereo. He felt a deep melancholy come over him. He felt so alone. And he might never chat to Ollie again. Things were so bleak.

"You're listening to FM-85, and I'm Ollie Bernard—the Sultan of Synth. Boy, have I got some tunes for you! Remember, if you want the hits, tune in for our two-hour megamix!"

Startled, Jimmy checked the tape was still playing and not the actual radio.

"Just messing with you," said Bernard through the foam of his headphones as if he was watching. It was a well-orchestrated prank, of course, pre-recorded. "Still the *private* mixtape, Jimmy. Have you thought any more about what we talked about?"

He had.

But there was something special about the mixtape, the radio show too. He could listen to the same song on another radio station, but it didn't have the same resonance. On the mixtape, the lyrics sounded as if they'd been rerecorded, as if the song was written for him alone. Words held a strange transcendency—they jumped out at him—like a special language intended solely for him. It was as if emotions and ideas were transmitted directly to his brain, in which they would gently dissolve, harmoniously acquiescing with his own thoughts.

The doctor burst through the door. "You lied."

Jimmy heard the accusation over Bonnie Tyler on his headphones; he took them off.

"Why did you lie to me?"

"I didn't."

"I have three nurses telling me they saw you chatting with the man I asked you about."

He shrugged.

"It's for your own safety. I'm going to have to take that radio away," said the doctor, pointing at his boombox.

"You can't."

"Watch me."

Jimmy held the stereo, his body a human shield.

"You can have it back next week, once this is all sort—" The doctor ceased his explanation as if censoring himself.

Two nurses arrived. It took all three of them to wrestle the stereo from Jimmy's arms, tearing the headphone's cord free, but amongst the frantic struggle, they'd not seen him eject the mixtape.

The precious mixtape.

How he slated them in his diary. He drew pictures of Dr. Jensen with knives in his eyes; he wrote spiteful little limericks about the doctor being infected with syphilis; he wrote stories in which the nurses were brutally raped.

Later, in darkness, with the door closed, Jimmy listened to the tape on the Sony Walkman he kept stashed beneath his diary together with the cigarettes and lighter in his bedside drawer.

He hated his life more than ever. *They* were supposed to be making him better, not worse. He felt so lonely. And angry.

The song was "Dancing in the Dark" by Bruce Springsteen. The Boss sang about that old cliché: you couldn't start a fire without a spark. But Jimmy had one. He had a light. First, he enjoyed a tab, blowing blue smoke in lazy rings in the little room's murk. But the lyrics—fire—fire—*fire*—they lit the kindling of an idea that spread, setting his mind ablaze with fantasies of revenge and destruction.

When he'd attempted suicide the last time, he had failed. But that was then. He'd show them.

Jimmy Simpson jammed a chair beneath the door handle, and, using his Hai-Karate deodorant as a flamethrower, he set his sheets alight.

By the time the doctors and nurses attempted to kick the door open, the room was a roaring cauldron of fire, poisonous fumes spreading, the flames licking the walls, setting the ceiling ablaze.

Still wearing his headphones, Jimmy danced alone. Fourteen years of pain receded, and a strange sense of relief washed over him. His lungs were filling with the filthy, coiling smoke, but that was okay because his head was full of music.

11.

"BY THE TIME FIREFIGHTERS REACHED THE BOY," SAID DR. JENSEN, "HE was dead. The fire was contained, but we did recover Bernard's mixtape and the boy's diary. There were other patients too. Other mixtapes. We had hard evidence."

"Shit," said Will.

"Bernard was a paranoid schizophrenic," said Dr. Jensen. "He believed he could infiltrate the minds of the other patients through his radio show. He believed he was sending subliminal messages to persuade other patients to commit suicide."

"You speak about him in the past tense," said Will. "Why? Where is he?"

"Dead," said Dr. Jensen. "He knew we were on to him. We found him in what is now lost property, hanging from the rafters in one of the old hospital towers."

"On to him? You *believe* Bernard had this...*this...ability*?" said Will.

"Of course not," said Dr. Jensen, his eyes darting between Will, Sue, and Dr. Barker.

"Then what did you mean?" said Will.

"Nothing," said Dr. Jensen, but the doctor had inadvertently shown his hand.

Will had never believed in the supernatural. But an impossible scenario unfolded in his mind's eye. He pointed to the computer-simulated brain on the screen and the indiscriminate eruptions of light. "Those lights, they're not chain reactions—they're not thoughts at all, are they?" he said, the epiphany hitting him.

"Then what are they?" said Dr. Barker.

"They're transmissions," said Will.

"That's impossible," said Dr. Jensen.

The doctor's irises were as clear as the bluest ocean, and Will could almost see the workings of his sharp intellect struggling to process the unfeasible.

"Impossible," agreed Dr. Barker.

"Is that brain scan possible?" said Will, pointing at the monitor. He directed his question at both doctors.

Neither answered.

12.

RYAN RUNS DOWN THE ENDLESS CORRIDOR TOWARDS THE SLANTING SHAFT of light, fleeing the predator on his tail.

He passes a soiled-looking wheelchair, an IV stand, a one-eyed teddy bear left to fester on the filthy tiled floor.

Despite his exertion, his heart is steady. He can hear every thick beat thudding in his ears, his cardiac ventricles collecting and expelling the blood in perfect sequence with the bleeping life-support machine that echoes so profoundly in the shuddering old walls.

Bleep…

It's as if he is inside himself, and somewhere there's a door. He must find it. That is his innate understanding.

Bleep…

At the end of the dilapidated corridor, he only finds another decrepit hallway, and another, each tunnelling deeper into the old asylum—deeper into himself, nearer to where the darkness lives inside him.

He tries to run faster. But in the catacombs of his unconsciousness, he is lost in a dream in which his limbs are slow and the enemy quick.

Bleep...

Broken neon signs adorn the shabby walls, the fizzing electrics as faulty as his own internal wiring. At first, the signs denote hospital departments: *inpatients, outpatients, phlebotomy.* Then as one corridor ends and another begins, the signs introduce years of decades that have long passed.

2008...

1994...

1987...

Music fills the corridors, too, the way a distant pipe organ announces the arrival of a summer fair, the timbre drifting on a faraway wind, teasing the ear with the promise of fun.

But somewhere, the needle scratches. The record plays: "Together in Electric Dreams". He can't pinpoint where the music originates. But he's heard this song before on that radio station that convinced him to take the pills, turn up the volume, and slip away.

He understands now: this frequency is deadly, like carbon monoxide in a warm house in winter, the music surreptitiously planting seeds of suggestion—poison as powerful as heroin. He'd been unwell already, of course, but perhaps the frequency needs insanity; perhaps the sane are immune.

He runs around another corner. Milly is standing at the far end of the corridor, outside a hospital room where thick black smoke rises from the gap under the door. Behind it, an out-of-tune, pubescent voice murders an old Springsteen hit. The song soon descends into a wail of agonised screams, and the door reddens, glowing with searing heat.

Ryan grabs Milly's hand, and they flee.

Yet they can't escape the music.

The DJ's voice booms like digital thunder, echoing in the corridors: *"You're listening to FM-85. Oh boy, have I got some hits for you!"*

The hospital isn't a hospital. It's a jukebox, and they are mice lost in its mechanisms.

"This is Ollie Bernard, and here's 'Small Town Boy' by Bronski Beat."

The beat begins seamlessly. *"Run Away,"* the song prompts them. And they hurry deeper into the maze of corridors. The music is so much more than sound, thicker than air, visible as a wraithlike mist.

They reach a door. It is unremarkable. Dirty. In need of paint.

Ryan is exhausted. He has run his whole life from every vile, fleeting thought that has emanated from his damaged mind. There's nowhere left to run. There is only the door.

But something follows.

He turns towards the tunnelling darkness behind him. A lone silhouette is backlit by the strobe of fizzing signs. Bernard steps out from the spectral mist, aviator shades shielding his handsome face, the white jacket wrapped around his lithe form.

Bernard flickers like broken neon. Blinking in and out of existence, he moves closer, running his hand through his slicked-back hair. The posturing is vain and contrived: a parody of the decade that refused to die.

"Stay?" says Bernard.

Ryan knows he *can* stay here forever, in this 1980s fantasia where the music hypnotises its victims like a pipe charming a snake. He can surrender himself and live in this immortal electric dream. He can exist in the frequencies that poison those that are most susceptible.

Bernard peers over his sunglasses, revealing eyes that burn as bright as lasers. "Stay," he orders, lighting a cigarette, his voice dropping several octaves.

His heart pounding, still gripping Milly's hand, Ryan turns back towards the door. The faded lime green gloss is chipped and scuffed. His hand grips the knob. The handle is smooth.

"You'll have peace here," says Bernard. He tells the truth, Ryan believes.

The music soothes.

But what is peace if it is fabricated, if it is synthesised?

Pain is real.

Ryan pulls the handle, and the door slams open, breaking hinges and cracking plaster. A black wind is released. It howls, visible as ghostly wisps, escaping the vast void behind...*the...the mirror*?

The dressing mirror is oval, four feet in height and covered in dust. Ryan wipes the glass clean with his palm—and discovers his reflection is absent; instead, an old man with bloodshot eyes and an empty bottle haunts the glass, returning his gaze.

The wind rushes, beating at Ryan's hair, his cheeks. Somewhere far away, Bernard calls, "Stay, Ryan. Stay."

The old man in the mirror silently mouths cruel obscenities... homophobic insults...racist slurs...

His whispered words echo in Ryan's mind: syllables that invade and metastasise, spreading ideas of hatred and fear.

Ryan winces. To look is to feel, and to feel is to hurt, and so he averts his gaze from the old man's rheumy eyes because the psychological burden is a wound too raw to bear. It's like trying to stare at the sun while radiation burns your retinas.

The void behind the mirror is vast, and the shadows that dwell there shift, taking insidious forms. Ryan wonders if that void is Hell, and he turns back towards the old man in the mirror.

Ryan's eyes lock with the old man's eyes.

Yellowed by years, maybe weakened by time, perhaps compromised by cataracts or glaucoma or macular degeneration, the old man's eyes are innately familiar: they are, of course, Ryan's eyes.

He faces himself.

It's hard to look at what he will become at the very end. But look Ryan does, and the mirror starts to crack like a frozen lake under the weight of his gaze, the fractures spreading from the centre outwards.

The old man regards him, his sallow cheeks tear-stained, his red, bulbous nose testament to decades of alcohol abuse that has apparently failed to quieten the rage within.

For all these years, Ryan has run from himself, and he knows if he refuses to accept himself for who he is, what he is, his cruel thoughts will consume him like cancer.

Ryan steps towards the mirror, his eyes all the time fixed on the old man.

The mirror shatters in an explosion of glass, shards spreading like shrapnel in a glittering shower of wind. Darkness floods the corridors; it spills from the broken mirror like an oil slick.

Sheltering his face with his hands, Ryan turns to Milly. But she is gone. So is Bernard, the corridors too…*the music*. He is alone with his thoughts.

For the first time he can remember, his mind is quiet, apart from the distant mechanical metronome bleep of the life-support machine.

Bleep…

Blind to the darkness, Ryan follows the sound, his footsteps the only other echo in the depths of his coma.

13.

WILL KICKED THE OLD DOOR SO HARD THE WOOD BUCKLED, THE surrounding plaster crumbling in an avalanche of dust. But the door to the old tower stood resolute. He kicked again, puffs of plaster erupting, the sole of his Adidas rebounding after each unrelenting attack.

"I have a key," said Sonny from behind him. The porter stood on the stairs below. Sonny tried the key. It turned. But the door was jammed.

Then Will heard it: music. It was faint, but he could hear the rapid, hollow beat of a drum machine and the electronic swarm of a synthesiser on the door's other side. Attached to the wall was an old fire extinguisher. Will unclipped it from its holster and slammed it against the stubborn door. The door swung open, revealing the bare-bricked wall of a cluttered attic.

The rising sun spilt through a small window, and in the constellations of swirling dust motes, for a fleeting second, Will thought he saw the shape of a thin girl, standing at the window and pointing towards the room's far corner, but the illusion evaporated as his eyes became accustomed to the dawn light.

In the corner, a neon sign fizzed: *On Air...On Air...On Air.*

Risking the faulty wiring, Will tore down the sign and smashed the fire extinguisher down hard on the flickering neon. It exploded in splinters of glass.

The door to the little radio studio was ajar, and Will could see the record turning on the old turntables amidst the red light emitted from the dozens of LEDs. The music played. And without comprehending the impossible for longer than was necessary, Will again lifted the considerable weight of the extinguisher and bludgeoned the decks beyond repair, the brittle old record breaking as easily as his son's sanity.

By the time he was finished, his brow and back were greased with sweat, the studio destroyed in a hail of violent destruction.

"I think we're done here," said Sonny, standing outside the studio door, placing a hand on his shoulder.

Amongst the dust churned by his exertion, Will nodded.

14.

"Shush," his mother said gently. "Everything is going to be fine. You'll see."

Ryan stared at the cracks in the ceiling. He was in a hospital room but not one he remembered. He could still hear the electronic bleep he'd followed from the depths of his coma to the surface of consciousness.

He tried to talk, but his throat felt dry. It hurt, as if a shard of glass had wedged itself in the soft lining.

"M...Milly?" he croaked.

His mother blinked. That's all it took for him to realise Milly had gone, one split-second, semi-autonomic closing of her eyes.

His dishevelled father appeared on the other side of the bed and gripped his hand. "Thank God," said his dad. "Thank fucking God." He never usually swore, not at least when he thought Ryan was listening. Tears streamed down his unshaven cheeks.

Ryan felt an unyielding, unapologetic love for both his parents then. That same second, fear flickered in his bruised and battered mind. He expected a flurry in the creative hemisphere of his brain for some terrible insult or profanity.

But none came.

15.

"I HAD SOME TERRIBLE THOUGHTS," SAID RYAN.

"As we all do," said Sonny, leaning on his broom.

They stood in the car park outside the psychiatric unit. Ryan was wearing his rucksack, the September sun warming his face, the early autumn shadows promising colder days.

He'd spent two days recovering in the general hospital following his overdose. Then he'd been transferred back to the psychiatric ward for three weeks. His improvement had been dramatic. Those were not his words; they were Dr. Jensen's.

He was finally going home. His mum was chatting to the young nurse on the hospital steps about his medication. Twenty yards away, his dad was firing up the car. Its radio was blasting Ed Sheeran, singing about a castle on a hill.

"You don't understand," said Ryan. "The thoughts were about you."

"And did you mean them?" asked Sonny.

"Of course not," said Ryan.

"Well then," said Sonny. He brushed back a dreadlock and smiled. "Remember we spoke about the frequencies? The good and the bad?"

"Yeah."

"Well, just because we hear the bad frequencies every now and then," said Sonny, "it doesn't make us bad people. The world's a complicated place, you know. And so are we all. We're all full of darkness and light and every shade between."

"Thank you," said Ryan.

"Most people are good, Ryan. *You* are good." Sonny held out his hand to shake, but Ryan hugged him hard, then pulled away.

"There's going to be times in your life when you think the worst things," said Sonny. "It's what you do that counts."

"Come on," shouted his dad from the car, beckoning him to hurry.

Ryan high-fived Sonny one last time.

The Ed Sheeran song finished, and the DJ on his dad's car radio was introducing the next track. A song Ryan recognised as an old eighties hit blasted from the speakers across the car park: Cutting Crew's "(I Just) Died in Your Arms".

His mother anxiously turned away from the nurse. His father immediately lowered the volume on the radio and gazed nervously in Ryan's direction.

Sonny smiled, and Ryan laughed. He walked to the car with his heart a little lighter, a little warmer, because a slice of darkness had been cut out.

As Ryan crouched into the car's back seat, he looked up to the hospital tower that he knew contained the little studio.

From the tower's small window, a pale face stared back.

The face was thin, the cheeks razor sharp, the breath a thin fog that steamed the dirty glass.

Ryan watched as a white finger slowly scratched letters into the window's dust. The words read, *Wired for Sound*.

RIDE THE NIGHT

"Look, old-timer, you've got an infection," said the carer whose name John couldn't recall.

"I know what I saw," said John from his armchair. "I'm seventy-seven, not ninety-seven. Don't patronise me."

The carer—Martin, *that* was his name—regarded him with amusement. "Try to stay calm." He smiled, but his eyes gleamed wolfishly.

"You're in on it too. *Aren't you?*"

Martin remained silent. Instead, he wiped the table with a filthy cloth. The too-warm communal lounge stank, the deodorising carpet cleaner and air freshener failing to mask the undercurrent of ammonia and incontinence. Martin's white tunic, too, was smeared with stains that might have been food or bodily fluids or both. John fought his rising nausea. He needed fresh air.

Finally Martin said, "The doctor did those tests, *remember*? She said you've got a urinary-tract infection. You're seeing things. Imagining things. It's common in older—"

"Listen. I saw that Polish *bastard* push Dorothy," said John, aware his voice was hushed yet strained and struggling not to erupt. "And she fell because he pushed her, not of her *own accord*."

"Whoa, John." He paused. "Serious allegation. You can't use

language like that, not here. These people want quiet—*rest*." The care assistant's expression was one of triumphant amusement, and he looked around at the passive, grey faces of the other residents who sat on the mismatching collection of beige couches, searching for a pricked ear or prying eye.

There was neither.

Hilda slurped from a spoon, her toothless, bird-like mouth dribbling porridge onto the tartan blanket on her lap. Porridge was all she ate. Gwen smiled at nothing and everything. Only Tom watched, but his eyes were impassive. The old man sighed, perhaps remembering some long-gone injustice of his younger years, perhaps not remembering anything at all.

Martin grinned. "And what you said was racist."

John was on the edge. Unlike the others, dementia or no dementia, he still had his dignity and his sense of right and wrong, and he refused to let this lie.

"I couldn't care if Fabian was Polish, German, Transylvanian, or a fucking Martian. Three times I've reported this." The withered cords of his old biceps tensed.

Martin again looked around the room, checked nobody was *really* watching, then pushed John back into his chair with force, holding his arms in a tight grip at the wrists against the armrests. His hands were strong, his eyes full of the fire, resentment, and frustration of a much younger man.

Care home, indeed.

"Listen, Mr Harper. You're not well. You have dementia. You have a urine infection. You're seeing things. Fabian is a good man. He was with Marcia too. He has a witness. Dorothy fell."

Abruptly Martin let go, never taking his eyes from John's. Then he turned and stormed out of the room, his face a strange wrangle of irritation and victory.

Dorothy walked in through the same door that Martin had left a second before. She was a scarecrow figure of neglect, her short hair standing on end, a dirty nightie clinging to her sallow skin. She looked at John and attempted conversation.

"D…dr…dri."

It was useless. He felt a sickening pity for her, but the gurgling sounds she made were nothing but the nonsensical, instinctual groans of a suffering animal.

But that didn't mean they had to treat her like one.

The duty nurse arrived in the lounge and escorted her away, gently whispering in her ear about getting dressed.

John looked out the lounge window, saw his faint reflection in the glass. His hair was so thin. It was already dusk. The old carriage clock above the fireplace ticked, its rhythm hollow and pointless but relentless and onwards.

"Are you feeling better now, young man? Martin said you were a bit uptight."

John was reading in his room. The door had been shut, but Fabian hadn't knocked. The Pole had walked in without warning.

"Leave me alone. You never heard of knocking where you're from?"

Fabian grinned, revealing the pointed, crooked teeth of a predator. The yellow light from the bedroom's dusty fitting bounced off his unattractive, angular head, shaved to stubble. His skull was flat and grotesque looking. His thin but athletic arms—protruding from the short sleeves of his tunic—were marked with crudely inked tattoos. Fabian worked the night shifts, and his deathly pallor reflected this.

"What do you mean, *where you're from?*"

John ignored him. He refused to take the bait.

"Oh, come on. What you reading?

"Leave me."

Fabian continued to smile. Martin now lurked in the doorway, too, with his coat on, ready to leave. Even from his chair with his chronically failing eyesight, John could see the shoulders of the dark jacket were thickly dusted with dandruff.

"Both of you, leave me alone."

"Night, Mr. Harper. You sleep now," said the Pole.

Fabian left the room. Martin remained at the door gesturing to his colleague for a cigarette but closed the door behind them.

John could still smell the rankness of the two men: cheap deodorant, sweat, and cigarettes. He longed for a cigarette now—another comfort age had forced him to give up.

He sighed deeply. How had it come to this, this excuse for an existence?

Thank God for the key.

Dorothy still occupied his mind. That monster *had* pushed her, and he'd seen the whole thing. She'd scratched him, yes. But the poor woman weighed six stone fully dressed. And she'd been frightened. She was also mentally ill, for God's sake.

The moment played in his mind on repeat: Fabian dressing her in a red cardigan; Fabian struggling to force her skeletal arms into the shrunken, too-tight sleeves; Dorothy's wails and screams, her arms whirling in a desperate cartwheel, catching Fabian on his face, blood blossoming on the Pole's cheek.

Then he'd seen the true nature of Fabian. His hooded eyes had glazed over. John had once read about the geometry of the eye in predators. Cats narrow their eyes to negate the sun's glare when attacking. This was like that. Fabian's eyes narrowed, and he'd erupted with violent rage.

A split second later, Dorothy was sprawled on the floor, holding her head, Fabian looming over her, poised like a sinewy beast. Before he rang the bell, the Pole had shouted, "She's fallen, she's fallen."

Poor Dorothy. Her word stood for nothing, but she'd not complained. And when John had, they'd closed ranks. After all, wasn't *he* demented too?

It was a terrible thing, losing your mind. Age took things slowly. That way, you had time to comprehend you were fading, that you were being erased one facet at a time, one indignity following another.

With his back protesting, leaning on his palms, John pushed himself out of his chair, walked to his bedside cabinet, and bent to open the bottom drawer. He glanced back towards the door. It remained shut. He could hear Fabian and Martin talking as they smoked at the nearby fire exit, their voices dulled by the thin walls.

At first, the drawer was a little stiff. He pulled harder on the small, rounded nub of the handle. Oh God, his back hurt. It had been a damp day in Bolton, and every joint ached. The cheap plywood drawer finally jerked open. In the centre of the drawer, waiting, was the Quality Street tin.

He picked up the tin and sat on the itchy, folded sheets on his hard bed. Over the years, he'd lost the dexterity in his fingers. His hands looked crippled and felt swollen, his fingers resembling chip shop sausages more than the nimble digits of his youth. He picked at the rim of the tin, trying to pry it open. After a time that seemed like an age, he managed to get enough purchase, and the lid opened with a metallic prang.

Inside the tin was the car key. He hadn't *really* owned a car in fifteen years. He'd lost his licence when his eyes had started to fail.

I'm sorry to tell you, Mr. Harper, you have extensive retinopathy due to your type-two diabetes. Time to pack in the beer and chocolate, I'm afraid.

Like hell he would. Small comforts were everything when there was nothing else left. The bottom had fallen out of his world a long time ago. If his vices killed him, so what?

But he still had *the key*. John pulled his legs up onto the bed. His legs had become thin. They were bird-like old-man legs. How could they look so skinny yet feel so heavy?

Sitting upright, with his stiff back pressed against the wooden headboard, he held the key in his hands and studied it, feeling the curve of its bow and the sharp cuts. Pressed into the metal was one word: *Chevrolet.*

Inside, hatred seethed in his veins, and he wondered if it was usual for such an old man to feel so bitter and angry. But he held the key, and eventually the feeling gave way to calm.

John closed his eyes and drifted, gripping the key. Sleep swept over him, and in the numb comfort of dreams, he was an old man no more.

It was another time.

He was another man—a shadow who rode the night.

THE GUN WAS ON THE PASSENGER SEAT, HIS FOOT FLAT TO THE FLOOR. THE Chevy thundered through neon streams of city lights below skyscrapers and smog. He smoked, and the car reeked of cigarettes, sweat, and coffee.

The cassette played, as it always did.

He waited for the name.

The man's voice rasped in stereo, but his instructions were clear: "I want him dead." The deep-voiced stranger on tape spoke slowly but precisely, with anonymous authority. "Kill Valdez."

He wound down the window, felt the warm wind ruffle his thick hair, and flicked his cigarette out into the encroaching night, watching a trail of sparks hit the highway behind, the road illuminated by the pink setting sun.

"He has a tattoo....on his tongue," said the man on tape. "The knife is in the glovebox. Cut out his tongue and send it to the address in the plastic bag under the seat. Dispose of everything. This tape too." A pause. "Leave no trail."

The cassette stopped.

He turned on the radio. A chirpy DJ announced that the day had been the hottest so far of 1987. The steady pounding of drums and electronic keyboard chords filled the car. He'd never liked Phil

Collins, but hurtling along California's Pacific Highway, it felt *fucking apt*.

The car careered along Malibu. Surfers, backlit by the now orange sky, carried their boards away from the Pacific, which raged against its name, waves crashing to shore in furious rolls of thunder.

Past Spanish-styled mansions, beach houses, and the ever-expansive ocean, he drove, the dying sun turning the world to red. Like Hell. Or some beautiful version. He regarded his eyes in the rear-view mirror and acknowledged their red rims. Too much coke. He snorted more anyway, the little mound of white powder packaged in a crumpled gas station receipt. That's what the yanks called them, wasn't it—*gas stations*? The coke surged, and he felt a dim kind of euphoria, his young body adrenaline-fuelled and alive, his other life another universe away. If this *was* Hell, or a road to it, so be it.

Drums.
Phil Collins could feel it coming in the air.
So could he.
Could Valdez?
On he drove, faster into the falling night.

HE SAT PARKED OFF-ROAD IN THE SHADOW OF TREES, HIS CAR HIDDEN ON A desolate road. He'd followed the map, turned inland and, miles from the coast, had entered the canyon where the road wound between sheet walls of cragged rock. Here, the dry brush of parched yellow grass grew on rocky, sun-baked terrain. But night had arrived, and the crickets sang.

Just in view, the corrugated metal warehouse lay some two hundred yards to his left, behind a row of trees. The building was painted white, or so he guessed. It was difficult to tell in the darkness at the foot of these black hills. Above, the stars glittered in the vast sky, and his place in the scheme of things suddenly felt infinitesimally small. The deadly weight of the gun in his hands, though, was a comfort, because the black and white photo of Valdez, taped to his map's top corner, made him nervous. The Mexican's cold-blooded stare burrowed into his mind, imprinting its image like a photo negative.

Sure enough, the bowie knife was in the glovebox. He attached the sheath to his belt, exited the car, and screwed the silencer onto the Remington's barrel. Shoving his car keys into his jeans pocket, he walked towards the warehouse, aware of every gentle crunch of his boots on the dry grass. The scorched, dusty ground was still warm; he could feel the heat rising from the land.

In the distance, voices erupted.

Laughter.

At the base of the rocky valley, every sound was amplified.

Branches scratched his bare arms as he crawled through and between small trees and shrubs. Somewhere near he heard a dry rattle. He checked his boots. No snake. Nothing.

A warning.

Valdez would get no such courtesy.

Again, laughter.

"Aquí, güey."

"Dale, cabrón."

He ducked, skirting the perimeter of the building, sticking to the shadows of trees.

There was a battered van parked outside. The engine was off. The silhouettes of two men entered the building through a door on the right. Both smoked. He could smell Marlboro fumes.

A scream split the night air. His heart thumped. Blood pounded in his ears. *Turn back. Turn away.* He squatted behind a mound of rocks, tried to quieten his breathing, and watched the building's door through long grass.

The high-pitched scream had been unmistakably female and had come from inside the warehouse. He turned off the gun's safety and, hunched over, dashed around the perimeter, making his way to the door from the building's far side.

With his back against the warm corrugated metal, arching his head around the door, he peeked into a long, dimly lit room. Wooden crates were stacked to the ceiling, seven high on every side.

"Pinche perra."

More Spanish, incomprehensible to his ears.

Then, abruptly, a woman spoke. "Bitch don't understand." Her voice was heavily accented, Mexican, and self-assured. Almost certainly, this was not the woman who had screamed seconds before. "If you're going to kill her, fuck her, whatever, get on with it," she said lazily. "Stop toying, güey."

Men laughed, jeered in Spanish.

Breathing hard, he arched his head further around the open door.

A young black woman was taped to a chair. She was hyperventilating. Two Hispanic-looking men stood over her. Both were lean, tattooed, and dressed in tight jeans and T-shirts. One lurched at her side, posturing with his left hand on his crotch and his right gripping a knife. In the dusky light, the blade faintly gleamed.

The other man, who wore a leather waistcoat over his T-shirt, stood observing, smiling. Neither man was big, but both possessed the slender, toned physique of a light-weight boxer.

But he recognised neither.

Valdez, in the mugshot, had a shaved head and long goatee. The smiling man had hair to his backside, tied in a high ponytail—years of growth. The knifeman, though, wore a much shorter brushed-back mullet but wouldn't turn his face around long enough for him to get a proper look.

The Mexican woman, who had still not revealed herself, spoke again. "These boys don't know what to do with you, lady. What were you doing here, alone, at night?"

From around the door he watched the black woman attempt to speak, but she was struggling to breathe let alone articulate a coherent sentence.

The Mexican woman walked into view. She was short, stocky, but attractive. Her hair was shorn in a pixie cut. She carried a pistol but looked too young to be involved with gangs and narcotics. "We came here for the dope. That's all."

"I d…didn't—" The black woman was shaking violently.

Even with his blood pumped with coke, he felt his hands tremble. But he *knew* why he was here, why the car had brought him. They were drug runners, gangsters. They would kill her. Whatever had brought her out here, whatever was going on, her coming here would likely be her last mistake. If he walked away, the cops would likely find her coyote-ravaged body in this barren gorge a week from now, if ever.

The first shot blew the long-haired man's scalp clean off. Aiming for the centre of his head, he'd felt the gun kick, heard the dull thud of the bullet, heard the wet spray of brains decorate the crate. The look in the man's eyes was one of slapstick disbelief, as comical as it was desperate.

He moved with shadow-like grace, his thoughts and actions as mechanical in their efficiency as a striking viper.

The man with the mullet moved with lithe agility too. He pulled the woman, and the chair she was strapped to, in front of him as a human shield, holding the knife at her throat.

It *was* Valdez.

A bullet ricocheted above his head, the Mexican girl firing and missing. He turned on her. The gun felt heavy now, like a powerful extension of himself, a siphon for all the hate in his heart. The springy trigger at first resisted, but when he fired, he caught her shoulder and then her neck with the second shot. She collapsed in a disjointed stagger—a newborn deer—one leg giving before the other, one side of her body still fighting, the other going limp. She died with both her brown eyes open, barely out of her teens.

He moved further into the building, pistol pointed ahead.

Shoot him now, he thought, but he couldn't get the shot.

Valdez's face was illuminated by the single light bulb, which swayed gently above the Mexican's head. Now, he could see his arms were pock-marked with needle tracks. Valdez's face looked jaundiced in the light. The floor was littered with drug paraphernalia. Syringes. A plastic-bottle bong. Cigarette butts. But Valdez was unmistakable. His hair had grown, and he now wore a wispy moustache instead of a longer goatee, but the ink identified him—a blue/green tear was tattooed under his left eye. On his knuckles, Chicano lettering covered the tops of his hands, his neck decorated with a grimacing Hispanic-styled devil.

"Back off, amigo." Valdez gestured with the knife. "Back off or I kill, *si*."

Valdez dragged the woman and the chair towards the back of the room, where there was a second door hiding behind stacks of wooden crates. The chair's legs screeched against the filthy concrete.

Thoughts raced through his mind, of the good person he'd once been, of the good person he *was*. Every time he did this, though, every time he took the car, he lost more, diluted some essential part of himself. *Dementia.* Did he *really* do this for good, to attempt to rid the world of bad men? Or was it for another reason, to get out of that piss-stinking pit of a bed and live, even for a few stolen hours?

Valdez stared with animalistic intent, and through the taut body of the struggling woman, the Mexican fired *one—two—three* times. He did this with the hidden gun, an indifferent smirk etched on his withered, crack-ravaged face. The dead look of apathy in Valdez's eyes was as terrifying as the bullets that exploded out of the woman in a torrent of crimson blood and fire.

He fired his own gun, and then the pain arrived. The shot tore through the already dead woman's shoulder, hitting Valdez in the chest. Valdez fell to the floor, and everything turned black.

FROM THE ROILING VOID OF SEMI-CONSCIOUSNESS, FACES FLIT IN AND OUT of John's whirling mind's eye. He watches a kaleidoscopic reel of loved ones, family, friends, and people whose names he never knew.

Whispers his mind can't quite grasp overlap and echo in the innermost region of his brain that he had once read was his hippocampus. These memories are a stream of simple thoughts, recollections of the fleeting, the small things. The little big things: his dead brother, a child once more, giggling as he lit bad farts on a hot day long ago; the coconut scent of his dead mother's perfume, her young smile; the loosening, cold grip of his dying wife's hand; the empty words of condolence that followed.

Dead. Dead. Dead.

One day his rapidly wasting brain would steal those memories too.

Then John is back in his bedroom, at *the* home. He knows this because he can see himself from outside, from above. He can see himself for what he really is, an old man lying sleeping and waiting to die, clutching a key on a piss-stained bed.

Was he even himself anymore? Was this all some terrible dream? How could everyone be gone? How could they be? How could they all leave him like this?

A shadow.

He feels for the key, not with his hands, but instead with his mind, and somehow he finds its tangibility, the sharp key digging into his thigh from his jeans pocket, the concrete floor sandpapering his cheek.

WHEN HE OPENED HIS EYES, HE SAW, IN HIGH-DEFINITION, THE TWITCHING beat of the wings of a fly as it lay its spawn in the meat of the dead woman. The creature's insectile buzz made his head pound, and the hot corrugated metal tomb stank, like a septic tank. The ground was wet, too, soiled with blood, piss, and shit.

He felt weak, light-headed. He pushed his palms against the splintered edge of a wooden crate, trying to get to his feet. The room spun, and the bare lightbulb dazzled his eyes. Black dots filled his vision. He leaned against the crate and waited for his eyes to settle. Eventually they did. But his returning focus revealed that Valdez had gone.

The chair to which the woman was strapped was capsized, her body still taped to it. She had small feet. She wore Converse. Of all things, those were the things he noticed. At some time that day, she had tied her laces for the last time, and now she was dead on the concrete floor of a squalid warehouse with gaping bullet wounds and flies circling.

He'd failed for the first time to protect who he was sent to defend.

The dead woman's eyes were open. She looked as terrified now as she had in those last moments.

Patting his blood-soaked body, he discovered he'd been shot twice. The first bullet had grazed his left shoulder, but the second, on his left side, was worse. A lot worse.

Time was short.

He heard a dry scrape, the sound like something heavy being dragged across the floor. Still holding his side, he followed the trail of blood leading back out the door.

Valdez was crawling across the floor, his arms outstretched, pulling his soon-to-be-carcass out of the warehouse, into the night and under a starlit sky. Perhaps that's where he wanted to die, beneath the pinwheeling constellations and not in the bloodbath inside.

Staggering, he made it to the Mexican. Using his boot, he kicked Valdez onto his back, like a helpless cockroach.

"Please." Valdez's voice was thick. Blood bubbled at the corners of his mouth. He was dying. But that didn't matter.

He unsheathed the knife.

Cut out his tongue…

"Open wide, motherfucker."

WHEN JOHN WOKE, BACK IN HIS BEDROOM, HE DISCOVERED HE'D DROPPED the Chevrolet key on the floor. There was no pain. No gunshot wounds. No sand on his shoes. No trace of the world he'd left.

He wiped the sleep from his eyes and put the key back in the tin, which he placed carefully in the bedside drawer. His head dully ached, as if he'd had three or four beers on an empty stomach before falling asleep. It was the way it always was—except, this time, he'd failed.

Like he'd failed to protect Dorothy.

The dead woman's eyes stared back at him from some deep recess of his mind where dreams lived. Part of him believed that's what it was: *a dream*. The manifestation of his dementia in sleep, convincing him he had special powers, that he could right the world's wrongs, travelling the night in an American muscle car. That had to be better than being a weak, vulnerable old man who spent his days wearing incontinence pads and shuffling around this filthy home. After all, dreams were real when you woke with sweat on your brow, gasping for breath, and clutching your sheets for your very life. But the nightmares only chased you as far as the unnatural luminosity of the bathroom where a splash of cold water would bring you around and the memory of the dream would fade, like the red Californian sky at the end of a hot summer's day. But the dream would not be forgotten, not entirely. You compartmentalised it, stored it in some back room of your brain in a box.

Or an old tin.

Was that what his subconscious was doing, attempting to control the degenerative state of his addling mind?

John walked to the window and pulled open the curtain. The action fanned the air and the mothball scent of his room into his face. It was dark outside. He had long abandoned keeping a clock in his room. He didn't need the reminder of time anymore, but it felt like the witching hour, that time when death creeps up on you and taps you on the shoulder, reminding you you're mortal.

The rain pattered against the window. In the dim reflection of the dark glass, John saw he was a frail old man. No, he didn't need a clock. It was late indeed.

DAYS PASSED WITHOUT INCIDENT. JOHN HAD BEEN SITTING BY THE WINDOW reading the paper in the evening sunshine for an hour, drinking tea from a poorly washed mug, when he heard the commotion upstairs. At first he ignored the loud bangs, but when he heard the screaming too he darted up quicker than he'd done in years. His back protested in an agonising spasm as he rose.

"Nurse," he shouted.

None came.

He shouted a second and third time. Still, nobody came.

The other residents in the lounge were oblivious. Only Tom, bushy eyebrows quizzically raised, smiled in his gummy way, as if the noise upstairs might mean the onset of an exciting party; the banshee-like shriek that followed confirmed it wasn't. John felt his spine tingle, his stomach flutter with nerves.

Dorothy was absent from the room. Worse, Fabian had come to work an earlier shift. The Pole and Martin were upstairs with her. *Alone.* He'd not seen the supervising nurse for twenty minutes or more.

John charged towards the stairs. This was the first time he'd used the stairs without the lift in nearly two years. Huffing and puffing, struggling for breath, John climbed, knocking over a Toby jug from a staircase shelf. When he reached the halfway point, he allowed himself three seconds to recover with his hands on his knees. His chest felt worryingly tight, his heart hammering hard enough so he could see his now sweat-drenched polo shirt visibly shudder with every beat.

Finally he reached the top. He was swaying now, holding on to the landing bannister to pull himself along, nearer to Dorothy's bedroom door.

And that's where they were, in the doorway to her room. Martin held Dorothy's arms against her body. Fabian's hand was clamped over her mouth. The old woman's hair was a tangled bird's nest. She wore a nightie. Urine gushed down her stick-thin legs. Dorothy's eyes were harrowing caves.

John shared her gaze for a split second, and then she bit. With the Pole's large hand covering most of her sallow face, his view was impaired, but John saw enough. Her cheeks visibly flinched. Fabian screamed. His hand turned red. And then he hit her on the side of her head with absolute force. The dull thud of the blow made John's guts rise.

The old woman fell to her knees and then faceplanted the floor. She did not raise her hands to break her fall.

By now, Martin had moved away from Fabian, had distanced himself from the culprit, was staring at his colleague with a confounded look of shock etched into his weasel-like features.

Fabian was aghast, was pointing to the unconscious woman on the floor and protesting with his unharmed hand. He held the bitten hand under his armpit where the blood blossomed and spread, turning his white uniform to red.

John was at Dorothy's side in a second. He cradled her head. Her body felt light, like a small child. When she opened her eyes, she smiled.

"Dorothy, Dorothy."

The old woman gestured back into her room with her eyes. She tried to speak again, but her voice was fading, too quiet to hear.

John lowered his ear to her mouth. He could feel her warm, shallow breath on his skin.

Dorothy groaned. Her words were lost on him, but he was aware she was desperately trying to convey something to him.

"*What?* What do you want?"

"Her tin," said Martin. "She wants the tin."

Before John had the chance to comprehend the care assistant's words, Martin had dashed to her bedside table where a small florally decorated tin lay under a bedside lamp.

"Here," said Martin, handing him the tin.

John took it with his free hand. The lid was loose enough that he nudged it off with his thumb. Still, Dorothy lay in his arms. She was dying. That much was obvious.

By now, Fabian was running away, hurtling down the stairs, knocking the South African duty nurse out of his way. He flew out the front door, which slammed shut behind him.

Inside the tin was a gold ring. Dorothy flexed her finger, as if telling John to slip the ring on.

He did.

Dorothy was practically mute, had been for years, but she opened her mouth then, with her brown tongue protruding from her split lip, and said, "Drive, John. *Drive.*"

YESTERDAY'S NEWS

"We spoke on the phone," said Gill, squinting in the sunshine through her thumping headache. "Gillian McKinley, *Evening News*."

The old man stood at the front door. The cottage overlooked a quaint little harbour where fishing boats slept in the sands of low tide. He smiled, his wild white hair blowing in the snatches of the warm September wind. Above, seagulls sailed, screeching in the salt air.

"Ah, of course, the reporter."

Gill flashed her ID.

"Glad you came. Please, come in."

The old man—she'd forgotten his name—led her through a narrow hallway and into an overheated lounge with an orange couch. Gill sat down. The décor was old-fashioned: brass plates; a fireplace cluttered with Toby jugs and old photos; an elderly grandfather clock that ticked too loudly, reminding Gill of impending deadlines.

"Nice place you have here."

"Thanks. I have been here ten years now. The old place had bad memories... Tea?"

"Thank you, but I don't really have much—"

"*Time?*"

Gill nodded.

"You have more than you know," said the old man mysteriously.

Gill ignored the bait, noticed the old man's right eye was badly bloodshot. "Deadlines, you see," she said.

"Oh, come on now. I can't talk without a drink."

"Okay, two sugars," said Gill, sighing. Maybe a drink would do her good. She couldn't stop shaking—low blood sugar perhaps. But she really didn't have long. She'd only agreed to call in on account she was passing the cottage on her way back from the council offices where she'd endured a two-hour planning committee meeting. The old man had called her earlier that morning, insisting he had the story of a lifetime. Usually Gill would have disregarded the call with all the other attention-seekers, busybodies, and nutjobs, but there had been something in the old timer's desperation that intrigued her.

Perhaps she should have listened to her instinct. The news desk had already texted three times, complaining she'd not tweeted enough from the meeting. It was no wonder local journalism was dying. How were you supposed to find the time to write considered, in-depth newspaper reports when all they wanted was constant throw-away social media posts? Or maybe she was a relic at forty—a dinosaur with a bad temper and a splitting headache.

"Unless you'd like something stronger? Wine perhaps?"

"Tea's fine," she lied. A proper drink was exactly what she needed. But the car was parked outside, and she would never take a drink and get behind the wheel again. Booze would have to wait.

After a time that seemed an eternity, Gill's host set a steaming mug of tea down before her on a wooden coffee table, together with a packet of digestive biscuits.

"I lost my wife," said the old man, sighing as he sat down, sinking into the other end of the battered old couch. "Eight years ago. She was never the same after we lost our son, our only son. He was nineteen."

His eyes veered towards a photo frame on a shelf. The frame was turned on its face.

"I'm sorry."

"*I'm sure*," he said.

"*Sure*?"

"When you get to my age, you're not sure of anything."

She let the matter go. He was old…confused.

"And when you get to my age, sometimes grief is all you have," he added, twiddling the ring with the green stone on his right hand.

So, this was what it was: a counselling session. Her phone vibrated angrily in her pocket again, demanding attention. "I don't usually do house calls unless I've discussed the story first," said Gill.

"Because of the deadlines?"

"Yes."

"I see."

"If you could tell me the crux of the story, that would be a good start," said Gill, taking a notepad and pen from her bag. "I always tell people to start with the basics—the who, what, where, why, when. It makes it easier initially."

"What about the *how*?"

"Well, yeah. Once we've established the initial facts. Then I can see if there's a story, or not." Right now, if Gill had to bet, she'd go with not.

"Oh, there's a story. It's whether you believe me."

"Go on. Try me."

"Okay."

"Right," said Gill, pen poised on her pad.

"Well, *the who*: me, Peter Wells."

Gill jotted down the man's name in shorthand and picked up her mug of tea.

"*What*: *well*, I've discovered"—the old man coughed, clearing his throat—"a portal in my garage that allows me to travel through time."

Gill's heart sank.

Seventeen years ago, on her first week with the paper, she'd received a four-hundred-page hand-written dossier, documenting the evening activities of extra-terrestrials at a popular dogging spot. She'd once sat in a house with a man who'd lined his walls with tin foil, claiming the police had hacked into his TV. She'd even interviewed a bloke who'd said a dragon was sleeping in the underground caves of a nearby mountain range. Over a decade and a half, she'd developed a radar that enabled her to screen out the loonies, saving her precious time chasing dead leads. But this one, it seemed, had slipped through the net.

"I'm sorry," said Gill.

"I can travel through time."

Gill put down the mug.

The old man continued. "*Where*: well, right here."

"You're serious?"

"*Why*: to visit my wife, of course."

"I'm sorry. This has been a mistake," said Gill.

"I haven't told you *when*—"

Dementia?

"—every day for the last eight years." The old man pointed to a book on the coffee table, *A Brief History of Time* by Stephen Hawking. "It's all in there. I know how this sounds."

"I'm sorry, Mr.—*Wells*. I'm busy. The paper has had two rounds of redundancies in the last three years. I don't want to be on the next list. I have to prioritise what I write if I don't want to be stacking shelves come—"

"You think I've lost my marbles, don't you?"

"Thanks for the tea," said Gill, rising from her seat.

"You think I'm senile?"

Gill started towards the front door.

"What if I'm telling the truth?"

"Look if you need a nurse, someone to talk to, I can call—"

"It's not as impossible as you think."

"Thanks, Mr. Wells. I'll see myself out."

"What if *you* could go back?" said the old man.

The blue lights of a police car whirled in Gill's mind's eye, lighting a country road on a dark winter's morning; lighting clouds of hot breath in the cold; lighting the darkest corner of her conscience that had festered for seventeen years—the insurmountable past that drink had failed to drown.

"Look, please. I'm asking for one minute of your time."

"Time that unfortunately I don't have," said Gill.

"I can show you." The old man spoke the words confidently, with an air of belligerence, his blue eyes twinkling with sincerity.

After a short second, Gill averted her gaze, her eyes settling on an ornamental vase, cracked porcelain that stirred memories of the split shell of a motorcycle helmet.

"Please, follow me," said the old man, rising to his feet and walking down the hall to the back end of the house.

Fighting every journalistic instinct, Gill followed.

The old man turned a corner and stopped at a short corridor, leading to a door. The door had a circular peephole. The passage itself was decorated in an odd fashion. A collage of hundreds of photographs covered every inch of the walls and ceiling. The photos were lined meticulously, picture to picture, one frame almost touching the next. Weirdly Gill thought of the Sistine Chapel. Black and white stills, colour Polaroids, and poor-quality digital prints denoted definite photographic eras. Every portrait was of the same woman, documenting her passage through life, from childhood to old age. The woman was attractive with wavy brown hair. In the later photos, her hair had turned grey, then white; even in these, while her skin was grey and thin-looking, her hazel eyes were bright and alive.

"Your wife?" said Gill.

The old man nodded.

The narrow hall was lined with six old grandfather clocks—three on each wall—that ticked out of synchronisation. Pendulums swinging, gears whirring, the clocks' precise kinetic mechanisms stirred within Gill visions of Victorian ingenuity. The hall was strange, though, because the museum of clocks and their onward, schizophrenic clamour were at odds with the photographic shrine and the pictures' inert stillness. The child, the girl, the woman, in every photo, she stared pointedly into the camera, as if she watched. She aged, staring from eternity into the quaint little house.

From his cardigan pocket, the old man took a pipe and a baggie containing dried leaves. He pinched a few leaves into the pipe and lit, and the hall was filled with thick sage-smelling smoke.

"To ease the transition of the mind," he said, inhaling deeply, eyes glazing, "I have to use the pipe. That door, it leads to my adjoining garage. But if I concentrate hard enough, it can take me back—anywhere I have been before."

Gill felt sorry for the old man. But she didn't have time for this.

"Give me a date," he said, setting down the pipe on a wooden sideboard.

"I'm sorry—?"

"Any date within the last seventy or so years."

Gill sighed and shook her head. She decided to indulge his fantasy. What harm could it do? "Okay. October 7, 1981."

The old man nodded curtly. "Wait here."

Peter Wells left her standing amongst the concurring commotion of the clocks. Shuffling as old men do, he walked towards the unremarkable door that led to the garage. On his way, he stopped, picked a photo from the wall, unhooked it, and regarded the picture of his wife aged around thirty. He then opened the door and disappeared, taking the photograph with him.

The clocks ticked more loudly, or so it seemed. The seconds passed slowly.

Then the door opened, and the old man emerged, looking dishevelled, looking marginally older. Gill noticed the old man's right eye was now completely threaded with burst capillaries. As well as the photo, he was holding a newspaper. A dew of sweat glazed his brow. He handed Gill the paper that felt stiff and fresh off the print. It was a copy of *The Daily Mail*. The old man placed the photo of his wife carefully back on the wall, gently patting it secure.

"Took me an hour to find a shop where I could pinch that," said the old man.

SADAT'S LAST SALUTE, the headlined stated.

Egyptian president Anwar Sadat shot dead at armed forces parade, the article reported.

A large portrait photo down the paper's right-hand side featured the dead president, saluting in a peaked military cap and regal uniform.

The date read, **Wednesday, October 7, 1981**.

"You must think I'm stupid," said Gill.

"Not at all."

"This is bull—"

"*The Mail*?" said the old man, smiling. "Right-wing propaganda. Not my cup of tea, but it was all I could get."

"You have a collection back there. You must have," said Gill.

"Of every newspaper printed…*ever*? You've seen the house from the outside. The garage barely fits my car."

The condition of the newspaper was pristine.

"Let me see," said Gill, almost barging the old man out of her way. Walking past the clocks, she opened the door—and found a dusty, old garage. Cobwebbed wooden shelves held garden tools, oil cans, and weed killer. Taking up most of the garage space was an old Ford Focus. The car, like the old man, had seen better days. Its passenger door was dented. Moss grew on the underside of the body. Rust corroded the wheels.

"The DeLorean it is not," said the old man.

"How?"

"It's all in that book. The one by Stephen Hawking."

"You expect me to believe—?"

"Are you familiar with Einstein's theory of general relativity?"

"For God's sake," said Gill impatiently.

"Look," said the old man. He snatched the newspaper back and held it horizontally. "Imagine space and time as a flat sheet where things can travel across in a linear manner. But if you put a large enough mass into the sheet, a force, it curves. It warps." The old man pushed the opposing corners of the newspaper towards each other, causing it to fold in the middle, creating a paper hump. "If you look beyond the sun through a telescope, you can see the stars behind. The sun consists of such mass that it curves space. It distorts, creating an orbit."

"And you're a professor of astrophysics at which university?" said Gill.

"The theory stands true. If you put a great enough mass into space it can distort time. Scientists understand the geometry, but the exact properties of the mass needed to create such a warp are not understood."

"Until now?" said Gill sarcastically.

"Right," said the old man.

"And what creates that mass in your garage, your Ford Focus?"

"My grief," said the old man, his eyes sparkling. "Nothing is more powerful than grief."

Or guilt.

"It can't be—"

The old man held up the newspaper. "And yet I'm holding this."

"A trick," said Gill.

"Do you want to try again?" he said, closing the door to the garage.

"Okay," said Gill, challenging the old man with her stare. "This time I'm coming with you."

"Doesn't work that way."

"Why?"

"*Another date*?"

Gill's mind scrabbled for a random date. But there was only one; the day, the month, the year, it scarred the ridge of the grey matter that was her hippocampus, reminding her of her terrible deed.

"February 4, 2005."

The day after. No. Hours later.

The words were out before she could take them back.

"Right," said the old man.

"Bring back a local paper," said Gill, steeling herself. "A copy of *The Evening News*."

The old man nodded and turned back towards the door to the garage. This time he took longer to ponder over which photograph of his wife to select; he eventually chose a more recent one in which she wore her hair in a silver bun.

The old man opened the door.

Gill tried to steal a look, but he moved quickly, and the door closed behind him, a thin cloud of dust puffing as it shut.

The clocks' mechanical oscillations sped, reaching a maddening cacophony of ticks and chimes.

Her palms greased with sweat, Gill waited. Then the door opened, and the old man appeared, looking worse for wear. His right eye was weeping red tears. He coughed—and handed Gill the newspaper.

The headline: **HIT AND RUN KILLS TEENAGE MOTORCYCLIST**
Police Appeal for Witnesses
By Gillian McKinley

Her heart beating thick in her throat, Gill read the piece she'd written seventeen years before. The words were eerily familiar.

"Let me try," said Gill. "I want to try your portal."

"You *can't* change things, you know."

"Then why?"

"You can *learn* things... Anyway, I'm not sure it would work, I mean for you," said the old man. "I've told you. It's my grief, you see."

But wasn't guilt as powerful a force? Didn't people shoot themselves, hang themselves, ply themselves with drink for years—*seventeen years*—in a bid to erase one night's drunken stupidity.

Surely the old man had to be fucking crazy.

But what if...?

"You'll let me try?" said Gill.

"Of course."

"Your eye?" said Gill, disgusted by the old man's bloody tears.

"It's nothing," said the old man.

Gill studied the old man's face for any sign of a lie: there was none.

The old clocks stood resolute in the hall, their wooden cases amplifying their gears and internal mechanisms.

This had to be bullshit. It was her hangover. She was drinking too much. Far too much. Her mind was coming undone at the seams.

But what if?

"You'll need this," said the old man, picking up the pipe. He pushed in some dried leaves. "Sometimes I can do it without, but this always makes it...*easier*."

Gill took the pipe. "What is it?"

"Salvia divinorum. You can get it online. It's used by Mazatec shamans, in Mexico, to meet God." He smiled gently. "I use it to meet my wife."

Gill was disgusted at the thought of sharing the old man's saliva but brought the pipe to her mouth regardless.

"Think of where you want to go. Take it slowly. It's strong stuff."

The old man lit the pipe. Gill inhaled. The thick smoke filled her lungs, burning her throat and chest. She coughed. At first, she felt a tingling sensation. Then the drug's potency hit. Gill's senses were scrambled. Her ego and sense of self shrank inside her, and the drug roared through her veins like a car thundering down a country road in the dead cold of a winter's night.

The old man gestured towards the door.

The clocks chimed.

Gill nodded and walked towards the door, unsteady on her feet. With sickening trepidation and regret pulsing through her veins, she opened the door—and stepped through.

It was like coming around in a strange bed after a heavy night, waiting for the incipient hangover to arrive like a black flower blooming—like it had every subsequent morning for the last seventeen years—and bloom it did again.

She was sitting in a familiar car. Beyond the windscreen, the line of black trees loomed against a night sky where pale stars glittered.

Bathed in the jaundiced glow of headlights, the bike lay on the road, the windshield smashed beyond repair, the wheels idling.

She stepped out of the car, under February stars. In the sky a jaundiced moon hung over the land.

The motorbike's engine tick, tick, ticked. Cold air grazed her cheek. Glass cracked, scrunching under her shoe.

The boy moved sluggishly, barely rustling amongst the prickly branches of hedgerow where he'd landed, his helmet cracked. From somewhere behind the visor, a mouth spoke wetly: "Helth me. Helpth thee."

Gill squatted above the boy who'd soon be a corpse, freezing in the bleak light of a winter morning next to a dead rabbit: *roadkill*.

"I'm sorry," said Gill. "I'm so sorry."

Was she? Not sorry enough. If this dimension of time held true, she'd be back here in eight hours with a photographer, reporting from the scene, chewing a mouth full of Trebor Mints to mask her booze-infused breath. She'd then hurry back to the office where she'd write the story, headline and all.

It had been a new job. A new start. She'd gone out for a few glasses of wine with the girls. She barely drank back then. *Not then.* But she'd been young. The pub was remote. She'd never planned to drive. Never planned for it to end the way it had.

"I didn't mean it," said Gill McKinley, staring at the helmet and the breath that steamed against the bloodied visor. On the boy's right hand was a ring with a green stone.

She had to get away. She hurried back to the car and its chugging engine. When she opened the door and stepped in, she anticipated falling back into the hall of the old man's house by the sea. But she did not.

Gill sat in the driver's seat and stared through the windscreen at the dying boy bathed in the bright headlights.

It was then she noticed the sky.

Beyond the haze of the headlights, the moon shone brightly. Narrowing her eyes, she considered its craterous landforms—and saw the dark crater at the moon's centre suddenly resembled the pupil of an eye. At closer inspection, too, she realised the dark lunar splotches brought to mind broken capillaries and burst blood vessels, branching across its continent-sized sclera. She remembered the peephole in the old man's door—and thought if ever she needed a drink, it was now.

IT REMAINS

"**B**lasted dog," said Jeff, draining the last of the brandy from his mug.

"Squirrel," said Ed, "or some animal. Must've been, the way she took off."

Outside, the cold wind howled, and the snow fell in brittle flurries, tick-tacking against the kitchen window. The storm swept through the forest surrounding the lonely little cottage, great gusts snatching at the groaning limbs of trees.

"Dad, you have to find her," pleaded Wendy. "Poor Pips. It's so cold."

It was. And eerie. Even at three p.m., there was a blue, Arctic quality to the light. Ed's fingers still burned from the cold too, despite him now clasping both hands around the warm mug of tea that Jeff had laced with brandy.

Jeff poured more brandy into his own mug and said to his daughter, "We'll find her."

"You promise?"

"I promise…first thing in the morning."

Wendy's eyes widened. "*No*, you can't leave—"

"*Honey.*"

"The snow is a foot deep. *Already*."

"She'll be fine," said Jeff. "She's a dog."

Ed looked beyond the still steaming kettle and out the window between the plaid-patterned curtains. She was right—a foot deep and growing thicker by the minute.

"We can't go back out in that, not now," said Jeff, his coat still dusted with snow. "It's getting dark."

"She'll die. If you leave her, she'll die."

"Look, Wendy…"

She glowered at her father.

Ed felt a pang of guilt. And shame. This was his fault. He had suggested they head back from the search. Pips would follow, he'd assured them. And he'd believed it too. He was less sure now.

"You said she could have ham for tea," said Wendy, looking at the gammon that waited in the cold pot on the unlit hob. "You said you were taking her on a short walk and she'd have a treat."

Short walk, indeed. When they'd set out on their expedition, they had no idea it would snow so heavily. They had been ill-equipped, wearing trainers, not boots. Their feet wet and the sharp wind chafing their cheeks, neither man was prepared for the dog bolting and the ensuing storm. They'd searched the vast woods for hours and had called and called, two middle-aged men bellowing in the forest at the foot of the Snowdonia Mountain Range. That had been three hours ago.

"We'll save Pips some ham," said Jeff. "She's a tough girl. Working stock."

Pips was a cross, one-part collie, and Ed knew herding dogs were prone to giving chase.

"Pips will be okay," said Jeff, bending so his tired eyes were level with his daughter's. "She'll come back, and if not, she'll bed down in the woods, and we'll find her in the morning."

But Jeff's eyes were bleaker than the weather. Pools of sorrow, Ed thought. He had aged beyond his forty-seven years. That's what losing your younger wife did.

Wendy stormed past her father, stamping her feet as if she was fourteen and not eleven, out of the kitchen and up the stairs. When she reached the upper landing, she stomped into her bedroom and slammed the door, causing the kitchen door to rattle in its frame. Ed noticed, not for the first time, that the door was afflicted with patches of blackish mould.

Now alone in the small kitchen, the two men listened to the cottage's old joists groaning in the blitz of the buffeting wind. Jeff sighed. "That dog," he began, then trailed off.

Ed nodded. He knew. Pips was also half lab and fiercely loyal. The dog had been the one thing in the world that had got Wendy through the loss of her mother. Pips had never left the girl's side, not through the tears, not through the screaming, and not through the terrible weeks of silence that followed.

"The cancer," said Jeff, looking up, "Rachael, she…" He rubbed his temple as if in physical pain.

Ed thought about the last time he had seen Rachael alive. He'd visited her in this very house. Tucked in a single bed in the dimly lit bedroom, she lay, shallow gasps escaping her frail form, Jeff at her side. Wendy had wept in the neighbouring bedroom while the carriage clock ticked too loudly—mockingly. Ed had sat beside Rachael and felt her impossibly light body rise as his weight settled on the mattress. The bedroom had been dark, the only light coming from a bedside lamp that painted eerie shadows with its warm fluorescence, and he remembered her hands, cold and thin, and a strange sense of her dissipating before his eyes as dusk turned to night and the shadows thickened.

Yet it was here they had chosen to remain.

At Christmas.

Tears welled in Jeff's reddened eyes. "It consumed her from the inside, and *still*…" He broke off. "Now I can feel this…*chasm* between Wendy and me."

Ed had felt it too. The house was a quiet place now. Unsaid things hung in the air amongst the ever-present, lonely hum of white noise, the frequency of sad thoughts, and the infinite void of death. It even seemed to retain a core of silence as the storm moaned and wailed outside. As trees creaked. As branches cracked and snapped, the whistling wind tearing tiles from the roof.

Ed patted his old friend on the shoulder, feeling his bulk, and Jeff wiped a tear from his cheek.

"I wish it had been me," said Jeff.

"You shouldn't feel guilty."

"*No?*"

"No, Jeff."

"Well, I wish it had."

"Things will—" Ed wanted to say get easier, but that seemed a betrayal of Rachael's memory, so instead he said nothing.

Jeff nodded anyway, momentarily looking up and regarding Ed with damp eyes. His eyes reminded Ed of Rachael's own, of how they had glistened, even at the end. They had been sharp blue eyes full of fun and empathy and not without mischief. The last time he'd seen her, her eyes still sparkled, even more so when she turned her head on the sweat-dampened pillow to see her beautiful, if ashen-faced, daughter standing at her bedroom door. How could that be, sharp blue eyes in the sockets of a grey-skinned wraith whom he was sure—at the very end—Jeff had willed death upon? Because she'd clung on so long—too long—more than Jeff could bear. The rot was as relentless as time. Rachael had been thirty-nine years old. Jeff had buried her on a plot of land at an old chapel cemetery not far away. That had been two seasons ago.

Jeff's lips trembled, and he tried to speak, but in the end, he simply let out a slow sigh as the snow continued to pitter-patter against the window.

"You did everything you could to help her, Jeff."

"*Everything,*" said Jeff, his eyes distant. "I did it for…for her…"

"Did what?" said Ed.

It was then Jessica returned to the kitchen. She had left to bring the men towels. She put her arm around Ed and kissed him, then reached out and squeezed Jeff's arm.

"Maybe I shouldn't have asked you both to spend Christmas out here with us," said Jeff. "Unfair. It was always going to be difficult the first year—"

"We're glad to be here," said Ed. He meant it. "As long as we're not imposing."

"Never," said Jeff, "not at all. Rachael loved it here. I couldn't think of a better place to spend Christmas, or with better people. I feel close to her here." Jeff poured the last of the brandy, topping up his mug and Ed's tea, which was now standing half full beside the kettle.

Jessica's eyes caught Ed's. Fleetingly she glanced at the empty bottle of brandy Jeff was holding. Ed understood—*the drinking*. In the two days they'd been here, Jeff had gone through at least two bottles, not counting wine. But Ed saw Jeff flinch, catching his and Jessica's brief exchange; the big man then, almost apologetically, produced another full bottle of cognac from the kitchen cupboard, together with a bowl-shaped glass with a short stem.

"I'm sorry," said Jeff, misunderstanding, offering the glass to Jessica. "Here, I was about to offer you one too. You must think I'm rude."

"No, really," Jessica protested. "I'm okay. A cup of tea will—"

But Jeff was already pouring a generous measure of brandy into the glass. Intervening, Ed took the glass from Jeff and poured the shot into his own mug. "Jessica will be fine with tea," he said, smiling. "Not everyone's a raging alcoholic, you know."

Jeff forced a smile. Ed sipped his potent drink and protectively laid a hand on Jessica's belly. She'd be three months on Christmas Day. It was their secret still. Jessica moved closer to him.

"You think Pips will be okay, in this cold?" said Ed finally.

"If she doesn't return tonight, I'll leave the porch open and a blanket," said Jeff. "She's a tough old thing."

"And Wendy?"

"Been difficult," Jeff said flatly. "But she'll have to be. We'll get the dog first thing in the morning. Right now, it's not safe."

Ed's gaze followed Jeff's, out into the snow. The trees whipped in blustering snatches. Somewhere, out there, in the forest below the mountains, Pips was lost. And in the howling gale, Ed imagined he could hear the dog, its lonely whine carrying in the wailing wind that rattled the frosted pane of the kitchen window.

"I better check on Wendy," said Jeff, finally taking off his heavy duffel coat and hanging it on a wooden chair next to the radiator. As he turned away, the back of the chair gave under the weight of the wet coat. Ed caught the coat and noticed the chair's top rail had snapped. On closer inspection, the wood was rotten and speckled with black-purplish markings—strange patterns of lesions flat to the touch.

"Your chair," said Ed. "What the—?"

Jeff turned. "*Again*." He sighed. "Just leave it. *Rot*."

"In your home?"

"Some kind of parasite, in the wood," said Jeff.

"Really?"

"Don't worry," Jeff mumbled.

But Ed saw Jeff's eyes dart to the wooden door frame. Sure enough, the markings were there too. And on the skirting boards. And on the top of the kitchen cupboards.

"As I said, dry rot. I'll get someone in after Christmas," said Jeff. Then head bowed, he left the dim light of the kitchen, walked past the small lounge and the twinkling lights of the Christmas tree, and trudged up the dark, narrow staircase, carrying snow on his shoes as he went.

No sooner had Jeff knocked on Wendy's bedroom door than he was racing back down the stairs. "She's gone," he said, barging into the kitchen, his face aghast.

"What do you mean?" said Ed.

"The bedroom window, it's open. She can reach the shed. She's gone."

Jeff threw on the coat he'd taken off a minute before and marched towards the back door.

"Wait," said Ed. "We'll need torches, dry clothes—"

"No time. Freezing out there. Get what you need and follow." He opened the back door, letting in a ferocious gust of wind and swirling deposits of thick snow. "Footprints lead that way." He pointed towards the forest path.

"I'll be right behind you."

Jeff nodded. He reached for the bottle of brandy on the kitchen worktop, tucked it inside his coat, and left, shutting the door and sealing the kitchen from the storm. Through the window, Ed watched Jeff's large frame hurry through the snow, towards the path, his hair ruffling in the violent bursts of wind.

Jessica looked up at Ed, her eyes searching his. They both knew he had to follow. He had to help his friend find his little girl.

"Hurry," she said. "I want you back before dark, all of you."

Ed knew that was unlikely because the days were short and dusk was settling, but he patted her tummy and said, "She won't have got far."

She smiled doubtfully.

"I should go."

"No, you'll help them more if you're properly dressed. You'll freeze like that."

She was right. The frozen snow on Ed's clothes had thawed in the warm cottage, and he was shivery and damp. Stripping to his boxers, he put on a pair of dry jeans, a shirt, jumper, and fleece, the only other coat he had with him.

Jessica packed a rucksack with a spare coat for Wendy. Ed found a torch and some batteries in a kitchen drawer cluttered with old boxes of matches, balls of string, and pens.

Now wearing a bobble hat and gloves, Ed kissed Jessica on the mouth, opened the back door, and followed Jeff's footprints out into the snow.

"Come back safe," she called. "I'll put on the ham."

He hadn't yet answered when the door blew shut behind him.

THE WIND RAGED ABOUT HIM, SNATCHING AT HIS CLOTHES. VISIBILITY WAS poor, the snow blowing in ghostly swirls, like dust devils in a desert storm. Pushing against the ragged gusts and following Jeff's prints, he reached the thick line of trees and shouted, "Jeff—Wendy!"

Only the late-December wind howled in response.

Ed looked back towards the cottage, could still see Jessica standing, watching at the window, and turned back towards the path.

The forest nearest the cottage was ancient woodland, crammed with deciduous native species of oak, ash, and beech.

The trees appeared skeletal against the darkening sky, their bare boughs burdened with snow. But after crossing a snow-covered meadow, though, the forest became a denser wood of pine and spruce where depleted numbers of trees had been replaced with quicker-growing evergreens many years ago. The dark here was thicker, the trees more plentiful and taller.

Ed followed the path, shouting for Jeff.

FIFTEEN MINUTES LATER, HE FOUND HIM LEANING AGAINST A TREE.

"I've been calling you."

"This was where Wendy was conceived."

Shining the torch's beam at his friend, he thought Jeff's skin looked yellow and jaundiced. He was again holding the bottle of brandy.

"That won't help you."

Jeff was swaying slightly and shivering. His eyes were wide and possessed a sick look. Then he turned towards the tree on which he had been leaning. "Can you see the carving?"

Ed could. The tree was an old oak, one of its kind between legions of tall pines. The carving was a crude heart with the letters J and R carved within. Beneath the heart, a W had been etched into the old tree's gnarled trunk. Jeff's finger was tracing the line of the letter, over and over. And Ed noticed the tree, too, was colonised with more of the purple-tinged markings that Jeff had described as rot.

Weird…

Right now, though, was not the time to discuss rot, dry or otherwise.

"We walked here in summer. I know it was here where we made her because I'd been working away and—"

"Jeff, we need to find her."

Jeff knocked back more brandy, then screwed on the cap. "She's headed to the chapel, to the cemetery."

"How do you know?"

"I heard the dog barking, that way. She would have heard it too."

"Then come on. Let's go."

Jeff tucked the brandy back into his coat. "Rachael's grave," he said, squinting in the torch's glare. "I can't stand to look at it."

Ed lowered the beam.

Then Jeff appeared to shake off the fogginess that Ed had mistaken for drunkenness; it evaporated as quickly as a frozen breath. "Never mind. C'mon," he said, his urgency renewed.

The sharp wind bit into the exposed skin of Ed's face as he walked, but he feared Jeff was showing signs of shock. The pained expression on his friend's face worried him. Although Jeff was marching through the snow with quick, purposeful steps, there was something else, something regretful in his demeanour, as if he feared what awaited them.

"Jeff, what's going on?"

But Jeff remained silent and marched on, in the direction of the chapel at the foothills of the mountain. Already the path was getting steeper, and the ascent was murder on Ed's Achilles.

"*Jeff?*"

He caught up and grabbed the larger man by the shoulder, spinning him around. Fear was etched into Jeff's thick features.

"Is there something you're not telling me?"

"The grave…"

"What about it?" demanded Ed, his patience at an end.

Jeff's eyes were rheumy and bloodshot. It was dark now. But the yellow light from the torch lit the snow that swirled about them, the flakes pinpricking the night like static on an old TV.

"I can't explain. I don't know how."

"Try."

"Rachael, in the end, she was in pain. A great deal of pain."

Ed nodded.

"Her grave, it's not right."

"What do you mean?"

"This is my fault," said Jeff, his hand again massaging his temple.

"What is?" said Ed.

"So much pain."

"*Look*, Jeff."

"She was screaming—"

"*Jeff*—"

"Sweating—"

"Calm down. Wendy needs you."

"Writhing, writhing in agony."

"What are you saying?"

"I helped her, Ed. I did. I had to. There was no other way."

Struggling to comprehend his words, Ed sighed, paused, then said, "When someone is that ill, overdoses are not un—"

"The morphine was gone," said Jeff. "I gave her all we had. I thought she had passed. But...she was *still* breathing." Slowly he raised both his hands before his eyes, regarding them with disgust. They were hands roughened by decades of hard work, scarred with old wounds and calluses, his knuckles as gnarled as the branches of that old oak. Hands capable of great strength... Yet Jeff had been nothing but gentle to his wife, nothing but kind. Ed remembered those same hands tenderly brushing away a strand of hair from Rachael's damp brow...stroking her pale cheek...

"I couldn't let her wake, Ed. I couldn't. She'd had enough. We'd had enough, *all* of us. I did it for all of us."

Ed could almost smell Rachael then, the ill-sweat stink of her deathbed, wafting in a room baked by fever.

"For *all* of us," Jeff repeated as if to convince himself as much as Ed.

The two men stood not a foot apart, their eyes locked, this long-kept secret between them, Jeff's sweet, slightly acidic breath a testament to his liver struggling to metabolize the constant boozing he'd been engaged in since Rachael had passed.

"She's gone," said Jeff. "The good part, the part we loved. But her suffering... it...it remains..."

The moment was broken by the distant shrill of a scream. A girl's scream. In the furious storm, it was a quiet sound but one that caused both men to hurry up the hill to where the chapel stood.

SCURRYING UP THE BROW OF THE HILL AND THROUGH THE PINE FOREST, the beam from Ed's torch was an erratic light in the dark, revealing snippets of the woods in juddering strobes.

Despite his apparent intoxication, size, and being three years Ed's senior, Jeff raced ahead, Ed struggling to keep up. But when they reached the top of the hill, even the winter night failed to disguise the state of the trees. They were dead. All of them.

"The hell?"

Jeff stopped, turned, and nodded knowingly at his friend.

It was dead of winter, the days when the fallen leaves of autumn froze on the ground and were buried by snow. But these trees were evergreens.

Were.

Now a forest of blackened trunks stood narrow and straight, every tree looming tall, but not one needle remained. Instead, the skeletal forms glinted purple in the torchlight. The scene was sad, ghostly, and somehow apocalyptic, like an atom-bomb nightmare. On the ground, a carpet of purpled pine needles glittered in the flashlight's beam amongst the freshly fallen snow.

"What?"

"There's worse," said Jeff and hurried towards the dim outline of the chapel.

The trees, or what remained of them, became sparse as they emerged from the forest.

Running, the torch beam a dancing moon in his fitful grip, Ed saw every bush and shrub was dead, bare-branched, and blackened as if a forest fire had raged through these parts a month before.

The derelict chapel stood before them, its small cemetery encircled by a low stone wall. The chapel was stone-built, too, and large enough to accommodate fifty people at most. While Rachael was buried up here—Jeff had fought hard for that—her funeral had taken place at a church some miles away.

"Wendy," shouted Jeff.

Ed shone the torch in the direction of the cemetery and saw the girl crouched and shivering beside a headstone. She was crying hysterically and petting the silhouetted outline of a dog. Jeff stumbled towards her, almost falling, and scooped her into his arms.

When Ed approached the grave, he saw the headstone was covered in black lesions, too. Like the trees, they glinted purple in the torchlight. And although the ground was covered in snow, he could see the strange malignancy that branched out in every conceivable direction from the grave.

But the worst thing was the face. The black mould had colonised the snow-covered headstone, its patterns corrupting the granite, its pigment forming the ghost of a gaunt human face, a deathly negative. Ed was reminded of the Turin shroud. But the face's identity was unmistakable. It was Rachael. Not the happy-go-lucky girl Jeff had married. It was Rachael at the end.

"Jesus," Ed muttered.

Ed saw the parasite, whatever it was, climbed the curbs of graves, was entwined around the architecture of every tomb and headstone. Even the chapel itself was tattooed with the markings.

Jeff crouched, hugging his daughter, and stroking their dog, now oblivious to Ed's presence. Bathed in the light from his torch, the little family was together again.

Ed had the urge to run then, to take off and run back to Jessica; she had a baby growing inside her.

"I'm sorry, Daddy," said Wendy, her nose streaming with snot and struggling to catch her breath.

"I told you not to come here anymore," said Jeff.

"I feel so alone."

"You're never alone," said Jeff, reassuring his daughter.

"Until you go too," she said, shivering violently, lips blue, staring at the bottle of brandy that lay at Jeff's feet, half submerged in the snow.

Jeff hugged her tightly.

The pair stood by the grave in a huddle, and Ed thought of life and what a delicate thing it was, the snow falling around him, the winter wind raging.

Ed looked at the markings. Was it mould? Fungus? Should they be worried about poisonous spores? It was everywhere. And here, in the cemetery, where it was most dense, the lesions were more concentrated and almost circular, swirling mazes of concentric rings, painting patterns over everything, infecting his thoughts like a creeper climbing a wall.

Infecting his mind with fear.

There was no doubt that the source of the infection *was* Rachael's grave. Everywhere else the lesions were flat to the touch, embedded in the molecular composition of whatever it infected. But Rachael's headstone was thick with it. The usually smooth granite had been roughened, was glittering a dull shade of purple, that face set in a mournful grimace.

Ed shivered, but not from the cold. The light from the torch was dazzling. He momentarily closed his eyes and sighed, but behind the screens of his eyelids, Rachael remained, glaring back at him amidst the swirling phosphenes and darkness.

Jessica was pregnant. In June, if not before, they were going to have a baby. They were going to be a family, three soft-bodied human beings bonded by blood, love, and their fragile existence.

A baby. A life. That terrified him most of all.

THE LAST GIFT

1.

Danny Shaw opens the door to the little hospital room and walks towards the dying man.

"*Grandad?*" he says, stopping short of the bed, his pyjama pants showing beneath his long parka.

The old man is a fragile husk, the hospital gown clinging to his skeletal frame. Pipes feed into his nose, and a machine beeps rhythmically beside him, counting down the final moments of his long life.

"Come closer," says Grandad in his Irish lilt. He's wheezing, and the whites of his eyes are yellowed. "Same old me."

Danny takes a step closer. He is frightened. He loves his grandad, but the room smells bad. Despite the ever-present antiseptic smell of the hospital, the air is cloying.

He notices the architecture of the old man's face has altered. At first, he can't fathom why, but then he realises his teeth are missing. He had always admired Grandad's white teeth. But now he knows. They had been false. Danny feels like he's been lied to, as if Grandad had pretended to be younger. The only thing that appears white now is Grandad's tongue, which is coated in an unhealthy-looking fuzz.

"Closer," says Grandad. He sounds different without his teeth.

The room is uncomfortably warm. But Danny keeps his coat on because he doesn't want to stay here long. With his hands dug deep in his pockets, he walks to the bed, fearing death is something he might catch. He smiles meekly, not knowing what to say.

"Why the sad face?" says the old man.

"I don't want—"

"Me to die?"

Danny nods.

"It's my time," says Grandad. His breath is shallow and ragged. "I've avoided it long enough. I'm tired."

Grandad's age is a mystery, but Danny knows he is old even for a grandparent.

"What year is it?" says Grandad without a trace of senility.

"Nineteen-eighty."

"Well then. Not a bad innings."

"Dad said you wanted to speak with me. Alone."

"I have something for you."

His grandfather has always been generous, buying him presents. He might have been old, but he knew what to buy. Only last month, Grandad had bought him a brand-new Darth Vader action figure.

"Is it a present?" asks Danny.

"Yes, a gift. My *last* gift. It's in the cabinet."

Danny turns to the bedside cabinet where a vase of flowers stands next to a glass and a pitcher of water.

"Top drawer," says Grandad.

Tentatively Danny slides open the drawer. Lying amidst a glasses case, a wallet, and loose change is something wrapped in khaki-coloured fabric.

"Go ahead. Take it."

Danny picks up the package. The fabric is prickly, most likely wool. The object contained within feels heavy and substantial in his small hands. Slowly he unwraps it—and reveals a pebble-sized, blood-red gemstone. When he turns the stone in his hands, he notices the ruby has been cut to the shape of a human skull. The rock and its sharp angles glimmer, and he feels the tiny hairs prickle at the back of his neck, as if an invisible current is travelling down the ridge of his spine. The stone is intricate in its design, beautiful yet somehow terrifying. Guessing the skull is perhaps of great value, he turns to his grandfather, questioning him with his eyes.

A glob of drool is dripping from the old man's unshaven chin. "A long time ago, there was an accident," says Grandad. "It was my fault. I can only pray God has forgiven me."

Coughing, his grandad gestures to the glass of water. Danny lifts the glass to the old man's lips, and he sips it like a baby bird, clearing his throat. Danny dabs his grandfather's mouth with the bedsheet.

"The accident, it happened during the war. Do you remember I told you I was a pilot?"

"Yes," says Danny.

"Well, I made a mistake…a terrible mistake. The odds of me surviving the war were small. Yet I did. Even though I *wanted* to die."

Shaking, Grandad cups his cold, bony hands around Danny's and closes the boy's fingers tight around the ruby. "I did something terrible. I would never tell you, but all you need to know is this stone kept me alive. I know the rock is valuable, but it's also lucky, and that's far more important. I want you to promise me you'll keep this rock safe for as long as you live."

Danny nods.

"*You promise?*"

"Yes."

"Say it, Danny," says the old man, his voice rasping with emotion. "Say you'll keep the stone safe."

"I'll keep it safe."

"Good," says the old man, "because it'll keep you safe too. We're all on the frontline, Danny, every one of us, every day, fighting on the fringes. Wherever there is pain, suffering, *war*…sickness, Hell is never far away."

Danny doesn't understand what his grandfather is talking about, but he nods again anyway.

"You mustn't tell anyone about this."

"Not even Dad?"

"Especially not Dad. He won't understand. You think you can do that?"

Danny isn't sure, but he knows what Grandad means. His dad is poor. He also knows old people have funny superstitions, but he sees the tearful desperation in the old man's eyes. "Yes," he says with conviction, then scratches his head, and a light brown lock of his hair floats to the floor as delicately as a feather.

The old man's bloodshot eyes widen, following the hair that drifts in the stagnant air. The hair lands at Danny's feet.

"I know, Danny," says the old man finally.

"*Know?*"

"About your treatment. You're here too, at the hospital, aren't you?"

Danny nods.

"Your father told me yesterday, before I was taken ill. He'd kept it from me. But I know now, and you're going to be okay," says Grandad. "I promise."

Grandad settles back down on the bed, noticing a tiny spider hanging from a thread. The spider dangles precariously close to the old man's nose.

"Always hated spiders," says Grandad wheezing.

"It's a money spider," says Danny, brushing the web away gently with his finger. "They're…*lucky*."

"You don't need any more luck, not now," says Grandad. He closes his eyes. "And neither do I."

A tear wells in Danny's eye.

"I love you," says Grandad.

"Love you too."

"Keep the stone with you, always."

"Yes," says Danny.

Danny inches away from the bed and dares to look at the precious rock in his hands. He runs his thumb over the skull's cranium. It is smooth and cold to the touch. While the ruby looks like the perfect imitation of a human skull, there is something off about it. The hollows of the eyes are angular and cruel looking, the teeth a little too sharp.

He lets the rock slip into the deep pocket of his parka. When he looks back towards his grandfather's bed, he realises that a silence now occupies the room that hadn't been there a moment before. The air is suddenly colder too.

"*Grandad?*" he says.

I love you…

The beeping machine sounds the alarm, and his parents burst into the room accompanied by a concerned-looking nurse. Danny grips the ruby in his pocket and watches as the nurse shakes her head, and his father begins to weep.

2.

April 1918 - RAF Detling, Kent

"WHO BROUGHT THE IRISHMAN?" SAID THE SOLDIER WITH THE THICK stubble, sitting to Shaw's left.

Shaw ignored the comment, knowing the other man was spoiling for a fight.

"Show some respect," said Captain Marshall. "*Lieutenant* Shaw is a damn fine pilot. You'll do well to remember that, as well as your rank, *Corporal*."

"Really…*sir*?" said the unshaven soldier.

"Yes, Brown, *really*," said Marshall.

Brown scowled, the lines forming miniature trenches on a face that was young yet already weathered. "Just as long as you don't expect me to take orders from a Mick," he said.

Five men shared the room. Serving as the airbase's main HQ, the red-brick hut was bare apart from the blackboard and the line of four chairs the men sat on.

Marshall stood near the door, occasionally glancing out towards the airfield. It was dusk, but the chugging propellers could still be heard from the repair sheds.

Shaw sat with his fists clenched, ready for a fight. But the soldier sitting to his right, another lowly corporal, squeezed his shoulder affectionately.

"Ignore him," said the soldier. "Brown's got the painters in. He gets highly strung when he's on the rag, you know."

"Watch your mouth, Jones," said Brown. "Last time the krauts had your number, who saved your skin?"

"Oh, shut up," said Jones. "We're all in this together."

It seemed so. When Shaw had been told he'd been selected for special operations, he'd expected an air mission. Yet these men were roughnecks, drafted from the frontline. Brown's impertinence would never have usually been tolerated. Yet the captain had let the matter go, perhaps because their army badges were unfamiliar. The Royal Flying Corps—or Royal Air Force as they had now been newly baptised—did not tolerate insolence.

Brown sat with his lips pursed, the vein at his temple pulsing.

Shaw had met quick-tempered young men like him before, and the war brought out the worst in many. But Brown had come from the trenches. War was in the man's veins, and a confrontation was probably best avoided. Yet part of Shaw wanted to fight. Just like he had done ever since the girl died.

The soldier sitting furthest to Shaw's right leaned over Jones and offered him his hand. They shook, and Shaw noticed the man's Sergeant Major stripes.

"*Walters,*" he said, crushing Shaw's palm. "Pleased to make your acquaintance. Don't worry about these two chaps. Lovers' tiff, that's all."

Then Marshall stood to attention, and the brigadier stepped into the room, trailing a thick plume of pipe smoke.

The four men stood from their chairs and saluted.

"*Gentlemen*," said the brigadier, addressing the men curtly. "At ease."

The four men sat. Marshall remained at the front of the room, near the door.

The brigadier was a lean man with a bearing as rigid as his cane. Beneath the peak of his military cap, his eyes were stern but eager. He picked up a piece of chalk and vigorously scrawled four words on the blackboard.

"Captain Manfred von Richthofen," said the brigadier, reading the words aloud.

His German pronunciation was guttural and precise, his clipped inflection evidence of his university education. Here was a man of high class and rank. Everything denoted that: the waxed moustache, the pressed uniform, the medals gleaming on his left lapel.

"I assume you're familiar with this name?" the brigadier asked.

Nobody answered.

"Well, you can all read, *yes*?" enquired the brigadier.

"Von Richthofen," said Shaw. "He's Captain of the Flying Circus, sir."

"Also known as the Jagdgeschwader," said the brigadier. "An elite air fighter squadron."

Brightly coloured aircraft appeared on the horizon in Shaw's memory. With Teutonic efficiency, the Flying Circus whirred over the decimated plains of northern France, sweeping aside wave after wave of British aircraft in a hailstorm of bullets and fire.

"Von Ricthhofen has singlehandedly taken down over seventy Allied planes," said the brigadier. "An extraordinary score."

"An impossible score," muttered Brown under his breath.

"Enlighten us with your thoughts, Corporal," said the brigadier.

He had been briefly facing the blackboard but had spun around and was now pointing his cane directly at Brown.

Marshall scowled disapprovingly from behind the brigadier. Brown squirmed in his seat. Clearly he had not meant his quip to be heard.

"N...nothing, sir."

The brigadier was now scowling too. "Spit it out, soldier."

"There're rumours, sir, on the frontline," said Brown.

"What kind of rumours?" said the brigadier.

"It's nothing, sir," said Brown.

"I order you to tell me, Corporal," said the brigadier. "*What kind of rumours?*"

"Of the...occult, sir," said Brown. "The lads are saying the baron has made an...*ungodly* pact."

"You disappoint me," said the brigadier, shooting Brown a look of disgust. "You're soldiers, not children. What is true is that this Flying Circus has created a legacy of fear on the Western Front. It is damaging morale."

Brown lowered his head, avoiding further eye contact.

"This so-called Red Baron has become a kraut national hero," said the brigadier. "*Circus, indeed.*"

He took a map from inside his long coat, unfolded it, and stuck it to the wall with a couple of drawing pins.

"The unit's operations have ensured German superiority over the Allied offensive. We know the squadrons are primarily based at occupied villages in the western Flanders Province, *here*." He slapped his cane against the map, pointing at the Belgium side of the French border.

"The squadron is highly mobile," he went on, puffing smoke. "While the units fly out of northern Belgium, they frequently establish improvised airfields, setting up camp in reach of their next engagement, east of the frontline in the Hainaut Province, *here*." Again, he tapped his cane against the map.

"These airfields are more strategic than the Germans would have us believe. If we knew where they were going to land, away from the protection of enemy support, we believe they would be vulnerable."

Clearing his throat, he eyed every man in the room with the intensity of a harrier hawk. "Many men have died to enable the mission I'm about to assign you," he said.

"You four men will form one of three special units assigned to operate behind enemy lines and seek out the camp of this much-maligned Flying Circus. Each unit, we hope, will be small enough to operate without detection. This mission is highly classified. Do you understand?"

"Yes, *sir*," answered the men in unison.

"This is a great honour," said the brigadier. "Each of you has been specially selected for the mission based on your skills. We are fighting a great deal more than the German army. We are fighting a nation, an ideology, a propaganda machine. The baron has become a symbol of the imperial war effort. In many ways, he cannot lose. If he dies in battle, he instantly becomes a German martyr. But his winning streak cannot be allowed to continue. We will end this fable of indestructibility. For good.

"Your orders: assassinate the baron and help dispel this...*legend*." He switched his attention to Shaw. "*Lieutenant*."

"Yes, sir."

"We believe a pilot would be advantageous on this mission, hence your selection. Sergeant Major Walters, too, has some pilot training. But your knowledge of planes and the dynamics of their operations will be vital when planning your method of attack...and escape. Indeed, if you can commandeer an enemy aircraft, you should seek to do so."

The room fell silent. So, there it was, a death sentence. They weren't coming home. Everyone knew it. Four men, not two *real* pilots between them. German fighters were mostly one or two-man vehicles.

The hard chair dug into the back of Shaw's thighs. The other men, too, shifted in their seats, wiping palms on knees.

"You, man," said the brigadier, abruptly breaking the silence, pointing his cane at Brown. "You need a shave. Come on now, smarten up, and get some sleep, all of you. You'll be fully briefed as and when." He puffed out another cloud of noxious pipe smoke. "You leave at first light."

SLEEP PROVED IMPOSSIBLE.

Shaw stood on the edge of the lake, his pockets filled with rocks, and contemplated suicide. The moon was bright and shimmering.

He'd woken up drenched in sweat and fighting for breath. Even whisky was useless. His mind raged with the memory of her.

Stepping into the ice-cold water, his feet burned with cold—then became numb. Whilst the mission *was* a death sentence, the end could not come quickly enough.

Tears welled in his eyes, the release of emotion allowing him the smallest of comforts and reminding him he *was* human and not some terrible monster made of war.

At night, the area around the lake came alive, frogs croaking, an owl hooting somewhere close by. The water rippled with the movement of some unseen creature, and Shaw's reflection morphed into the girl's. Pale faced, she stared back from the concentric circles on the lake's surface.

"What are you doing out here?" asked Marshall.

The captain had crept up on him quietly, the end of the cigarette in his mouth an orange ember.

Shaw felt suddenly ashamed, wiping tears from his eyes.

"Just cooling down, sir," he replied.

"Well, don't cool down too much," said Marshall, a silhouette against the barracks. "You have an assignment tomorrow, *remember*?"

"Yes, sir."

A moment's silence, then:

"What's bothering you, Lieutenant?"

"Nothing, sir."

"Don't give me that bollocks. You've not been the same since you returned from that flight a fortnight ago."

Shaw remained silent.

"*Well*? I'm asking you a question. I order you to answer me, Lieutenant."

Shaw closed his eyes. The girl's face materialised within the phosphenes on the screens of his eyelids, haunting him. He remembered her standing among the coal-scuttle helmets of the enemy, face cast in terror, bullets tearing her to bloody ribbons. When he'd squeezed the trigger, he'd not known the krauts had harboured civilians amongst their legion. From the sky, the soldiers had been a compact unit, the girl hidden.

He had not disclosed the incident. But now he felt compelled to follow orders and share his burden.

"I shot a civilian, sir," he confessed.

"I see."

"A girl—*a child*—she was hidden within their battalion. It happened so fast. I saw her…go down."

"Lieutenant, we're at war. People die every day and—"

"That doesn't make it right."

"No, it doesn't. But it doesn't make you culpable either. If you're going to blame anyone, blame them, the enemy, for harbouring civilians within their ranks."

Shaw studied Marshall's face. It had been hardened by war. Three years ago, Shaw had left Ireland to enlist in the Royal Flying Corps. In that time, the captain had aged considerably. They all had, those who were left.

Originally enlisting as an air mechanic, Shaw had been sent to France as the driver of an observation balloon. Then came pilot training. His squadron had been largely assigned on reconnaissance missions, flying from Essex, photographing enemy lines. The work was dangerous, and every day brave men died. But as the war progressed so did aviation, and the dogfights became a strategic feature of the Allied offensive. Killing German fighter pilots, though, was one thing, an innocent child another. Only monsters did such things.

"You know, you might be dead soon anyway," said Marshall bluntly.

Shaw could only hope. The life expectancy of the average pilot fighting on the Western Front was two weeks. Yet here he was. Years later. The perverse thing was that, in the clouds, he felt free of the horrors and torment that plagued his sleep and every waking hour.

"Stop blaming yourself," said Marshall again. "Every time you fly, you save lives, maybe hundreds. That child might have died, but you *will* save another, I promise you. I expect to see you ready at first light." The captain gripped his shoulder. "Get some sleep," he said.

Shaw watched Marshall walk away and felt torn between war and suicide: between committing atrocity and the ultimate atonement. His thoughts interrupted by a sudden rustle, his eyes darted to the shrubbery over on the far bank of the lake.

A frog croaked, hopped, and dimpled the surface of the water, and in the wavering reflection the girl appeared again, made ghostly by moonlight.

Alone.

He stared down into the cold lake.

She had been just a child.

You know, you might be dead soon anyway.

Yes, he could hope.

THE FOUR MEN LEFT THE BARRACKS AT SUNRISE. THEY WERE DRIVEN BY armoured car to the port of Dover as the birds tweeted their morning song. The sky was clear, the gentle breeze ruffling the treetops.

After a choppy journey aboard a ship crammed with newly enlisted, propaganda-fed soldiers, they met their guide at Calais. Wilkes was a dishevelled-looking corporal who chain-smoked Wood-bines. "I'm to escort you to the frontline," he said, by way of greeting.

"*Frontline?*" said Brown. "We're going to the front—?"

"Corporal Brown," said Walters, "*enough*."

"Look," said Wilkes, revealing a mouth full of rotten teeth. "Don't know nothing more, I'm afraid. Eat and rest as much as you can. You have a three-day march ahead."

And march they did, advancing with the jovial battalions, limbs aching under the weight of their kit.

They passed through leafy hamlets where cheering villagers lined the streets, waving them through with Gallic gusto. Pretty girls blew kisses. Bakers threw warm loaves of bread. There was even wine, bottles passed from soldier to soldier. They ate and drank and smoked, their momentum set by the flanking cavalry and horse-drawn carts.

On the second day, the landscape changed. They saw buildings burning and black plumes of rising smoke. Planes whirred above, and great tanks rattled and shook the ground, spitting mud from their tracks, barely moving quick enough to pass the march.

As they neared the front, the trees became fewer. Carts lay on their side, wood splintered, wheels idling in the breeze. A horse lay dead beside the road, its unravelled intestines attracting flies.

"They all seem so happy," said Jones, acknowledging the horde of soldiers resting on the grass bank of a cobbled road. "I don't think they know."

"Know what?" said Shaw.

"That they're all about to die."

Half an hour later, they were back on the road. Shaw had changed into his spare socks. His feet were bleeding profusely. Although the dry socks helped a little, his boots might as well have been made from razor blades.

That night, they slept beneath the stars on their thin groundsheets. The light rain didn't bother them, and Shaw was grateful for his exhaustion. It provided sleep.

The next day passed quickly, and Shaw felt almost comforted by the stiffness in his limbs and the blisters on his heels as they marched. The physical pain of exertion masked deeper psychological wounds.

The girl, though, still haunted him. Now and then he would catch her watching, shimmering amidst the flames of a burning farmhouse; peeping through the gaps in the barbed hedgerow; giggling from the bough of an old oak, beckoning him to the frontline, leading him towards Hell.

The trenches were close.

Bombs burst like firecrackers in the distance, and filthy smoke clouded the horizon. They passed soldiers who appeared anything but jovial. The battle-worn men rested on the ground, some smoking and chatting. Others sat alone, flinching at every distant explosion, their eyes darkened hollows.

One livelier group played football, the goals made from rifles stuck in the earth by their bayonets. Shaw wondered if those bayonets had pierced human flesh, robbing some newly enlisted Bavarian of his young life in a flash of brutal violence. He doubted it. Those who went over the top were cut to pieces in seconds. He'd seen it from the sky.

The severely injured were a stark reminder that this was no boys' club. Stretcher upon stretcher was lined with men bleeding from every conceivable injury: patched eyes; severed limbs; gunshot wounds. All too often the men simply bled out, coughing, spreading sickness, waiting for a cart to take them away. But there was little medical provision. The ambulances Shaw had seen were few, and the air was thick with the hum of flies.

As they entered the support line of the trench system, they encountered the duckboards above the sinking mud.

"This way," said Wilkes, leading them.

Shaw saw Brown grab Walters' arm and pull him back. "He's taking us back to the front, the *very* front."

"I would have thought that was obvious by now," said Walters.

"*I can't*—"

Walters shook his arm free. "*Orders*, soldier. Keep going."

They trudged onwards through the maze of mud—and arrived in Hell.

Emaciated soldiers cowered beneath the lip of trenches. The sky rained bullets. Sandbags absorbed much of the gunfire. Frantically men dug amongst the corpses of the fallen, repairing walls while others slept apparently oblivious, wrapped in their soaking blankets. One man fried his rations on the lid of his mess tin as the bullets zipped inches above his head.

It was now dusk, and the sky strobed, the ground shaking beneath the unending peals of thunder. The enemy artillery churned the sinking mud, disturbing rotting bodies. The swarms of flies fed, and so did the corpse-fattened rats. Everywhere they scuttled, spreading disease. Shaw watched as the vermin gnawed at the fingers of a hand emerging from the mud, belonging to somebody's son or husband or father.

The smell was the worst, though. The knee-high water that filled the trench carried the stench of the flooded latrines. A turd floated past Shaw, brushing his knee. But even the scent of piss and shit was preferable to the reek of death, which clung to everything and infused the air like gas.

"Not far," said Wilkes as the sun slipped below the horizon. "Make sure you duck low here—otherwise you'll lose your head."

The five men ducked beneath the lip of the trench where a sign read: DANGER, scrambling along the narrow channel like dogs as bullets whirred like angry wasps. After thirty yards, they reached an alley of sandbags.

"In here," said Wilkes, darting right into a dugout that materialised in the now inky darkness.

A small corridor had been burrowed through the mud. Timber

joists supported the low ceiling that shook with every exploding shell. A series of bunks lined the walls, beyond which they emerged into a room the size of a large kitchen. Shadows danced and rippled in the lamplight.

They were greeted by a thin officer with a neat black moustache. His dark eyes glowered from his weasel-like face. "Finally, you've arrived," he said, saluting. "I'm Captain Curtis. Here, put those on." He pointed to a wooden table piled with grey-green uniforms and German helmets. "You leave at midnight."

THEY WERE ORDERED TO REST. BUT SLEEPING ON THE HARD BUNKS WAS difficult. Twice they'd received the call to put on their gas masks, and they'd been woken by the agonised screams of a young soldier, shouting for his mother.

In all, Shaw had slept for no more than a few minutes at a stretch, and was exhausted. He'd spent most of his time staring at a wooden beam where a spider fed on a fat fly. He'd always hated spiders. The way they wrapped up their prey and feasted upon their liquified remains was repulsive.

He had just drifted into sleep for perhaps the seventh or eighth time when Curtis shook him awake. "It's time," said the captain, his eyes steely in the lamplight.

The men assembled in the dugout's main room where a map was spread on a small wooden table.

"We've been working on a tunnel," said Curtis, drinking tea from a tin cup. "It's highly classified, of course, and guarded twenty-four hours a day at the entrance. Last thing we need is the krauts finding their way here." He gave a hollow laugh.

"The ventilation is poor. It's a highly claustrophobic environment. The tunnel burrows beneath a relatively shallow point of no man's land and emerges in an abandoned, highly compromised section of the German trench system. The krauts have given up repairing it because the wall has been blasted to oblivion, leaving it exposed. Ordinarily, you'd be at great risk of being hit by friendly fire at this point, but we will, of course, ceasefire...*briefly*. The tunnel has been trialled, and we believe the point from which you'll emerge is hidden from enemy eyes."

"Believe?" repeated Brown incredulously.

Curtis ignored him. "We'll keep a lookout. Once you've made it through, we will resume firing, concentrating our attack *here*." The captain tapped the map. "This should provide a distraction, allowing you to slip unnoticed into the enemy trench system. From here on in, you're on your own."

The captain again pointed at the map. "You'll need to memorise its networks." He traced his finger along a wavy contour marking the German frontline. "Make your way to the support line, *here*, and then to the back."

Shaw saw Brown swallow hard enough for Walters to glance at him, and for the two men to share a brief, nervous exchange. Seeming to pick up on what the other two men were clearly thinking, Jones said, "Is *that* it?"

"Yes," said Curtis.

"How are we supposed to make our way to the back unhindered?" asked Jones.

The men had already changed into the German uniforms, but the helmets remained piled on the table. Curtis picked one of them up and showed it to the four men. The helmet had a red cross on a white background painted on the front like a St. George's flag.

"Medics," said Curtis. "Pick the lightest man and stretcher him through."

"And if we're apprehended?" said Brown, his scowl returning. "If the krauts address us, we'll be done for. I don't know a word of German."

"That's where Herr Walters comes in," said Curtis. He dared to smile as if their plan was fool proof, not something half-baked and potentially suicidal.

"Ich bin etwas aus der Übung," said Walters.

"And what the fucking hell does that mean?" said Brown.

Curtis frowned at Brown's choice of language.

"I'm a little rusty," said Walters.

Curtis waved a hand as if dismissing their misgivings. "Once you reach the back—and you *will*—you must slip away into the country-side. Each of you has a map included in your kit as well as civvy clothes. Make your way south. There you'll wait in proximity to the airfield."

"This is madness," said Brown.

"War is madness, Corporal," said Curtis. "While you were sleeping, I ordered a fourteen-year-old boy to go on a recovery assignment. He did not return. Doubtless the rats are gnawing at his eyes as we speak. We are living on the fringes of Hell. But needs must, gentlemen. I have every confidence you'll succeed."

THE CAPTAIN ESCORTED THEM THROUGH THE WARREN OF SANDBAGS towards the tunnel's entrance. Shell after shell bombarded the line, scattering rubble and debris in huge eruptions of mud, burying men dead and alive.

Shaw stepped over a young man's corpse. The fresh carcass' eyes glistened as the heavens strobed, and he felt ashamed because some small part of him envied that man; the fear, at least, had left him.

The men passed another Danger sign, crawled under another low-lipped wall, and emerged before a black hole surrounded by sand-bags. The tunnel was guarded by a single teenager who wore a helmet two sizes too big. The boy crouched beside the entrance and its supporting joists, holding his rifle tight against his undernourished body. He slapped at a louse scaling his cheek.

"Dark down there," said the teenage soldier, gesturing towards the tunnel's opening. "Don't envy you."

"That's barely large enough for a twelve-year-old boy," said Brown. "How are we going to crawl through there with full kit?"

"And a stretcher?" finished Jones.

"*Manage,*" said Curtis, checking his wristwatch. "There's little time. In eleven minutes, we will cease firing for three. That should give you ample time to reach the tunnel's other side and get behind the German defences."

A shell exploded nearby, collapsing a wall of sandbags. The dirt around the tunnel's entrance crumbled.

Shaw peered into the thick subterranean darkness.

Another flash of blinding light preceded the quake, but the thunder from the explosion arrived a split second too late to warn of the avalanche.

Time slowed. Shaw roiled on the brink of unconsciousness, lost under a cloak of darkness, his mouth filling with mud, his ears ringing. When his comprehension returned, he found himself buried beneath the earth, fighting for his life, struggling to breathe.

"Dig," shouted Curtis from somewhere distant. "Dig, man. Dig."

Shaw felt strong arms wrap around him, and he was hauled back into a world lit by the strobing sky. Again, the men threw themselves to the floor as the world shook.

"You have to go," said Curtis, still face down in the mud. But when he looked up at the tunnel entrance, Shaw saw the young guard now reduced to something from a butcher's slab. The blast had unhinged his lower jaw. His tongue twitched uselessly like a fish in its final throes. His scorched uniform was tattered, revealing seared flesh. The boy's organs spilled like foul fruit, his steaming body heat rising into the cold air. Yet he still lived. So did that louse, scurrying across his mutilated face. The boy's eyes pleaded with the other men, looking to them for some impossible comfort.

Curtis staggered upright and drew his pistol. He pressed the barrel against the boy's temple—tipping that too large helmet aside—and fired. In the briefest flash of gunfire the captain's features were transformed from man to monster.

"Bastards," shouted Curtis, holstering his pistol. "You need to go, all of you…*now*."

Ducking into the mouth of the hole, Shaw crawled forwards, pushing his backpack before him. His uniform was wet with mud, and the numbing cold burned his hands. But he felt sweat prickling his brow. The air was thin, and his chest tightened as the ceiling crumbled around him, claustrophobia sapping his strength. He felt faint.

"Move, you Irish bastard," said Brown from behind, his voice laced with panic.

Shaw hauled himself forwards through the stinking mud, feeling it fill his fingernails and his nostrils, tasting the bitter earth.

Another shell hit, and again the ceiling crumbled, the tunnel filling with more soil.

"For fuck's sake," screamed Brown, "*move*." The military training Brown had endured had clearly left him. Shaw could feel the man writhing in the mud behind him, overcome by hysteria.

"Stay calm," shouted Walters, only a few yards behind, but his voice distant and muffled in the cramped shaft.

The darkness was unyielding. Shaw's eyes struggled to adjust from the strobing sky outside to the near total blackness. His vision was still flashing with colour, due to the retinal afterburn from that last blast. The darkness, though, was a blank canvas for his over-active imagination, which conjured the girl into being. She stood before him in the tunnel, her nose wrinkling, her white dress billowing behind her, as it had the day when he'd gunned her down, her body collapsing, white dress erupting with red.

He rubbed his eyes, smearing them with mud.

"Would you get a fucking move on?" bellowed Brown, striking his leg.

Shaw blinked, and the girl was gone. He pulled his body through the sludge, his conscience a raw wound.

The passage birthed them on the fringes of no man's land, the exit hidden by a pile of heavy sandbags. Shaw helped drag out the other men one by one, Jones emerging last with the stretcher. Curtis had said this section had long been abandoned. That much was obvious because the kraut soldier who greeted them was skeletal, his bones picked clean by rats.

Brushing clumps of thick mud from his German uniform, Walters whispered, "They've stopped firing."

He was right. The gunfire from the Allied side had ceased. But the boom of cannons and the intermittent rat-a-tat of German guns continued.

"We're out of sight here, but not for long," said Walters. "*C'mon.*"

Fifty yards further along it became apparent why the Germans had abandoned this section. The trench wall had completely collapsed, and for thirty yards, there was no protection at all. Clambering over fallen sandbags and rubble, they found themselves on a level with the grim vista of no man's land. Lit by the flash of enemy fire, strewn with bodies, mud, and barbed wire, it was a wasteland too desolate even for ghosts.

They navigated the system from memory, wandering the maze of sandbag alleys and crossing more canals filled with stinking water.

"Stop," said Walters at last, halting before a crossroads within the trench system and pointing to a breach in the wall ahead where more sandbags had fallen. "Once we're through there, we're in enemy territory proper. We'll be visible, which means *no English* from here on. Wait for the shelling to begin. The noise should excuse us from any German chatterboxes." He smiled and pointed to the stretcher. "Jones, you're the smallest. Hop aboard."

Brown took the stretcher's rear and Shaw the front. As the bombs arrived on cue, they dashed for cover, throwing the cot carrying Jones over the wall of sandbags. Again, the world trembled as if invisible giants were stomping across the ground, shells lighting the skies like some apocalyptic storm.

Then planes dived overhead, careering towards the Allied defences, guns blazing, the land churned by bullets.

Amidst the frenzy, a trio of German soldiers appeared from the gloom, screaming. Any audible communication with the enemy was redundant. The cacophony of cannon fire and the screaming engines of the planes ripped the sky apart. Shaw felt his innards vibrate.

The German soldiers assembled the machine gun, fixing it above a mound of dirt, building a wall of sandbags as they worked. The tallest of the men manned the gun and squeezed the trigger, his face cast in an insane grimace of hate, fighting the recoil, scowling across the wasteland separating them from the enemy.

Walters nodded. Brown and Shaw lifted the stretcher, and they made their way behind enemy lines, Walters leading the way.

The trench system was much like the Allied lines. The wounded fought side-by-side with the weary, knee deep in their own shit. It was a warren of bodies and decimation.

Shaw's gaze skittered from soldier to soldier, meeting the eyes of the enemy. He could feel his hands shaking from the strain of the stretcher, the handles burning his palms. He feared capture. Such a fate, he knew, would be worse than death. He doubted the krauts would be so kind as to merely shoot them.

A gaunt-looking German soldier sat in the sludge with his back resting against sandbags, nibbling a biscuit, his gaze vacant.

They passed the soldier slowly, the boards under their feet sinking in the mud. The gaunt man ogled them, his grey eyes reading their every step. He was looking at their boots. Shaw's boots were caked in mud. Yet the man, he had no doubt, had noticed some small difference. They passed the soldier without incident, but Shaw looked back over his shoulder and saw the man watching them sidle away.

They reached a support line leading away from the front. Even though the shelling was still deafening, the cacophony of battle was punctuated with snippets of soldiers' conversations. Listening to the curt Germanic dialects, Shaw wondered if Walters was truly capable of convincing a German soldier that he was kin.

Eyes down, he thought. *One step at a time…*

Those steps were becoming harder, though. Jones was heavier than he looked, and the stretcher was more cumbersome with every muddy yard.

Ahead, a group of soldiers sat in a huddle frying cured sausage on a tin lid. Another thin soldier, this one with dirty blond hair and a moustache, regarded them and shouted something in German. Shaw's heart thudded in his chest. They ignored the man and walked on.

But the soldier shouted again. "Hey du, stehen bleiben!"

Walters stopped.

"Mein Freund ist verletzt dort drüben," said the soldier, pointing back the way they'd come. His tone was gruff, his inflection harsh.

Shaw had no idea if the man was angry or if his brisk manner was simply an intricacy of a language that was completely foreign.

"Wir bringen ihn nach hinten," stuttered Walters in reply, gesturing to Jones, who remained on the stretcher, eyes shut.

The German stared straight at them, his sharp cheekbones streaked with dirt, his eyes sunk in deep hollows. After a moment, though, he nodded and they moved on.

Nearing the rear of the trench system, Shaw realised how much more dire their predicament became the further they moved from the din of battle. Hordes of German soldiers were resting away from the furore of the frontline. Here, the men sat or lay on the ground in profusion, sleeping, eating, drinking, some chatting labouredly. Shaw wondered what these young men were talking about. He guessed it was the same as the British—their wives and girlfriends and children, their reminiscences of home, anything to distract them from the terrible conflict in which they were embroiled.

But one word was all it would take from any one of these hundreds of enemy soldiers. *One word,* and a sequence of events would be initiated that would ultimately result in death by torture.

Shaw's heart pounded. He'd read the reports of what the krauts did to prisoners. They gouged out eyes; they cut off hands; they pressed hot irons into flesh.

He had heard other things too: women raped; babies bayonetted; children given hand grenades as toys... The Germans were a cruel race. You only had to listen to their language to know that.

Walters nodded, gesturing towards a troop of horses. The animals were reined and tied to several carts carrying ammunition and supplies. Once they rounded the carts, they were hidden from the eyes of the enemy.

A low wooden fence separated the men from a cornfield. In the distance, the black outline of a forest loomed against the night sky.

Jones had one leg over the fence when a German soldier appeared from around the cart.

"Deserteur," said the soldier, pointing at Jones.

Shaw turned and saw Walters approach the dark-haired kraut.

"Deserteur," said the soldier again, still pointing at Jones.

"Nein, nein," said Walters, who reassuringly slapped the young German on the shoulder—and pushed his knife up into the man's throat.

The soldier fell gasping for breath, the ragged tear spurting a geyser of blood.

"Quick," said Walters, and the men jumped the fence and disappeared into the corn, leaving the trenches behind and the soldier bleeding in the dirt.

THE MEN MARCHED THROUGH THE TREES AS THE SUN ROSE, FEARING THE enemy at their back.

Surely, it was only a matter of time before the legion discovered their comrade dead—and sent a party seeking vengeance.

The straps of Shaw's pack cut furrows into his aching shoulders, but at least the land was flat, and the forest of deciduous oak, willow, and beech was thick enough to conceal their tracks. They were still in range of the decimated battlefields, yet the vegetation was lush, the ferns and grasses untouched by war. Despite the distant echo of booming cannons, birds twittered in the trees and searched for insects to feast upon.

Walters crouched beside a blackberry bush and studied the map, swatting gnats and picking berries. Whilst they were conscious of the need to move swiftly and efficiently, they needed to stay on course.

Walters traced his finger along a blue line. "We're somewhere around here, in the Hainaut Province," he said, pointing to a minor river on the Belgium side of the border. "Mons is not far. But we need to head away from the city." He pointed to a blot on the map marking a small settlement. "We head here, find somewhere to rest, and wait. According to the information we have, the airfield is here." Again, he tapped a section of the map. "Pastures, most likely cattle grazing, but the land is perfect for a camp."

"How far?" said Brown.

"Maybe a day, a day and a half," said Walters. "We're okay where there's cover." He traced his finger southeast of Mons. "But once we break into the fields, we'll be exposed, and there will be people."

He was right.

Three times they crossed fields under the suspicious eyes of farmers. They'd long ditched both the German uniforms and stretcher and could have passed for Flemish peasants, taking turns to push their rifles and kit on a small cart they'd stolen.

Despite their disguise, they were vulnerable out in the open. None of the men spoke French or Dutch, and they were acutely aware of the soldier they'd left behind with his throat slashed.

Later that day, they ducked under hedgerow when a convoy of armoured German vehicles sped past, and ventured back into the forest when a group of children spotted them mulling at a crossroads.

After sleeping in a deserted barn, they arrived on the outskirts of a tiny village early the next morning.

"What are the odds?" said Walters.

"Fuck me sideways," said Brown.

The planes looked like toys from a distance.

Crouched under the hedgerow, the four men passed Walters' binoculars back and forth, taking turns to view the line of huge tents in the near distance. The Fokker triplanes—red and green and blue and yellow—looked too brightly coloured to be war machines, though each was stamped with the intimidating insignia of the Iron Cross.

It was difficult to gauge the exact number of planes, due to the flatness of the land and their poor vantage point, but Shaw counted at least ten large tents and twenty planes. There were also several much smaller conical-shaped tents, like white witches' hats, positioned at the furthest end of the field.

"You think he's in there, *the baron*?" said Jones.

"Every chance," Walters replied.

They were close enough for the voices and laughter of the enemy to carry over to them. With the binoculars, they spied five pilots sitting around a stove, sharing a bottle of wine. The faint aroma of cooking meat wafted across, causing Shaw's stomach to rumble with hunger.

"We wait for nightfall," said Walters.

THE GERMAN PILOTS DRANK WELL INTO THE SMALL HOURS, PERHAPS celebrating some victory or other. Sitting around a campfire, they cheered and heckled one another. Other men tinkered with the aircraft, their tools clinking, the planes' propellers spluttering to life amidst the drunken exuberance.

Shaw crouched at the field's edge with the three other men. Each held their unfastened bayonet. They had hidden their rifles and gear beneath the spiny branches of a gorse bush. They were each armed with a pistol but had agreed not to use them. Even a gun equipped with a silencer could wake the camp. They were vastly outnumbered and would rely solely on speed and stealth.

"Starting to get light," said Jones, squinting at the faint blue glow on the horizon.

Shaw was cold, his limbs stiff and cramping. "We can't do this in daylight," he said.

"Time yet," said Walters. "You really think these men will be up early? We'll be done and away while they're still asleep."

Half an hour later, the camp was silent, the paling stars still glittering in the early morning sky.

"*There*," said Walters. "I'm pretty certain that's the baron's tent." He pointed to a conical tent adjacent to the red plane.

"*Pretty certain*?" said Brown.

"Has to be, *Corporal*," he said, reminding the other man of his inferior rank.

"And if we get him, then what?" asked Jones. He pointed at a two-seated biplane, most likely used for reconnaissance. The plane was positioned away from the fleet of smaller one-man fighters. "The brigadier said we should commandeer a plane."

"Speaking frankly, the brigadier doesn't give two shits whether we come home or not," said Walters. "Once we start one of those planes, we'll wake half the province."

"Then what?" said Jones.

"We head to the forest west of here," said Walters.

Jones scowled. "Do you have any idea how far—?"

"Our best chance," said Walters.

"This is a fucking suicide mission," said Jones.

"King and country, Corporal," said Walters.

TWO GUARDS PATROLLED THE MAKESHIFT AIRSTRIP.

Shaw and Walters skirted the camp's perimeter, sticking to the shadows, encroaching on the conical-shaped tent nearest the red Fokker.

They watched as Jones darted from plane to plane, weaving between and rolling under the brightly coloured aircraft. The guard at the field's furthest end was taking a piss when Jones' bayonet opened his throat. The guard fell silently into the hedge in which he'd been urinating.

Jones gave a low hoot to let the other men know his job was done. The sound, though, was enough to alert the second guard, who stamped out his cigarette and reached for his holster. Brown lunged from the shadows and pushed his blade through the back of the man's neck.

"Okay," whispered Walters to Shaw, pointing to the small tent. "You're my eyes."

Shaw nodded.

"Hoot for trouble. *Got it*?"

"Aye, sir."

Walters winked, then crept towards the tent, disappearing between the canvas flaps.

The rest of the men waited, the seconds after Walters had entered the tent seeming to stretch interminably. Then the spell was broken by the unmistakable crack of a pistol echoing across the meadow.

Walters staggered out of the tent, holding his stomach, and the pistol cracked again. Blood and brains erupted from the back of Walters' head, splashing grass already wet with dew.

A moment of unnerving silence preceded a volley of German expletives echoing across the camp.

Jones was now running towards the opposite side of the field, heading to where their rifles and gear were hidden. But already the Germans were spilling out from every tent, shouting.

A half-dressed pilot fired his machine gun in short, controlled bursts, causing Jones' body to spasm in a death dance.

Watching from behind the tent, Shaw was powerless to intervene.

Another kraut aimed at Brown, who had drawn his pistol. The German pilot stood composed, locked in concentration, his feet planted evenly, the distinctively shaped Luger pistol extended in his grip. He fired once, twice, three times, hitting Brown in the chest.

"No," screamed Shaw.

The German spun around, spotting Shaw too, which gave Brown enough time to point his own weapon from the ground and fire. The German fell.

Shaw raced towards where Brown had fallen and found him bleeding profusely from his chest and abdomen, grimacing in pain.

"You need to get the fuck out of here," said Brown, spitting blood.

"This way," said Shaw, pointing to the hedgerow at the fringe of the field. He slipped Brown's arm around his neck, lifting him.

"I'm not going anywhere," said Brown, wheezing. "Even a fucking Irishman knows that."

Shaw did. Blood was spouting from Brown's chest in pulsating gouts. The trauma would be fatal. They both knew it.

"Get me to the red plane...*the baron's plane*," said Brown, pointing to the nearest fighter. "I'll start her up for you."

"We'll head that way. There's cover," said Shaw, pointing again towards the field's boundary and a line of trees. "Come on. That's an order."

"I don't take orders from a fucking Mick, *remember*?" said Brown, grunting with agony. "*Red plane. Now.*"

Shaw had craved death. His guilt and sense of fair play demanded it because he had killed a girl. But how could he look a dying man in the eye and deny him his final wish? Brown *needed* to die for something. He didn't have long. Shaw's arms were already slick with Brown's blood. Its metallic reek turned his stomach.

"Fuck them," said Brown. "Fuck their Kaiser. Fuck their Flying Circus. Fuck the baron. You take the *red* plane."

Amid the commotion, they were yet to be spotted again by the startled Germans, and they staggered towards the Fokker like two men tied together in a three-legged race.

The sun rose above the horizon, painting the field in a vibrant pink hue, and the cool mist hung low across the grass in spectral wisps, cloaking the planes in an ethereal sea. The aircrafts' wings and noses jutted from the vapour like the fins of sharks in dark waters. And maybe it *was* this trick of the light, an illusion, but the baron's Fokker appeared wraithlike, pulsing with otherworldly energy.

Shaw left Brown bent over and bleeding at the plane's nose and climbed into the cramped cockpit. Despite his gratitude, the situation was too urgent for sentiment. The first thing he noticed was the red gemstone embedded in the dashboard, skull-shaped and grimacing. But there was little time to consider the ruby's strange allure.

The baron emerged from the small tent, his pistol drawn.

Myth and legend were usually reserved for the dead. The living grew old, got fat. Mortality was ugly.

The baron had no such flaws.

In his split-second glimpse, Shaw saw the young baron was the perfect Aryan specimen: cool blue eyes; cheekbones carved from stone; and a cruel, downturned mouth that suggested cold-blooded ruthlessness.

The Iron Cross was pinned to the neck of his double-breasted military jacket, and he stood wreathed in mist and swathed in black leather, face as implacable as the red skull on the plane's dashboard.

"*Go,*" shouted Brown, spinning the plane's propeller.

Shaw wasted no time. He set the mixture lever to rich and gunned the engine. Slowly the propeller turned, and turned again…then it caught, and the plane spluttered to life.

Brown nodded curtly. Then he was gone, a bullet burying itself in the side of his head. He fell to the ground, his eyes wide open and glistening in the early morning sun.

"Halt!" cried a German guard. "Halt!"

The baron reloaded his pistol, his eyes flashing like blue fire.

Shaw willed the plane to move. The camp was a hive of commotion. More pilots spilled out of their tents and into the field, half dressed, holding their pistols.

Bumping over mounds and molehills, the plane taxied forward, at first slowly then picking up pace. A bullet whistled past Shaw's head. He glanced back as the baron fired again, another slug glancing off the propeller.

Shaw adjusted the wing for take-off and gently pulled back as the plane picked up speed. Rushing forward, it bumped and rose and lifted into the sky, and as it climbed, Shaw made adjustments, straightening the Fokker to bring it in line with the horizon and watching as the field shrank beneath him.

Perhaps hungover on French wine, the German pilots were tripping over themselves. A man fell flat on his face as he dressed, his leg caught in his trousers. Another pilot frantically waved his arms in the air, as if that might cause Shaw to turn around and apologise.

The baron, though, slipped into the cockpit of a blue Fokker plane like a serpent into water. Even amongst the clamour, he was calm, composed, together. His goggles came down, and the blue plane ascended.

Shaw's plane was quickly gaining speed and altitude. The Fokker was slower than the Allied planes he was accustomed to, but it moved easier, its rudder offering a slicker level of manoeuvrability.

Again, he glanced back. The baron was nowhere, gone like the mist beneath them. Shaw's plane was equipped with a compass, and the fuel gauge told him the tank was full and good for at least one hundred and eighty miles. His aim was to make his escape across the border and over the Western Front, though that was easier said than done when you had the ace of aces on your tail.

Shaw hit the blip switch on the stick, cutting the engine, allowing him to dive and point the plane westwards. As the plane drifted, the first machine gun bullets whistled past his head, missing him by inches.

He pulled back, and again the plane soared. He looked over his shoulder, to see the baron tailing him, their conjoined slipstreams cutting the early morning sky to ribbons, the clouds now golden and iridescent in the diffracted light of dawn. The sunrise was heavenly, the beams of light casting shadows amongst the heavy clouds. He wondered about heaven—not a place for child killers. He could see the girl's face in the abstract patterns of a cloud. He'd heard other pilots discuss something called...*pareidolia*, was it? The tendency for the mind to perceive things in the inanimate.

Another round of bullets snapped in his ear, jerking his mind from its momentary lapse.

The baron was closing, yet Shaw knew that if he could get enough altitude, he could shake the baron and his bullets.

He pulled back, gaining height, breaking through clouds and feeling the currents of air ruffling his hair and rippling his skin. He checked the altimeter. He was approaching four kilometres and rising, the earth disappearing beneath him, the details of the land shrinking.

Without gloves or goggles, he was ill equipped for flying. His hands and face burned with cold to the point of frostbite, yet his ascendance *was* somehow cleansing. Despite the bullets, despite the personification of death on his tail, he suddenly felt freer, closer to the celestial. And as the oxygen depleted and his strength waned, his thinking slowed and he felt almost drunk, his sins slipping away.

Still the baron came.

Higher and higher, the Fokker ascended, and again Shaw checked the altimeter:

Four and a half kilometres...and rising...

The air was so thin. His heart felt rapid in his chest, his vision clouding.

Still rising...

Shaw knew he was close to losing consciousness. His every movement was drunken and laboured. Yet still the plane climbed, and his senses were enriched with a rising awareness of euphoria.

He looked back.

Gone was the baron on his tail. Gone was the war. Gone was the girl and his shame...his guilt, his culpability.

He was the sky.

HE WAS UNSURE AT WHICH POINT HIS HEAD FINALLY CLEARED, BUT WHEN he came to the plane was sailing at a safer altitude, the tank half empty. His head was pounding, and his legs were starting to cramp. The physical stress on his body due to oxygen depletion was also causing his mind to play tricks. The dawn sky was crimson, the topography of every cloud a four-dimensional image of the girl's face, cast in that terrible moment when the bullets had cut her to pieces. And when the wind whispered, so did she, damning his soul to Hell for eternity.

But this couldn't be Hell, could it?

Drifting aimlessly west, the plane whirred hypnotically. He piloted the aircraft in a dreamlike state, wondering if he had indeed perished and was steering the Fokker towards the afterlife.

When he looked down, he saw the rising smoke, the smouldering buildings, the ravaged land. The war below raged. Entire platoons of men were nothing but meat, to be churned out by the machineries of war. The Western Front was a graveyard, haunted by the dreams of despots, who built empires from the ruined bodies of husbands and sons and fathers…

And little girls…

Shaw was considering where he'd put the plane down when the blue bird dipped on the horizon before him. The Red Baron was still here. And he had Shaw in his sights.

This time, though, the bastard faced him head-on. Shaw considered ascending to a higher altitude, but he had been left weak by the last ordeal. His limbs held all the strength of paper, and the enemy was already hurtling towards him.

Shaw gripped the stick, gritted his teeth, and waited for the opposing plane to appear between the barrels of his machine guns.

When it did, he fired, bullets spitting in perfect synchronisation through the whirling arc of his propeller.

Feeling every judder of the machine gun's violent recoil, he saw the baron in a series of quick-fire flashes. Even through his goggles the German's expression was one of murderous concentration.

The planes passed one another, barely two inches between their wing tips. The baron swooped around, tearing through the clouds, eyebrows inverted and forehead furrowed in a scowl.

A hail of bullets rained down on Shaw's plane, and he felt a dull thud at his shoulder, erupting in a hot flash of pain. Grimacing, he pulled back the stick but found the plane was descending rapidly.

He fought for control, then looked out and saw the right wing was shredded and vibrating violently. Again, the baron came, firing in controlled bursts, lead pockmarking timber.

Hurtling towards the ground, Shaw felt his stomach lurch as he continued to wrestle for control, attempting to guide the plane down gently. But to no avail. The ground rushed up towards him, and everything went black.

HIS SENSES RETURNED SLOWLY: THE ROUGH FEEL OF HIS DRY TONGUE, THE smell of burning fuel, the crushing weight on his legs.

When he opened his heavy eyes, the world pulsed in red and black flashes in rhythm with the thin beat of his heart. The sky was still a deep red too, the girl's face an hallucinogenic tapestry amongst the troposphere where his plane had glided moments before.

Maybe this *was* Hell?

Or some barren no man's land between life and the eternal enemy. Had the borders between dominions been blurred by mankind's appetite for death and destruction? Were Hell's fires fuelled by war?

Had the girl led him here?

The red Fokker lay in ruins, the nose crushed and aflame, the wings smashed. The wreckage lay next to an abandoned trench system where slack-mouthed corpses hung on coils of barbed wire and black smoke rose in lazy curls.

His legs were trapped under the wreck, the plane's dashboard crushing him. Lying amidst the hot, hungry flames, he closed his eyes and waited for death. That was when he heard the low scraping sound. He opened his eyes and looked to his left. Belly down, the baron was crawling through the mud towards him, away from the smouldering wreck of his own plane.

Did I shoot the German down? Shaw thought.

Somebody had.

Blistered skin peeled from the right side of von Richthofen's once-handsome face, revealing white bone. The baron's black leather jacket was alight, licked by flames.

"Schädel," he groaned, one leather-gloved hand clasping hopelessly, pawing at the hot air. "Sk…skull."

Shaw gazed at the red gemstone inset into the dashboard and realised what the dying man desired. But behind the baron he saw something else, something worse.

Beyond the shrouds of drifting black smoke, he saw a dark hole in the earth. A young guard wearing a helmet two sizes too big was sitting beside the entrance, his face a nest of lice, his jaw hanging loose on his chest above his spilt and steaming innards.

"Dark down there," he slurred, tongue flapping like a fish.

The creature that came for the baron scrabbled out of the hole like an arachnid, darting through smoke and shadow.

Squinting through his concussion, Shaw saw that the thing's abdomen consisted of a lumpen congealment of human heads, wearing gas masks or helmets, each empty expression like a testament to the abomination of young men slaughtered before their time. The thing's legs were made of splintered swords and rifles; the claws were sharpened bayonets.

The thing hissed, its makeshift body scraping and clattering as it dragged the screaming baron into the hole.

A foul wind blew, and the clouds above shifted, twisting the girl's face so that it wore a cruel smile.

Shaw didn't begrudge her celebrating his imminent demise. She deserved her victory. He looked again towards the hole where the baron had been dragged—and saw the creature readying itself.

Dark down there…

From the black hole, the eyes of the thing gleamed, all eight of them, and wet jaws made of shrapnel and bomb shards and bullets twitched hungrily.

Panic raced through him, and all at once he realised he did not want to die, not like this. Why had the baron desired the skull? Because it was valuable? Or was there something more?

He remembered the brigadier's words:

Seventy Allied planes…

Brown's words:

The lads are saying the baron has made an…ungodly pact…

An extraordinary score…

An impossible score…

Unsheathing his bayonet from his belt, Shaw dug the blade under the skull's jaw and prised the ruby out of the dashboard. The second the rock was in his hands, he felt its raw power, spreading like streams of cool mist over his skin, sending shivers down his spine. Among the rippling flames, the gem glowed red.

The girl in the crimson clouds scowled.

He looked back towards the hole into which the baron had been dragged. But now there was no hole. No mutilated guard at its entrance. No terrible creature of war waiting to feed upon him. And the baron's body now simply lay in the mud, flames burning holes in his leather jacket, his face a mask of death.

Shaw told himself he was experiencing hallucinations. He was badly concussed, suffering from hypoxia, bleeding heavily from his shoulder…

He gripped the skull tight—and saw the helmets of Allied soldiers bobbing on the horizon, men moving towards the plane.

What were the chances? he thought—and fell into the numb comfort of dreams.

3.

"HE GAVE YOU THE SKULL?" SAYS DAD.

Danny shifts awkwardly in the pew in the little hospital chapel, fiddling with his Darth Vader action figure with its telescopic lightsabre.

"It's okay, Danny. I know."

"You do?" he says, looking away and out of the window at the brooding January sky. The clouds are as thick as soup.

Dad smiles. "I was about your age when I heard the story. My uncle told me. I've heard stories that your grandfather was a great pilot, but he would never talk about the war. French soldiers found him in a stolen German plane. He'd crashed it somewhere along the Somme."

"The Somme?"

"It's a river," says his dad. "Your grandfather believed he only survived the crash because of that rock."

"You believe that?"

His father smiles again, a tear welling in the corner of his eye. "What's important is that Grandad believed it."

He squeezes Danny's shoulder hard enough that it almost hurts. But Danny doesn't mind. It feels good to have his father with him.

"Dad, I'm worried."

"What about?"

"My chemo."

Dad takes Danny's hand and holds it tight. "It's going to be okay. I know it, son."

"Are you sure?"

"Yes," says Dad, but a flicker of uncertainty flashes in his eyes.

"The rock, it looks expensive."

"I don't care about that. I care about you. It's what your grandad wanted."

"He told me to keep the stone with me—always."

"It can't hurt."

No. Losing Grandad, that's what hurt.

Danny looks out of the window. The sky is a uniform grey. The amorphous clouds threaten snow. But within their twisting shapes, he can almost see the face of a little girl, smiling. He wonders what there can possibly be to smile about on such a dark winter's day. Closing his hand around the gemstone in his pocket, Danny finds himself smiling too.

ABOUT THE AUTHOR

Richard Clive is a horror and science-fiction writer who lives in the medieval town of Conwy, North Wales, with his wife, daughter, and pet Labrador. When not writing fiction, Richard works as a journalist but originally studied film and scriptwriting in Manchester. Richard's work has been published in numerous horror anthologies.

Find out more about Richard at www.richardclive.com.

Printed in Great Britain
by Amazon

87120347R00162